THE AFFAIR

By Danielle Steel

The Affair • Neighbours • All That Glitters • Royal • Daddy's Girls
The Wedding Dress • The Numbers Game • Moral Compass • Spy
Child's Play • The Dark Side • Lost And Found • Blessing In Disguise
Silent Night • Turning Point • Beauchamp Hall •In His Father's Footsteps
The Good Fight • The Cast • Accidental Heroes • Fall From Grace
Past Perfect • Fairytale • The Right Time • The Duchess • Against All Odds
Dangerous Games • The Mistress • The Award • Rushing Waters • Magic
The Apartment • Property Of A Noblewoman • Blue • Precious Gifts
Undercover • Country • Prodigal Son • Pegasus • A Perfect Life
Power Play • Winners • First Sight • Until The End Of Time
The Sins Of The Mother • Friends Forever • Betrayal • Hotel Vendôme
Happy Birthday • 44 Charles Street • Legacy • Family Ties • Big Girl
Southern Lights • Matters Of The Heart • One Day At A Time
A Good Woman • Rogue • Honor Thyself • Amazing Grace • Bungalow 2
Sisters • H.R.H. • Coming Out • The House • Toxic Bachelors • Miracle
Impossible • Echoes • Second Chance • Ransom • Safe Harbour
Johnny Angel • Dating Game • Answered Prayers • Sunset In St. Tropez
The Cottage • The Kiss • Leap Of Faith • Lone Eagle • Journey
The House On Hope Street • The Wedding • Irresistible Forces
Granny Dan • Bittersweet • Mirror Image • The Klone And I
The Long Road Home • The Ghost • Special Delivery • The Ranch
Silent Honor • Malice • Five Days In Paris • Lightning • Wings • The Gift
Accident • Vanished • Mixed Blessings • Jewels • No Greater Love
Heartbeat • Message From Nam • Daddy • Star • Zoya • Kaleidoscope
Fine Things • Wanderlust • Secrets • Family Album • Full Circle • Changes
Thurston House • Crossings • Once In A Lifetime • A Perfect Stranger
Remembrance • Palomino • Love: *Poems* • The Ring • Loving
To Love Again • Summer's End • Season Of Passion • The Promise
Now And Forever • Passion's Promise • Going Home

Nonfiction

Expect a Miracle
Pure Joy: *The Dogs We Love*
A Gift Of Hope: *Helping the Homeless*
His Bright Light: *The Story of Nick Traina*

For Children

Pretty Minnie In Hollywood
Pretty Minnie In Paris

Danielle Steel

THE AFFAIR

MACMILLAN

First published 2021 by Delacorte Press
an imprint of Random House
a division of Penguin Random House LLC, New York

First published in the UK 2021 by Macmillan
an imprint of Pan Macmillan
The Smithson, 6 Briset Street, London EC1M 5NR
EU representative: Macmillan Publishers Ireland Limited
Mallard Lodge, Lansdowne Village, Dublin 4
Associated companies throughout the world
www.panmacmillan.com

ISBN 978-1-5290-2145-5

1 3 5 7 9 8 6 4 2

A CIP catalogue record for this book is available from the British Library.

Printed and bound by CPI Group (UK) Ltd, Croydon, CR0 4YY

To my so greatly loved children,
Trevor, Todd, Beatie, Nick,
Samantha, Victoria, Vanessa,
Maxx, and Zara,

May you have lives and times of great joy,
courage in the hard times,
and may each of you
have the happy endings you wish for,
and I wish for you.

With all my love and
prayers for your happiness,

Mom/ds

THE AFFAIR

Chapter 1

Heads always turned when Rose McCarthy walked into a room. Nearly six feet tall, she was ramrod straight, and impeccably put together with faultless style, long graceful legs, and her snow-white hair cut in a chin-length rounded cap. Her piercing blue eyes missed nothing. She could terrify anyone with a few well-chosen, soft-spoken, eloquent words, or comfort and delight a young employee with generous praise. For twenty-five years, she had been the legendary editor-in-chief of *Mode Magazine*. Gentle, polite, supremely competent, she ran it with an iron hand, with the ultimate grace and discretion. She was known for excellent judgment, wise decisions that always benefited the magazine, her dedication, and love of fashion.

She always wore a touch of color somewhere, or an interesting, eye-catching accessory, a ring she had found at an ancient, dusty jewelry shop in Venice, a bracelet from a Moroccan bazaar, a scarf, a pin, an unusual piece of some kind. Her elegance was in her bones.

She usually wore black, but then would surprise everyone with a strong color occasionally. No one could ever manage to emulate her, although they tried. No one looked as perfectly turned out as she did at nine in the morning, or any other hour of the day. She was wide awake and alert the moment she got to the office, and never stopped all day. She pushed her employees hard and expected the best from them, but she was infinitely harder on herself than on anyone else.

Her background was fascinatingly contradictory. Her father had been a much published, highly respected British historian, who had taught at Oxford. Born and raised in London, she attended Oxford for two years at her father's urging, but never liked it. Her Italian mother was a well-known expert on the paintings of the Italian Renaissance. She was from a large aristocratic family. Rose's daughters teased her that she was Italian at home and British at work. There was some truth to it. Rose's mother had been as emotional as her father wasn't. Rose had learned from them, and flourished as an only child, with love and support from both her parents. She loved visiting her mother's warm family in Rome frequently. She spoke fluent Italian, French, and English, and after two years at Oxford she had attended the Sorbonne for a year, which she liked much better. Her passion and instinct for fashion had surfaced at twenty, when she was living in Paris. She returned to London then, became an intern at a well-known British magazine, and within months had fallen in love with an American banker, Wallace McCarthy. On an impulse, at twenty-one, she moved to New York for him, got a low-level job at *Vogue,* fought her way up through the ranks, and became an associate editor by the time she was thirty. Eleven years later, at forty-one, she was offered the position of editor-in-chief of *Mode Magazine,* and had made it the vast success it currently was. She was the soul and spirit of the magazine, and set a high standard. Twenty-five years after she took over, *Mode* was one of the most influential magazines in the fashion world. Its success was unquestionably credited to Rose. Her husband, Wallace, was proud of her, and always supportive of her career. Their marriage was important to both of them, rock solid and a priority for her. She was a powerhouse in the office, and a loving wife at home.

True to her British upbringing, she never said a word about her personal life at work. She rarely mentioned Wallace in the office, although he was the center of her life at home. And in the midst of her steady rise to stardom as a fashion editor, she'd given birth to four daughters who she privately admitted were the joy of her existence. She hardly ever talked about them during her daily life. She was a consummate professional, had taken a minimum of time off when she had them, and returned to the office, ready to work. When she came back from maternity leave, she was as slim and stylish as ever, with every hair in place, ready to focus on the magazine again.

Her forty-year marriage had been stable until her husband's death four years before.

Only her faithful assistant, Jen Morgan, who had followed her from *Vogue* and was still with her, ever knew anything about her personal life, or how truly heartbroken she was when Wallace died after a shockingly brief illness. More than ever afterwards, Rose was extremely close to her daughters and spoke to them often, but as had always been the case, when she was at the office, she was all about *Mode,* and nothing else. Her career had always been her passion, but it became her refuge too, once Wallace was gone. Her two lives never intersected. She had created an incredibly successful magazine, and a family of four young women who were very different, but immensely close to each other and to her. She was proud of them and the lives they led as adults.

She had always made time for her husband and their daughters, but now that she was widowed and the girls had grown up, she dedicated herself even more to her work. Sometimes it seemed as though she never left the office. She was often there when everyone else came in. An early riser, she liked getting a head start, and left the office late every night. She had compartmentalized her time for years between husband, children, and job, and now her work had her full attention and took up the lion's share of her time. She adored her daughters, but they were busy with their own lives, which she felt was as it should be. She didn't interfere with them, nor make demands on their time. She filled her days and nights with what she did for *Mode.* She lived and breathed the magazine, and every detail and issue had her full attention. Nothing escaped her notice.

She looked around the table on that particular May morning with a cool smile. The important senior editors were at the meeting, as well as the full creative board. She always listened to what they had to say, but Rose had the final word. If asked, all of them would have said that she was fair. She didn't impose her opinions on them, but when they heard her reasoning, they often recognized that her instincts for *Mode* were right. She loved it almost as a child, like a living, breathing human being, which it was to her. She didn't guess.

She *knew* what was right for *Mode,* and in twenty-five years, her mistakes could be counted on one hand.

They were having an early planning session for the massive September issue they published every year. All the major fashion magazines did, but *Mode*'s September issue was the most coveted by all. It became a collector's item every time and was as iconic as Rose herself. She was a fashion legend and everyone wanted to see what *Mode* was telling them about the styles for the coming winter season. Women redesigned their whole look and wardrobe according to what *Mode* told them about their makeup, their health, their hair, and what they should wear. *Mode* didn't impose anything on them. Their readers begged for what *Mode* had to offer.

They normally got an early start and began working on each issue three months in advance. But they began working on the September issue even earlier. There was so much to think about, and discuss, starting with who they put on the cover. And beyond that, the theme, the editorials, the articles, and the placement of the ads of their advertisers, who paid a fortune to be highlighted in the September book.

They already had three options for the cover, but none of them excited Rose. They seemed tired and obvious to her. She wanted someone on the cover who would grab their readers' imaginations and make a big splash. One of the senior editors had suggested a female rock star of major importance. They'd done her several times before, and there was nothing new or different about her, although she was a fabulous-looking woman. They had also considered an Oscar-winning actress, but Rose wanted someone younger. The beauty editor wanted to see the First Lady on the cover. She had won America's hearts with her good deeds and sharp mind. She was an attorney, and had championed women's causes since her husband had come to the White House. It was a noble thought, but she had a ladylike, somewhat prim, conservative style, and with the First Lady on the cover, it would be hard to make it about fashion.

"She's my age," Rose said with a dissatisfied look. "We can't do that for September. We can use her later."

Their most hard-edged senior stylist, Charity Bennett, had another suggestion, and made herself heard shortly after the meeting started. Rose frequently had run-ins with her, but respected her style and quick mind, and Charity often took them the extra mile to something truly avant-garde. She was young and daring. Rose always kept a leash on her so she didn't take them too far. Charity had jet-black hair, a sharp ivory-white face, and was never afraid of going toe-to-toe with the editor-in-chief. Rose admired her for it, and listened to what she had to say. Even if Rose wasn't crazy about her personally, the pepper and spice she contributed to their editorials were a good wake-up call to help them stay ahead of current trends.

"What about Pascale Solon?" Charity suggested. "She's twenty-two years old, spectacular looking, and she just won every prize there was at the Cannes Film Festival for her new film. She's having a white-hot affair with Nicolas Bateau, who wrote the book the movie was based on. He's forty-two, nearly twice her age, and they were the big item in Cannes. He made it very obvious that he's having an affair with her. He's married of course, and the biggest bestselling author in France. Everyone says she's going to win an Oscar for the film, and for sure a Golden Globe," the award given by the foreign press, which often presaged how the Academy would vote for the Oscars. "She's young, she's new, and one of the most sensational-looking girls I've ever seen. She's so sexy, she has an almost innocent pornographic quality to her. She makes Lolita look like Minnie Mouse. What do you think?" She looked straight at Rose, who sat quietly, expressionless, thinking and not reacting for a minute. At times, Rose was inscrutable, until she wished to share her thoughts.

"She's a possibility," was all Rose would concede. When there was something about an idea she didn't like, she became Sphinx-like. To those who knew her well, she was obviously not sold on the idea. And if they couldn't get Rose on board, they all knew it wasn't going to happen. Rose had to believe in the decisions she made.

"If we don't get her, *Vogue* will," Charity said, knowing that that might make Rose want to grab Pascale before someone else did. Charity knew that Rose never let *Mode* stoop to tabloid journalism, but they were not above touching lightly on some tantalizing detail of a subject's personal life, without taking it too far. Rose had rules and set boundaries she expected her editors to respect. She would only agree to what they wrote if it was confirmed as fact, and would not tolerate editorials in the magazine that were handled in a sleazy way. She hated filth and idle gossip. The magazine was about fashion, not peeping into their subjects' occasionally unsavory lives. If they were famous, they usually had secrets. Charity Bennett always tried to push Rose beyond that line, and when sufficiently annoyed by it, Rose didn't hesitate to push back. This time, she didn't comment, she just pursed her lips, which everyone in the room knew was a warning sign to back off.

"We can't base our interest in her on an affair with a famous writer," Rose finally commented. "By the time the September book comes out, it could be over anyway. The film just came out. Four months from now she may be sleeping with someone else, and we'll be old news and look foolish." She hated publishing gossip, as they all knew, and steered clear of it whenever possible. They did serious articles and interviews about the direction of their subjects' careers and lifestyles, and an affair with a married man, even a famous one, was not enough to convince Rose to put Pascale on the cover. But there was no question, Pascale Solon had become a major star overnight, in a tough role that she had handled brilliantly. And Nicolas Bateau had been the co-producer and director, and had apparently been coaching her in his spare time. He had gotten a fabulous performance out of her. Rose hadn't heard about the affair until Charity brought it up. It was just the kind of salacious information and innuendo that Charity thrived on. Rose wanted a fashion story on the cover, not a tell-all piece.

"The affair may not be over as fast as you think," Charity persisted. "There's a rumor that she's pregnant, so we may be right on target with the story in September." She was smug, as another editor rolled her eyes.

"Oh please, don't give me another cover of a naked star with a big round belly on the cover. I'd rather see the First Lady in one of her navy blue suits and a white blouse with a bow. We can't do another pregnant star," Rose said, starting to seem annoyed.

"It won't show if we shoot her now." Charity gave her a quelling look, as Rose went down a list of someone else's suggestions, none of which grabbed her either.

"What about Michaela Lim?" Rose said, distracted. She was another new young star, and had just delivered a brilliant performance in a recent movie.

"Next year," Charity countered. "No one's heard of her yet. She's not nearly as glamorous as Pascale. And she really is too young. She just turned nineteen. She needs to be more seasoned before we put her on September." Rose nodded agreement. She had a valid point. "Let's face it, Nicolas Bateau is a hunk, and if he leaves his wife for Pascale Solon, it's going to be news around the world, and our September issue is going to be the hottest issue on the stands. I want to grab that," Charity said with dogged determination. Pascale was heartbreakingly beautiful, and there was no denying that she would look fabulous in anything they put her in. It was a no-brainer, but Rose didn't like it.

"It will also seem as though we endorse infidelity, and men cheating on their wives. This is America, Charity. Americans don't like men who cheat. This isn't France." Charity had worked for a French fashion magazine before coming to *Mode,* and it came dangerously close to tabloid journalism. Rose's face was expressionless and her tone cold when she turned her electric-blue gaze on the senior stylist who was so determined to put Pascale on the cover. "We're not a tabloid or a movie magazine," Rose reminded her sternly. "There are plenty of other magazines to cover that. Let's not forget who we are." Charity looked frustrated, and they went on to other details of the issue that had to be decided in the coming weeks. When the meeting ended, they hadn't agreed on the cover yet.

"I think he's fooled around before," Charity said, as the meeting came to a close. "I forget who he's married to, someone ordinary but nice looking. I think she's a writer or a journalist or something."

"She's a well-known interior designer," Rose corrected her. "And they have young children. I don't like the story." She stood up, which was the signal for all of them to go back to work. The meeting had lasted for two hours, and they had covered considerable ground on other points. There were a million component parts to their big issue. In the end, the final decisions would be made by Rose, but they all knew that without exception, Rose did what was best for *Mode,* and had unfailing instincts for what that was, whatever her personal opinions. They respected her for it, even Charity, who didn't agree with her in this instance. Their other options all seemed like such a bore to her. She was the youngest of the senior staff, and on most occasions, Rose liked the spice she brought to it, but not this time.

Rose left the conference room quickly after the meeting. She knew there would be a mountain of emails and messages on her desk. Jen Morgan would handle as many as she could, but most of them would require callbacks from Rose to reach resolution. The proverbial buck stopped with her. She never complained about it. Even her rivals agreed that she was one of the best editors in the business, and courageous about the stands she took. She was a strong defender of women's rights. Integrity and honesty were important to her, vital in fact, and were at the heart of every interview and editorial.

She flew past Jen's desk, barely looking at her, clutching a thick stack of files from the meeting to her chest. She had appointments lined up all day long and was in a rush.

"Do we have a cover?" Jen smiled at her.

"Not yet. I have to make a confidential call. I'll probably be on for fifteen or twenty minutes. Hold my calls till then," she said, as she reached her office and paused in the doorway. Jen sat just outside.

"The stack on your desk is already pretty bad," Jen reminded her. "Another twenty minutes and you'll be buried."

"Can't be helped. I've got to make this call. There's a storm brewing." She offered no explanation as to the nature of the storm.

Jen raised an eyebrow but didn't ask. She knew not to, and also that Rose wouldn't have told her what it was about anyway. She rarely confided in anyone at work, even her trusted assistant. "I'll hold back the invading armies," Jen promised. She was good at her job, and Rose appreciated her for handling the million tiny details of her position so well.

Rose walked into her office and closed the door, then sat down at her desk. She saw that Jen hadn't been exaggerating. There was a tall stack of messages, printed emails, and other material on her desk. She tried not to look at it as she dialed the familiar number.

She knew she wouldn't be able to reach Olivia at that hour, so she didn't call her. At thirty-nine, she had recently been appointed a superior court judge and would either be on the bench or conferring with lawyers in chambers. Olivia was Rose's third daughter and Rose was proud of her, and the others. Olivia had an enormously responsible job now. She was married to Harley Foster, a federal court judge, who was twenty-one years older than she was. He had been one of her law school professors. They had a fourteen-year-old son, Will, and were a very serious, conservative family.

Athena, her oldest, was never her first choice to call with a problem. She had a laid-back, philosophical, ultra-positive California take on life, and always told her mother that everything would be all right, even if it was obvious that it wouldn't. Her perspective was entirely different from her mother's and her sisters'. She had made other choices in her life. Athena was forty-three years old, had lived in L.A. for fifteen years, was a TV chef, had written the definitive vegetarian and vegan cookbooks, and owned her own vegan restaurants. She had lived with the same partner for thirteen years. Joe Tyler was a chef too, owned his own very successful restaurant in L.A., and was five years younger than Athena. They weren't married and had no wish to be. They lived together and were happy as they were. They shared a flock of dogs that Athena referred to as her "babies." She said they were the only ones she wanted. Athena said that marriage was a man-made invention that just didn't work most of the time, and children weren't for her. She was great with them, but content to play with other people's children when she had the chance. That was the only "kid fix" she wanted, and Joe agreed with her.

Rose had called her second daughter, Venetia, forty-one years old, a stunningly successful fashion designer who had set up her business fourteen years before, with the sound financial advice of Ben Wade, her venture capitalist husband. Venetia was a remarkable, creative woman, and always had been. She was fearless in running her business, and the designs she created always made a sensation. They were as odd and zany as she was, and she came up with creations that looked like trailer park meets Paris and Las Vegas, on steroids. When Rose first saw her designs, she couldn't imagine who would buy them, unless they were as odd and eccentric as her daughter. But the clothes worked, and seemed to fulfill nearly every woman's fantasy of how they wanted to look. There were sequins and leopard prints in expensive Italian fabrics, serious little Chanel-style jackets in white mink and denim to wear with jeans. She had priced them high to place them in the luxury market, and much to Rose's amazement they took off and were a major hit. A year after she started her business, *Mode* did a feature article on her, and so did *The Wall Street Journal*. She was as tall as her mother, and her dark-haired, green-eyed, movie-star-handsome husband, Ben, was even taller. Venetia had a striking figure and went to the gym at five A.M. every day. She combined discipline and creativity, a blend that had made her a success. She had a wild mane of long curly red hair. The press called her the Golden Lioness, because she also had the Midas touch and a great head for business.

She had gone to both Parsons School of Design and Columbia Business School. She and Ben had three very appealing although somewhat wild children, two boys, Jack and Seth, and the youngest, India, a girl. Venetia said she wanted more, but hadn't convinced Ben yet. Somehow she managed to do it all, work, marriage, motherhood, just as her mother had. Unlike Rose, however, Venetia had a townhouse in New York that usually looked like a bomb had hit it, but she looked great, and so did the kids. They were all bright and lively, and her five-year-old daughter had her mother's creative streak. She wanted to design sneakers with sparkles on them when she grew up.

In spite of how busy she was, Venetia always took time to listen to her sisters' or her mother's problems, and gave them impressively good advice.

When her assistant answered, Rose asked to speak to Venetia. She came on the line a few minutes later, happy to hear from her mother.

"Sorry, Mom, I was in a design meeting. What's up?" Rose never called her at that hour. They usually talked when Venetia was on her way home from work in an Uber, which was often the only time she got to herself. Once she got home, she helped the boys with their homework and the kids would monopolize her for hours.

"I just heard something in a meeting that worried me, and I wondered if you know anything about it," Rose said in a solemn tone.

"Hemlines are getting shorter? If mine get any shorter, my customers will get arrested." She laughed. But she realized then that her mother sounded serious.

"It's about Nicolas," her youngest sister Nadia's husband. "He's supposedly having an affair with the girl who starred in his current movie, Pascale Solon. Has Nadia said anything to you? I haven't talked to her in several days. I've been wrapped up in the September issue. I hope it isn't true. Apparently, they outed themselves at the Cannes Film Festival last week. Doesn't Nadia go there with him?"

"Yeah, usually. She was installing a house in Madrid, so she probably didn't go with him this year or she only stayed for a day or two. I haven't talked to her. We've been playing phone tag. I saw something about it on the front page of a tabloid at the grocery store."

"You buy your own groceries?" Her mother sounded shocked. "What don't you do?"

"It was my turn to cook for the kids, and I stopped to buy frozen pizza." They had a housekeeper and a nanny, but Venetia tried to cook for them once a week.

"I feel better." The women in the family were famously poor cooks, except for Athena, who made up for all of them and was a genius in the kitchen, if you liked vegetables.

"I was hoping it was just the usual tabloid crap, since she wasn't there. What did you hear in the meeting?" Venetia sounded worried too.

"That Nicolas is having an affair with Pascale Solon, and she might be pregnant."

"Oh God, I hope that's not true. Maybe the whole thing is just Hollywood hype, to promote the movie," Venetia said hopefully. She didn't want her little sister to get her heart broken. Nicolas had been a flirt when he was younger, but not recently. It was just part of the culture, since he was French, but Venetia didn't have the feeling it went further than that. Nadia had never complained to her about it, or said he cheated.

As she thought about it, Venetia was wearing one of her creations, signature leopard capri pants, a turquoise sequined sweater, and bright green alligator Hermès high-heeled pumps, with an armload of emerald and diamond bangles on one arm, a bracelet with a huge chunk of turquoise on the other, her red mane pushed up on her head with a diamond chopstick through it. They were standard work clothes for Venetia, and somehow on her it all worked. She was a beautiful woman and could get away with it. She was an icon in fashion and had a style all her own. She had been outrageous with what she wore since she was a teenager, and had made a successful career of it as an adult.

"I hope it's not true," Rose said fervently. "I just turned the girl down for the September cover, and I'm sure I haven't heard the last of it. Especially if the rumor is true, about the affair. I don't even want to think about a possible pregnancy."

"That just sounds like tabloid crap, Mom," Venetia reassured her.

"What do we do now? I don't want to pry and upset Nadia if she hasn't heard the rumor," Rose said thoughtfully.

"I'm sure she has. It's probably all over the internet." Venetia clicked on her computer, and there were half a dozen articles to choose from, and some paparazzi shots. "It might be true, about the affair at least," Venetia said sadly, sorry for her youngest sister. "Call her, Mom. I'll call her later. Let me know what she says. I can't believe he'd be that dumb. He has a beautiful wife, a great marriage, they adore each other, two great kids, and he's making an ass of himself with a starlet half his age? Pathetic. And way too French. Flirting is one thing, but this is awful for Nadia, if it's true."

"I'll call her. I'll catch you tonight," Rose promised Venetia, who went back to work a few minutes later, worried about her little sister.

Rose sat at her desk for a minute, thinking of her youngest daughter. Nadia had done her junior year at the Sorbonne, following in her mother's footsteps. She had met Nicolas then, out with friends one night at a nightclub, and they had fallen madly in love. He was six years older than Nadia and a graduate student in political science, and by the end of her junior year abroad, she said she was too in love with him to leave him and come home to New York. Her parents hadn't been happy about it, but Nadia had been adamant and stayed in Paris with Nicolas. Nicolas was studying political science but wanted to be a novelist. Nadia transferred to the American University of Paris, and never came back to live in the States again. She had taken decorating classes in Paris after she graduated, and got a job as an intern working for a fancy decorator. She and Nicolas had married eleven years before, when she was twenty-five and he was thirty-one, after living together for several years. She had Sylvie, who was ten now, a year later, and then Laure, who was seven. Nadia was thirty-six and had her own successful business as an interior decorator. And Nicolas's dreams had come true. He was the biggest bestselling novelist in France. He had been a political journalist for a while, until he wrote his first successful novel. He was charming and very bright. His parents had died in an accident shortly after he and Nadia married and he inherited everything as their only child, including their château in Normandy, which Nadia had helped him restore at the same time she opened her own decorating business.

In some ways, Nadia was different from Rose's other daughters. Like Venetia, she was artistic, although she applied it to homes instead of fashion. And she had a good head for business. But she was quieter than her sisters, and had inherited some of her mother's British restraint. The others were all outspoken about their opinions. Nadia usually kept her views and plans to herself, until she did them. She was shy, but self-confident, and her clients loved her for her gentle ways, her discretion, and good taste. She never forced her opinions on them, but always managed to convince them of the choices she preferred and thought best for them, with stunning results. The houses she decorated often appeared on the covers of the best interior design magazines.

While her sisters had argued with each other when they were younger, Nadia quietly forged ahead fearlessly in the direction she felt was the right one, and Rose had always been impressed by how brave she was. She rarely consulted anyone about her decisions, didn't waver, and trusted herself even when she was very young, as with her decision to stay in France with Nicolas, and she had never regretted it.

He had been good for her, and once they married and started a family, Rose respected how strong their relationship was. Nadia handled Nicolas's fame with poise, as well as her business and their family. She ran his family château with ease and made it a beautiful home for them, seemingly effortlessly, despite her youth. Nadia always made her mother think of the adage "still waters run deep." She was one of the most competent of Rose's children.

Rose often thought Nadia had the perfect life, a happy marriage, sweet children, a husband she adored, and who clearly loved her passionately. Every time Rose saw them together, he could hardly keep his hands off Nadia. Rose liked her son-in-law, and there was no question, he was a talented writer. He'd written five bestsellers in France so far, and was published abroad in translation as well. This was the second movie based on one of his books, and he was well known in France, and even in the States. He had everything he needed to be a happy man, and now he was having a flagrant affair with a young movie star.

It broke Rose's heart to think of it, and how Nadia must feel. It was a sure way to destroy the marriage that had been so happy and satisfying for both of them for eleven years. She had no idea what had gotten into him. At forty-two, he was old enough to know better, and too young for a midlife crisis, in Rose's opinion. And Nadia wasn't one to complain if she had a problem.

Rose dialed Nadia in Paris, after she and Venetia hung up. She wasn't sure how to broach the subject. Nadia was so private that Rose wasn't sure she would open up to her. After asking about the children, and Nadia telling her about a new client in the South of France, Rose decided to take the plunge.

"I heard something that worried me today," Rose began gently, and there was silence at the other end. Nadia was smaller than Venetia and her mother and had dark hair. Athena and Olivia were blond, as Rose had been. Nadia and Olivia were much shorter than their sisters and mother. Nadia was a beautiful girl, the only dark-haired beauty in the family. Despite her dark hair, she had her mother's blue eyes and creamy white skin. Her sisters used to say she looked like Snow White.

Nadia sounded hesitant and subdued, and finally let out a sigh that sounded like air being let out of a balloon in a slow leak. Rose could almost feel her daughter's shoulders drooping as she did. "I know what you heard, Mom. It's about Nicolas. It's in all the tabloids here. He made an ass of himself at the Cannes Film Festival, and the press is having a field day with it. I didn't have the heart to call you." She hadn't called her sisters either. She was too upset.

"Was he drunk?" Rose couldn't imagine what had gotten into him.

"Maybe. I don't know. I wasn't there. I was working in Madrid. He says he got involved with her when he was making the film. She's a beautiful girl," Nadia said sadly. "I've been busy and he got carried away."

"You're a beautiful girl too," her mother reminded her, furious with her son-in-law. "Did you know, or suspect something?"

"No, I never thought he'd do that. I trusted him completely. It all came out after Cannes, when I saw it in the papers. I feel like an idiot. Maybe it's partially my fault. I've been working a lot, and very hard."

"Was it some kind of one-night slip?" Rose asked her. Not that she found that acceptable either. She had never cheated on her husband, nor he on her, to the best of her knowledge, in forty years of marriage, in spite of her career. One-night stands were not acceptable to her, but they were better than a serious affair.

"No. He says he's in love with her, or infatuated, or something. At the same time, he says it's not serious. He's confused. He promises he'll get out of it, and he says he loves me and the girls and doesn't want to leave me. He expects me to sit and wait." As an only child, Rose knew he had been indulged and spoiled in his youth. This was more of the same to an extreme degree, at her daughter's expense.

Rose was deeply unhappy at what she heard from Nadia. "Has he done this before?" She was trying not to sound unduly shocked, or too judgmental, so she could be helpful to her daughter. Righteous indignation wouldn't get them anywhere, although Rose was livid with him for hurting and betraying her daughter.

"Once," Nadia said honestly. "When I was pregnant with Laure. I don't know what happened, some kind of panic and insecurity about his book not doing well and the responsibility of two children. He went crazy for about a month, and then he got out of it. It was with his editor at the time. He changed editors after that. That was eight years ago, and everything's been fine since then. I never told you because it was over in a matter of weeks and it was some kind of aberration. It never happened again. He promised he'd never cheat again, and he hasn't. Until now. This time, I guess the temptation of working with Pascale Solon was too much for him. I think it went on during the whole filming of the movie. And of course everyone knew but me. Then somehow he lost control at the Festival. Now the whole world knows. She's a big star so it's hard to keep it quiet. How did you find out?" She sounded tired and sad as she talked to her mother. It made Rose's heart ache for her.

"One of our stylists proposed her for a cover and mentioned the story."

"Does she know I'm married to him?"

"No, she doesn't. I didn't say anything. I just came out of the meeting and called you."

"Do my sisters know?" she asked miserably. The whole situation was not only painful and breaking her heart, but with everything on the internet, it was deeply humiliating.

"I called Venetia before I called you. I was afraid to upset you. I know you don't like to talk about things if you're upset and I didn't want to intrude on you."

"It's okay, Mom. The stupid thing is I love him. He's a good husband and a wonderful father and we love each other. At least I think he loves me too. He says so. He's upside down at the moment. It's like he forgot he was married, and now he's up to his ears in the affair and the press is all over him because they're both so well known. I know it's wrong, but people do that here. They have mistresses and affairs, and women do it too. Usually, they're disenchanted with their marriages. He says he isn't. He just couldn't resist her. Nicolas is very clear that he doesn't want to leave me for her."

"Do you want to leave him?" Rose asked. She wondered if she should. She didn't like the situation, and "confused" was a poor excuse for prolonging the affair. He was indulging himself and hurting Nadia while he did.

"I don't know," she said cautiously. "I don't want to lose him or give up on our marriage, but I'm not going to hang around while he has an affair with someone else. I'm not so much shocked as hurt. I was furious at first. Now I'm just sad about it. Some of my friends here have been in this situation. Most of the time, they don't get divorced. Some of my women friends have had affairs too. They say it keeps their marriage 'fresh.' Anyway, that doesn't apply here." There was nothing fresh about the situation. Nadia sounded wilted and depressed, understandably.

"Do your daughters know?" Rose asked her.

"Not yet. But someone will tell Sylvie at school sooner or later. I'm sure their parents all know. Nicolas is famous in France. And it's all over the internet."

"Which means he needs to be that much more circumspect. He can't go around having affairs with starlets and expect you to live with that and stick around," Rose said angrily.

"He feels terrible about it," Nadia said protectively. She almost felt sorry for him, except that she was so miserable herself. She wanted to hate him for it but she didn't. She just wanted the affair to be over and to have their happy life back. She didn't see now how that could happen. And he hadn't given up Pascale, despite their tearful discussions about it.

"Is he going to get out of it?" Rose asked, angrier by the minute. Nadia didn't deserve this. She was such a loving wife to him, and he had been loving to her too. What was he thinking?

"He says he will get out of it, but he wants to do it carefully, so he doesn't make an even bigger fuss in the press about a breakup." It sounded like an excuse to Rose, but she didn't say it to her daughter, to avoid upsetting her more.

"Do you want to come home with Sylvie and Laure for a while?" Rose suggested. Getting away sounded like a good idea to her. But "home" was no longer home to Nadia. Paris was.

"No. There would be even more talk then. The press would say we're getting divorced. This is bad enough. I'm just trying to keep below the radar and avoid the photographers when I go out. I've told the girls it's because their father's movie is such a big hit."

"Why don't I come over to see you? I can come for a weekend," Rose offered.

"Are you going to put Pascale on the cover?" Nadia asked, thinking about *Mode Magazine*.

"Not if I can avoid it," Rose said. For the first time, she was letting her personal interests come before those of the magazine. "I can't hold back the tide forever if this becomes a huge story and lasts, but I'll do what I can to discourage it. The stylist who suggested it was pushing hard. Let's hope Nicolas gets out of this quickly, and then you can decide what you want to do about it. You can't be married to a man who cheats on you every few years. Twice in eleven years is two times too many." Nadia nodded, with tears in her eyes, grateful for her mother's call. She'd been embarrassed to tell her, and she hadn't known for long. Nadia was still reeling from the shock herself.

"I feel so stupid. I'm the one he doesn't want." She started to cry then, and Rose felt as though someone was ripping her heart out of her chest as she listened. She wanted to strangle Nicolas for the meanness and stupidity of it, and the selfishness. It was all so public, in the tabloids and on the internet.

"It sounds like he's out of his mind at the moment," Rose said, still trying to understand it, "which is no excuse. I know people who've survived worse things in their marriages, but this is bad enough. He needs to end it quickly, and get out of it, and then people will forget. But if he carries on with her, it's going to be a huge mess."

"I know. He knows that too. He's obsessed with her," Nadia said. It was every wife's worst nightmare, her husband in love with a gorgeous movie star twenty years younger than he was.

"Exposing it at the Cannes Film Festival with all the press around was insanity."

"I guess he is insane at the moment," Nadia said, but she sounded better and stronger while talking to her mother, and more confident again. There was something about her mother that always made her feel grounded. She had felt lost in the jungle alone without a compass since finding out about Pascale. Her mother was a beacon of light in the dark, and always had been, for her and her sisters. And her father had been too. He had been the perfect, equally solid male counterpoint to Rose, and a father they could always count on. They all missed him. He was conservative, but not unreasonably so.

"I'll figure out when I can come over," Rose promised, and then had to hurry off to her next meeting. She was twenty minutes late, which never happened to her. But this was more important than meeting with the art department to talk about the look of the September cover and which photographer they wanted to use.

She felt flustered thinking about her daughter, which was rare for her. She didn't want to give her bad advice, or influence her about something as important as her marriage, but she wanted to throttle her son-in-law for what he'd done, and was still doing. And if Pascale was pregnant, as the press was insinuating, it would be even worse. She wondered if Nadia had heard that rumor too, but as down as she had sounded on the phone, Rose didn't want to ask, especially if it wasn't true. False rumors were the tabloids' stock-in-trade. And they had a fearsome way of ferreting out racy tidbits, or were without conscience about inventing them, to spice up their headlines.

Rose rushed out of her office for her meeting with the art department, and Jen handed her a fresh stack of phone messages.

"Legal wants you to call them about a recall of a beauty product in the last issue. They need you to sign off on it."

"I'll call them when I get back," she said smoothly, trying to force her mind to the present and not think of Nicolas's affair, but it was all she could think of, and how sad and defeated Nadia had sounded on the phone.

"Everything okay?" Jen asked, looking at her carefully. Rose looked stressed and harried, unusually so.

"Fine." Rose smiled smoothly, in just the way she was famous for. The world could be coming to an end, and Rose always remained calm and unruffled, or appeared to, but she didn't feel that way now. She never let on when she was upset, and thought it undignified to do so. But she felt like a lioness whose cub had been injured by a hunter. She was out for blood, Jen could see it in her eyes. "I'll be back in a while." The meeting lasted longer than expected, followed by a slew of phone calls, and others she had to return. It was eight o'clock by the time she got home, and eight-thirty when she called

Athena in L.A. She sounded as she always did, happy and relaxed, when she answered the phone. It was five-thirty in the afternoon for her, her show had gone well, she was going to one of her restaurants shortly, and then she was going to meet Joe later to go out to dinner. They had a casual life, she lived in clogs and her chef's jacket all the time, and appeared on TV in exercise clothes sometimes. She had never aspired to her mother's elegant, fashionable style. She was heavier than her sisters, and had never worried about her looks and weight the way they did. She was almost as tall as her mother and had a full, lush Rubenesque body, which Joe said he loved just the way it was. She had wanted to be a chef since high school. She loved food and the art of preparing it. Her theories were unorthodox and her recipes easy to follow, which had made her popular with the masses, first in California, and then all over the country.

Athena had never been the student her sisters were, she had her own tempo and lifestyle. She had studied cooking in Paris, Barcelona, Rome, and Milan, and became fascinated by vegan and vegetarian cuisine. Her cookbooks were a huge success, her TV show even more so. Her fans felt as though they had a personal relationship with her because she was so personable, and they wrote her adoring letters.

There were half a dozen dogs barking in the background when Rose called her. Two of them were rescue dogs, two were strays, and she had two others she'd gotten from breeders. Most of them were mixes, and one of them was huge.

"Stanley, get your feet off the kitchen counter," she said in a firm voice as she answered the phone, and was pleased to hear her mother at the other end. They chatted for a few minutes about what she was doing, and she said she was going to be taping a show in Japan at some point. Rose told her about Nadia then, and Nicolas's affair with Pascale Solon.

"Wow, that's awful. Is she going to leave him?" Athena sounded worried about her.

"She hasn't figured it out yet. I think she's in shock, and he's still involved with Pascale."

"How terrible for her. . . . Stanley, what did I just say?" Talking to Athena was always a three- or four-way conversation, which included several dogs, workmen, and people delivering groceries. Rose could never understand how four women could be so different. Athena's world had nothing in common with her sisters'. They didn't even like dogs. But Olivia, Nadia, and Venetia all had children, and Athena didn't want any. At forty-three, she was perfectly content with her life as it was with Joe. He was a respected chef too, although he was less well known than Athena. She always seemed larger than life, and she lived in friendly chaos. "Maybe she should come here with her girls for a visit. I'll suggest it to her. What's happening with them this summer? Will he be with the girlfriend or with her?" Just asking the question turned her stomach. Athena didn't like the situation either.

"I didn't even think to ask," Rose admitted. "The whole story is so unnerving, and I feel so sorry for her."

"Maybe they should try couples therapy. We did a few years ago, when we started fighting about the restaurants, mine and Joe's. The therapy really helped."

Her mother smiled at the idea. "Nicolas is French. Can you really see him going to therapy? Men don't rush into that in France, or even here sometimes."

"Yeah, but I can see it if he wants to save his marriage."

"Maybe he doesn't," Rose said. "He's not promising to break it off anytime soon. He wants Nadia to give him time."

"For what? So he can continue sleeping with the girl? I don't think so. She ought to lower the boom on him now, and see what he does." It was a simple, direct approach. Rose didn't disagree with her, but it didn't sound like Nadia was willing to do that. For now, with Nadia still off balance, he had the upper hand. She hoped that would change soon.

"I'll text her later. I don't have time now. I'll tell her to come out this summer. It would be fun, for me too." Rose was touched by Athena's and Venetia's reactions of unequivocal support for their sister. Particularly Athena, whom her sisters referred to as Mother Earth.

Olivia was more vehement when Rose got hold of her after Athena. They had just finished dinner at nine o'clock. She and Harley both worked long days on their court cases.

"She should divorce him. Immediately," Olivia said without hesitating. She was the toughest and most hardline conservative of the four sisters. She saw everything in black-and-white, according to the letter of the law. They had a fourteen-year-old son, Will, who was a brilliant student, and Olivia treated him like an adult, and always had. It had seemed odd to Rose when he was younger. "She needs to contact a lawyer, now. I don't know if they have no-fault divorce in France, but she needs to take action, protect her separate property, and go after him for whatever she can. Does he own any other property in France? Do they own the château jointly?"

"I doubt it. He inherited it when his parents died." As an only child, he had inherited everything. "I think inherited wealth is separate," Rose said.

"Well, she needs to divorce him as soon as possible. She has her own income and he needs to be accountable for his actions." Everything she said made sense, but Rose could tell from talking to Nadia that she was too stunned to make a move, although Rose was sure she would eventually. The situation was untenable. Nicolas was having his cake and eating it, while Nadia's heart was breaking.

Olivia reported the conversation to her husband, Harley, after she hung up, and he agreed with her. He was just as tough with his opinions as Olivia. They were a good match and had an excellent marriage. Their careers were similar and complemented each other, and they agreed about most things, even about their son. It had given Olivia a somewhat skewed view of the world. She assumed that most "normal" people were as conservative as they were, or should be. She was rarely tolerant of people with a different point of view. It worried her mother at times that she had such a narrow perspective.

Being married to a much older man had suited her, from the moment she and Harley had fallen in love while she was in law school. He had been married and widowed years before, and never remarried until he met Olivia. He was inordinately proud of Will, their only son, who was a straight-A student. They shared their opinions with him liberally, and he didn't always agree with them, but rarely said so. He knew what was expected in their home, and who you had to be to get along. His parents would never have tolerated it if he voiced his differences, so he didn't. Rose worried about him and thought him almost too compliant and accommodating, and couldn't help wondering at times if that was who he really was, or if it was a persona he pretended to be in order to please his parents. They made it very clear that no straying off their path would be acceptable to them. Olivia was almost more rigid in her ideas than her husband, despite the difference in their ages.

Rose lost the battle for the cover, and conceded regretfully, in June. She called Nadia as soon as it was decided, to warn her. She still hated the idea of putting Pascale Solon on the cover of the September issue. It tacitly endorsed behavior which she found abhorrent. Others were caught up in the romance of it, swayed by how in love they seemed, and how physically attractive Pascale and Nicolas both were. Rose almost wondered, if they had been less beautiful, would people have been less tolerant of the fact that he was still married, living with his wife, had cheated on her, and fallen "madly in love" with someone else?

Charity Bennett almost crowed over her victory when Rose backed down and gave in about the cover. Pascale was the girl of the hour, and they were the "It" couple. Their love affair was out in the open by then, and Nicolas wasn't even publicly apologetic about it. He was more so to his wife, privately, and insisted he didn't want to lose her, which enraged his mother-in-law, given his flagrant behavior and the pain it was causing Nadia. It was as though he and his fans had forgotten that he was married, Nadia existed, he had children, and that his passion for Pascale was forbidden fruit. He was living out every man's fantasy, to have a beautiful young woman at his feet and a wife to meet his more practical needs at home.

Within days of their deciding to put Pascale on the cover of the September issue, Pascale admitted publicly that she was pregnant. It upset Rose even more that Nadia had to deal with that too. Nadia made no comments to the press, and was unavailable to discuss it with anyone. As soon as the news was out, Rose made a reservation to go to Paris and spend the weekend with her daughter. She couldn't think of anything else to do except be there for her. And Rose also felt that it made the magazine seem less than respectable to endorse their affair with a cover story.

Rose had had no contact with Nicolas since the affair became obvious at the Cannes Film Festival, and she hoped she wouldn't see him in Paris, although she knew from Nadia that he still spent time at the house, stayed there frequently, and hadn't moved out. He visited his daughters daily. They knew nothing about Pascale and the baby, which seemed miraculous to Rose, given the furor in the press. But at seven and ten, they were sheltered and knew nothing of their father's behavior, and their mother didn't tell them, and was keeping them off the internet.

Rose was planning to urge her daughter to consult a lawyer as soon as possible. Rose had never felt as conflicted as she did now in her role as editor of *Mode Magazine,* delivering what their readers wanted, satisfying their curiosity about two people so publicly enamored with each other. She knew that contributing to the feeding frenzy would hurt her daughter deeply and make her feel even more betrayed.

Rose had a heavy heart as she boarded the Air France flight on Friday night after she left the office. All of Nadia's sisters were up in arms on her behalf. They didn't criticize their mother for the upcoming cover and interview with Pascale that would appear in *Mode,* but they hated Nicolas for what he was doing to their sister, and they closed ranks around her to support her.

Rose had said nothing at the magazine about her personal connection to Nicolas Bateau, and no one except her assistant, Jen Morgan, remembered. Others vaguely recalled that she had a married daughter who lived in France, but not for an instant did they suspect the heartbreak it was for Rose.

Rose was quiet and pensive as the plane landed early the next morning at Charles de Gaulle airport. She wanted to see her daughter now and comfort her. She had left her role as editor of the world's most influential fashion magazine behind in New York. All she was in Paris was Nadia's mother, and she hoped her presence would be enough to give her daughter strength to face the nightmare she was living and the grief that lay ahead.

Chapter 2

Nicolas came home for dinner on Friday night, as he still did several times a week, to be with his children and see his wife. He didn't always spend the night, and slipped away after the girls were asleep so they didn't know that he had left. They thought he had left for work early the next morning. He still spent some nights at home, though not many, because he wanted to keep up appearances for his daughters as much as possible. And he wanted to see Nadia too. Absurdly, he didn't want to lose her, despite what he was doing and the way he was behaving. He was loving and kind to Nadia and the girls when he came home, which somehow made the situation even more painful for Nadia.

She was willing to cooperate for the girls' sake, at least for a while. He had always been a devoted father and adored his daughters. He had been a good husband too, with the one brief exception eight years before, and nothing untoward since. He and Nadia had a solid, loving relationship, or so she thought, until very recently, when she discovered his affair with Pascale Solon.

Since he'd been on location for part of the shooting of the fateful film that had destroyed their marriage, she had been unaware of his spending his off hours, or nights, with Pascale. He had been managing it carefully once they got back to Paris. Nadia had suspected nothing. It had all exploded at the Cannes Film Festival, when he had been openly amorous with Pascale. He told Nadia it was as though he had forgotten who he was for those few days, and the press jumped on it immediately. He confessed everything to Nadia after Pascale told him, while they were there, that she was having his baby. He had lost his mind for a few days. For months before that, he had been excited, and terrified to be discovered. He thought he was in love with her and said he was flattered that a girl so young and beautiful would want him. He had thought it was a passionate interlude that would only last while they were making the movie, and Nadia would never know. He never wanted to hurt her and told her he had had no intention of ever doing anything like it again, with Pascale or anyone else, and he didn't want to risk his marriage. He had wanted to end the affair when the filming of the movie ended.

He knew that Pascale had a habit of becoming involved with whomever she was working with, which was not unusual among actors and producers or directors. And he assumed she would want to end it too. There was an otherworldly kind of atmosphere on a movie set, and then you came back to earth and went back to your own life. He had tried to do that with Pascale, and had counted on Nadia never finding out, and leaving the affair behind him on the movie set. And then Pascale had begged him to see her again, once they got home to

Paris. He had, and discovered that their physical passion became addictive. He knew he had to stop, and wanted to, but discovered he couldn't. She wouldn't let him. Pascale appeared so lost and vulnerable, suddenly cast into the pressure and demands of major stardom, it made him want to protect and take care of her, just until she got on her feet.

She had been so overwhelmed and terrified at the Cannes Festival, it had been endearing, and he believed he was in love with her. Then she told him about the baby, and he realized that they had created a new life together, which touched him profoundly, as it had when he and Nadia first conceived their babies. It made his bond to Pascale suddenly real. It was almost as though he forgot he had another life, and a wife and children. All he could think of was this delicate, gentle young woman, and the child that would be theirs forever. Her beauty wasn't what drew him to her. He thought Nadia just as beautiful, which he told her, though she didn't believe him. But the new life growing inside Pascale now had made him suddenly willing to risk everything so he could be with her and protect her, at least until the baby came.

And then after the Festival, he woke up when he got home. Within days, he knew the terrible mistake he had made having the affair, letting it show in Cannes, admitting to the affair publicly, and telling Pascale that he loved her when she told him about the baby. It was almost like being in a movie, only it was real. Now everything and everyone he loved was on the line. He was faced with the consequences of his actions. He told Nadia honestly everything that had happened, even that the affair had gone on for months, all during the filming of the movie. Hearing it was like a dagger being plunged into Nadia's heart, particularly for a woman who was so honest and pure and faithful. Her quiet dignity as she listened made it even worse.

In the beginning, he hadn't faced what his passion and elation could cost him later, and now he was trying to hold the torn shreds of his marriage together, and not lose Nadia, while trying to work things out with Pascale in some reasonable way. He had a responsibility to her too now, which he didn't want to shirk. He had never tried to dodge his obligations, and never wanted to fall short with the people he loved and who counted on him. Even now, he wanted to continue to be a husband to Nadia, but she said she just couldn't do that, not after being publicly humiliated for the past month and especially now that he was having a baby with another woman. His clandestine indiscretion while making the movie would have repercussions for the rest of their lives, whatever they did. Nadia had told him that Pascale's pregnancy was the final blow to their marriage. It devastated him to hear it, and know it was true. He was going to lose everyone and everything he loved most. And he knew he deserved it.

He had told Nadia that Pascale wasn't asking to marry him. She felt she was much too young for marriage, but absurdly, not for a child. She said she had wanted a baby for the past two years, and she couldn't think of a better father than Nicolas, and she fully expected their affair to peter out eventually. She didn't expect or even want a long-term future with him, and he had risked his family and marriage for her and a moment of passion. He had allowed himself to be lulled into not worrying about her getting pregnant and gotten careless. Now, until after the baby was born and the affair ended naturally, Pascale wanted him to leave Nadia and live with her. At twenty-two, and given her casual, unorthodox, modern philosophies about life, she wasn't a long-term prospect for him, and he wondered if she understood the forever responsibility of having a child. It wouldn't be a baby she could cuddle forever like a doll, it would be a child, a person, with illnesses and problems, needs. It would have to have an education, and would become a troublesome teenager one day. She was only thinking of the present moment, and he had been unable to convince her what the future would look like. She was in no way prepared for what she had undertaken, and she assumed that he would be the responsible party, while she would be there to have fun with the baby, which he knew wasn't how it worked.

She had grown up haphazardly herself. She had never known her father, or even who he was, had a mother who came and went after having her at sixteen, and a grandmother who had raised her and died when Pascale was seventeen. She'd been on her own ever since. And she assumed that any child would survive since she had.

Nicolas was willing to hold up his end with the baby since he had conceived the child with her, and he loved her to some degree, and Pascale insisted on having it. But he knew he would never love Pascale as he did Nadia. Pascale was ephemeral. Most of her charm and appeal were in how fey and childlike she was, but he couldn't imagine her taking on the role of mother. Pascale didn't pretend that she was going to love and stay with him forever. She had spoken to her mother, who had agreed to raise the child, since she was older now, and that way Pascale would be free to pursue her career and her life, meet other men, have other children, and do whatever she wanted. Pascale was a free spirit.

So he had thrown away his future and a solid life and marriage for something that glittered for an instant in the sunlight and blinded him briefly. And now he had to pick up the pieces of his shattered life every day. He couldn't think about writing right now, couldn't concentrate, and although he realized that his current anguish might make a good book one day, he didn't want it to be a modern-day tragedy. He wasn't ready to end the affair with Pascale, it wouldn't be right with her pregnant, but more than anything, he didn't want to lose Nadia and their marriage. So he was running between the two women, trying to placate both, begging Nadia's forgiveness, so she wouldn't give up on him before he had time to clean up his mess. He thought that he'd be able to ease out of the relationship with Pascale sometime after the baby was born, if Nadia didn't divorce him first. And whatever Nadia did, he knew the affair with Pascale wouldn't last, but the baby would.

Pascale wanted him around to play and sleep with, until they got tired of each other, which she fully expected to happen sooner or later. As she put it, you don't choose a partner for life at twenty-two. But he had at twenty-six, when he'd met Nadia, and it had worked wonderfully for sixteen years, eleven of them married, until he ruined everything with the affair with Pascale. He was an interlude for Pascale, a chapter. Nadia was his life. He told her he realized that more than ever now. But extricating himself from Pascale wasn't easy. She fully expected his constant presence now, at least until the baby came.

He and Nadia talked about it again on Friday night, after she put the girls to bed. Dinner had been strained, although Nadia was determined to put a good face on for the girls for as long as she could bear it, but it was becoming harder each day, knowing that Nicolas was still with Pascale, at least some of the time. She had inherited her mother's stiff-upper-lip genes, never airing problems in the presence of others. Sylvie had asked her recently why she cried so much and was in such a bad mood, and she had said that some of her decorating clients were giving her a hard time. Sylvie had asked her then if she and Papa had had an argument. Nadia had smiled through her tears and denied it, and made an extra effort to seem cheerful and pleasant when Nicolas came home for dinner that night.

Nicolas appreciated what she was doing, and knew full well that another woman would have thrown all his belongings out on the street, although they both knew that many French women put up with their husbands having affairs and mistresses. It was part of the culture, even for some people their age. And many wives in France weren't faithful either. After eleven years of marriage, many of the men they knew cheated on their wives regularly, and some of the women did the same. It wasn't how either Nadia or Nicolas wanted to live, and wasn't their vision of marriage. After his one earlier slip, Nadia thought that that was over for him, which made this all the worse now. This had blindsided her completely. She thought they were happy and settled forever, and now their whole life had blown up in their faces.

Nadia was having a hard time getting through it, and he felt terrible about that too. She looked tired and strained, had dark circles under her eyes, and had lost at least ten pounds, which she couldn't afford. She looked sick. She was still working as hard as ever and taking care of their daughters admirably.

"I'll spend this weekend at home. We'll do something together," he promised with a mournful look. Guilt was his constant companion now, whichever woman he was with.

"You can't," she said in a small sad voice. She knew she should be angrier at him, and at times she was, but most of the time, she was desperately hurt. Anger hadn't had time to set in. At first she had been shocked and numb, and now she felt crushed by what he had done, living with it every day, as he went back and forth between the two women like a metronome.

"Why can't I?" He looked panicked. So far Nadia hadn't forbidden him to come home or spend the night, although she had threatened to, but she did make him sleep in their guest room now when he stayed, and warned him not to let the girls see it. She refused to share a room with him, and they had had no sexual contact since she learned of the affair after the Film Festival. And Nicolas wisely didn't try to approach her.

"My mother is coming for the weekend. She's arriving early tomorrow morning," she said simply. He groaned.

"Oh Christ. Why now?"

"Why do you think?" Nadia gave him a dark look and he nodded.

"She knows, of course," he said glumly, as they sat at the kitchen table.

"Obviously. The whole Western Hemisphere knows. It's been in every tabloid in the world and on the internet. There are dozens of pictures of you with Pascale. We're just lucky no one has told the girls yet." But sooner or later, it would happen. His books were sold and successful in translation in many languages and countries around the world. And Pascale had already become famous with her previous film, which was why they had hired her for his latest one. So they were fodder for gossip around the world.

"Did you tell your mother?" he asked her.

"I didn't have to. She heard it in an editorial meeting, when they wanted to put Pascale on the cover of the September issue, along with an interview with you."

"I told you, Nadia, I won't give any interviews. I know I started this horrible mess, but I don't want to make it any worse than it is." It was too late to stop the tidal wave of press, but he didn't want to contribute to it. He was still hoping she would forgive him one day. But he also knew that although Nadia had lived in France for half her life, and in many ways had become very French, at the root of it, she was American and so were her sisters, and the four women were extremely close. He felt sure they must be trying to convince her to divorce him. He couldn't really blame them, given how it looked, but he was still hoping to stem the tides of disaster, although that didn't look promising at the moment.

Nadia had retreated into her shell since the announcement of Pascale's pregnancy, and was saying very little to him about her plans. They were living in a tenuous status quo at the moment, and he doubted it would hold for long. Just long enough, he hoped, for Pascale to have the baby, and for him to make some kind of arrangement or agreement with her, then return to the fold with his wife and daughters before their life burned to the ground. He knew it was a race against time as to how long Nadia would put up with the misery he was causing her. He was fully prepared to try to make it up to her for the rest of his life, but he didn't know if she would let him, or if the damage was reparable for her. She wasn't letting him near her, and avoided him when he came to the house, except when their daughters were in the room. Then she pretended to be friendly with him, although not affectionate, which they had always been before. Nadia was a warm, kind, gentle woman, and their relationship had been very close. He wondered now if it ever would be again, no matter what he did to make amends. She was a forgiving person, but he knew he was asking for the extreme. She was living with personal pain and public embarrassment of the worst sort for any woman, her husband openly involved with another woman and having a child with her. He himself cringed when he thought about it, as sanity returned.

Everything about their life had seemed so perfect until now. She always talked about how lucky they were to have such a good life. They lived in a beautiful apartment overlooking the Seine on the Quai Voltaire on the Left Bank, in the seventh arrondissement, with the spectacular monuments of Paris spread out before them like a movie set, and the Eiffel Tower visible from their terrace and sparkling on the hour. Nadia had decorated the apartment with her usual exquisite taste, with a combination of unusual modern pieces and family antiques Nicolas had inherited. It was a warm, comfortable home, and at the same time a showplace when they entertained. They and the children had been happy there.

Nadia had cut herself off from everyone they knew the minute his affair with Pascale hit the papers. She didn't want to have to defend him, or share her pain. And he was lying low too. Suddenly, after living a full life before, they were living in a vacuum, with only the paparazzi for company. They had lost so much because of him. Knowing how close they were, he was sure she was talking to her sisters for support. Her mother's visit was the first sign of it, and he dreaded seeing her. Rose could be glacial or brutally eloquent when she felt betrayed, and she was a lioness with her cubs. She was a remarkable businesswoman and opponent, but in her private life, she was a fierce advocate for her children, and loyal to all those she loved. She was old-fashioned and conservative in her values. He had crossed every possible line and he wasn't looking forward to seeing her. He could guess what her reaction would be, deservedly. Pascale was in the South of France with friends for the weekend, and he had told her he wouldn't go so he could see his children. He could still call her and say there had been a change of plans. He could catch a commuter flight to Nice at Orly late that night, since Nadia didn't want him with her mother, and he was grateful to avoid her.

Despite the agonies between them, Nadia and Nicolas were still a beautiful couple to look at. She was petite, with dark hair, and fair English skin that she inherited from her mother, and her mother's blue eyes. Nadia's were darker blue, like sapphires. She was always elegantly dressed in a quiet way that he had been proud of. She looked more French than American by now, and had always felt at home there. She had fit right in, from the moment she arrived at the Sorbonne. Her sisters were more American in their style and points of view. Nadia had always been more European, and in a way more like her Italian grandmother, who was warm and funny. Nadia didn't have her mother's cool, restrained English demeanor, or her sisters' more open, outspoken American style. She was very French in her manner and way of seeing things, after living there for sixteen years. She was also a woman of dignity who kept her sorrows private, and he had exposed her to public scrutiny in the worst possible circumstances.

In contrast, Nicolas was fair, with thick blond hair and a chiseled face. She had always loved his looks but couldn't bear to see him now. He was taller than most French men, broad shouldered and athletic, and looked like a movie star himself. They made a striking couple and, if anything, they had gotten even more attractive in the eleven years they had been married. In a subtle, quiet, distinguished way, Nadia wasn't obvious or showy, like Pascale, who had dazzled him at first, blinded by her beauty and overt sexiness. Nadia was beautiful too, and infinitely smarter.

His success as a novelist had delighted Nadia, and she had been proud of him. He gave her all his manuscripts to read while they were in progress. She gave him helpful suggestions, which he followed most of the time. And now, in his own disarray, he couldn't write a single sentence. He was too upset about both women to think about writing or anything else.

Her own decorating business had flourished, with projects in progress all over Europe. She was trying to keep it all going now and avoided discussing the scandal of his affair with her clients.

It was even more painful since they had talked about having a third baby for the last year or two, but decided they wanted to wait another year or so, hoping they'd be a little less busy. And now Nicolas was having his third child with someone else. It was another blow, which went straight to Nadia's heart.

Their values had always been the same, or she had thought so, although he was more forgiving of his friends' infidelities than she was. She always said it was a disgusting thing to do, and death to a marriage, and she told her women friends the same when they confessed their indiscretions to her. It was the one thing she didn't like about French life, and she was outspoken about it. Now it had happened to her, and she either had to eat her words and tolerate it, or leave him and divorce him, American style. She was torn between her two cultures, and most ravaging of all was how much she loved him and wanted to turn the clock back to before it had happened. She couldn't see how their marriage could ever be the same after this.

"Does everybody know?" Nicolas asked her miserably before he left the apartment. He always made a point of not looking at the tabloids.

"My client in Madrid called last week to tell me how sorry she was to read about it online, and then asked me if we're getting divorced. She assumed we are," Nadia said quietly and he nodded. "My clients in London all read it first, and they were nervous I'd move back to the States."

"And would you?" he asked, panicked.

"I don't know, Nicolas. The *Titanic* has hit the iceberg and I haven't decided what I'm going to do about it." She no longer felt at home in the States and hadn't for years. She was much happier and more comfortable in France, or had been until now. She couldn't imagine going back there to live, and she had a booming business, but Paris had suddenly become an agony for her. Everyone knew about Nicolas's affair, even their grocer and dry cleaner, because Pascale was so famous. It was hard to live with. And she had the same horror as her mother of exposing her personal problems in her professional life. She felt naked to the world now. And he had done that to her. She didn't want to run away, but his bad behavior hung over them like a toxic cloud. He had polluted their marriage, and their life.

He didn't try to kiss her goodbye when he left. He knew better. He said good night. The girls were sleeping by then, and he slipped quietly out of the apartment and went to Pascale's to throw some of his clothes into a bag so he could get to Saint-Tropez. He was living out of suitcases, which he hated, with one foot in each camp.

He thought of Nadia and was sorry to leave her, since he had hoped to spend the weekend with her and the girls, but he was relieved not to have to see his mother-in-law. That was a meeting he wasn't looking forward to. And he knew that whatever she said to him, no matter how harsh, when they finally saw each other again, he deserved it.

For everything he had done and exposed Nadia to, he expected to be punished in the future. All he wanted was not to lose her, if he hadn't already, even if he wasn't worthy of her at the moment, given what he'd done.

What he needed was time, just enough to let things wind down gracefully with Pascale, after the baby came. But he had no idea if Nadia would give him that, or what she still felt for him. And Rose arriving in Paris terrified him. She was like a dark angel flying in to save her daughter, and he was sure she would be urging Nadia to leave and divorce him. He wondered if Nadia was going to listen to her mother and sisters. All he could do now was pray that what they had before would carry them through this disaster.

Her family were his enemies now, no longer his allies. He had lost their allegiance. He had never felt so alone in his life as he took a cab to Orly, thinking about both women. He tried to focus on Pascale and meeting her in Saint-Tropez for the weekend. But all he could think of was the pain in Nadia's eyes whenever he saw her now, and he knew Rose would see it too, and hate him for it. He hoped that Nadia wouldn't give up on him and would resist her mother's pleas, but he had little hope that she would, as the tears slid down his cheeks. And he suddenly dreaded the weekend with Pascale in Saint-Tropez. His marriage was a high price to pay for his brief affair, and their baby. And what chance of happiness would that child have with such a tortuous beginning? He felt guilty for that now too.

Chapter 3

Rose's plane touched down at Charles de Gaulle Airport at eight A.M. After a brief spell in the bathroom on the plane, she emerged as perfectly coiffed as always, with just a hint of makeup, in a fresh crisp white shirt, black slacks, and a black linen blazer. She looked neat as a pin, and as though she had just stepped out of the pages of a magazine, and not flown all night on a plane. She was carrying a large, well-seasoned black alligator Hermès Haut à courroies bag that she always traveled with. Even in the airport, heads turned when she walked by. Between her height, her stark white hair, the way she carried herself, and her innate elegance, it was obvious that she was not just any traveler, with a VIP representative from the airline hurrying to keep up with her. Rose was eager to get to Nadia's apartment and see her daughter.

There was a car and driver waiting for Rose when she got her luggage, and she gave him the address on the Quai Voltaire in her flawless French. She always spoke to her granddaughters in French as well. It was more comfortable for them, since Nadia was fluent and spoke to them in French too. Sylvie and Laure spoke English with a French accent, and managed when they had to.

The ride from the airport took less than an hour early on a Saturday morning, and Rose was pensive as she looked out the window at the familiar landscape. She came to Paris often on business, and was always happy to see Nadia and Nicolas and the children when she did. This time was different. She was here exclusively to support her daughter. Pascale's announcing publicly that she was pregnant had made their current drama that much worse. Pascale and Nicolas were all over the press, and she could only imagine how devastated Nadia was. She wanted to see for herself. She was worried about how noble and decent Nadia was being, and thought her daughter should fight back. And divorce was certainly an option, perhaps even the wisest course, although Rose didn't take divorce lightly.

Sylvie and Laure were having breakfast in their nightgowns when Rose arrived and rang the bell. Nadia buzzed her up, and when Rose got upstairs, Nadia stood looking at her mother for a moment with a smile and tears in her eyes.

"Thank you for coming, Mom," she said in English. Her mother looked as perfect as ever. Nadia's long dark hair was tousled and hanging down her back. She was in a pink cotton nightgown that made her look barely older than her daughters. Rose set down her small suitcase and the alligator bag, hugged Nadia, and followed her into the kitchen where the girls were eating and laughing with each other. They looked up in surprise when they saw their grandmother.

Their mother hadn't told them she was coming, to surprise them, and they leapt out of their seats and ran into her arms. They babbled happily with her for the next half hour, until their mother sent them to their rooms to get dressed and reminded Sylvie to help Laure do up her buttons and tie her shoelaces.

"They look fine," Rose said, studying her daughter's face. She looked tired and thin, with circles under her eyes, predictably.

"They don't know what's going on," Nadia said quietly, and handed her mother another cup of coffee. Rose looked as though she was dressed for a meeting. Nadia was happy to see her.

"What about you? Anything new?" Rose watched her carefully.

"He was here last night. He wanted to spend the weekend with us."

"That must be confusing," Rose said, frowning, wondering if Nadia was still sleeping with him. She hoped not but didn't want to ask. She was respectful of her children's privacy and the sanctity of their relationships, which were none of her business, although Nicolas was proving to be the exception to the rule. His life had become the business of the entire world.

"I didn't let him stay, obviously," Nadia said with a sigh. "He keeps telling me how much he loves me, and that he'll make a graceful exit after she has the baby. Apparently, she considers herself too young for marriage."

"Or too French," Rose said with a disapproving glance, and Nadia laughed. Her mother still had some of her old British prejudices about the French, but she had loved and trusted her son-in-law until recently. "So what *does* she want? She's too young for motherhood too."

"She wants to live with him for as long as it lasts. I'm not planning to stick around for that, for the next few years, while he has two households, with a foot in each, or riding two horses, as the French say."

"Even modern French men don't do that anymore. They have kids and don't marry, but juggling two women is no way to live, especially for you. You deserve better than that."

"I know," she said sadly. "I thought he'd end it with her before it came to this, but the baby changes all that, and I think he's secretly happy about it. He loves kids." Her mother rolled her eyes.

"Please, this isn't about his love of children. It's about his having a sloppy affair, making a spectacle of himself at a highly publicized event, and letting it get out of hand. It's about his wanting to have fun with a hot young girl, not his love of kids. It's feeding his ego, and not much else." Nadia didn't disagree. "And what are you supposed to do in the meantime?" She strongly disapproved of how weak and selfish he was being, like a boy half his age.

"I have no idea," Nadia said. "I keep thinking about what I should do. I want it to have never happened, but it did."

"Have you called a lawyer yet?" Nadia shook her head and didn't want her mother pressuring her about it. Her sister Olivia had called her and insisted she file for divorce immediately, but Nadia didn't feel ready to do that yet, and wasn't sure when she would. It had to be on her timing, not theirs.

"I haven't had time," or the heart to do it. "He comes to see the girls all the time, which is good for them."

"Where is he living?" It sounded confusing to Rose.

"Here, some of the time, in the guest room, and with Pascale the rest of the time. He hasn't moved out yet. I don't think either of us is ready for it. Some of the time I want him to, the rest of the time, I don't. We're doing it this way for the girls, for now."

"Or because you're both too frightened to let go? You're letting him have his cake and eat it too," Rose said pointedly.

"Not really. I'm just not ready to do anything radical yet. This is all very new."

"I'd say having a baby out of wedlock with a twenty-two-year-old actress, and being on the front page of the tabloids is pretty radical, wouldn't you?" Nadia smiled and nodded. Her mother always got right to the point without wasting time.

"Yes, it is. I just want to be sure, before he moves out and we tell the girls we're getting a divorce."

"Can you see yourself taking him back after this?" her mother asked her, shocked. She couldn't imagine it herself, and Nadia shook her head.

"No, I can't. I'll never feel the same about him again. But divorce is a big word, and it lasts forever."

"I thought marriage was supposed to last forever," Rose said primly, more so than she would have at the magazine, where she had to be more modern and open-minded, but this was her family, and she hoped they had the same values she did.

"I thought so too," Nadia said as the girls reappeared in denim shorts, pink T-shirts, and pink sneakers. Sylvie had done Laure's hair in pigtails, and they were sticking out at an odd angle, and Sylvie had forgotten to brush her own, which was a tangled mass of thick blond curls. Laure had dark hair like Nadia's and was the image of her mother. Sylvie looked more like Nicolas, with a hint of her aunt

Olivia, which Nadia noticed occasionally, but Sylvie had a sunnier disposition than her somewhat daunting aunt.

Nadia went to get dressed and do their hair while Rose settled into the guest room with the view of the river below, and a few minutes later, Nadia came to ask her if she wanted to go to the park with them.

"That's what I'm here for," she said as she put on ballet flats and jeans, and a few minutes later, they went for a long walk. They stopped for lunch on the terrace of a café on the Boulevard Saint-Germain on the way back, where Nadia picked at a salad, and Rose and the girls had sandwiches. They walked back to the apartment slowly after that. It had been a relief not to talk about Nicolas while they were out. His name didn't come up again until just before dinnertime, when he called to talk to the girls, and Nadia handed them her cellphone. It was obvious that they were happy to hear from him, and he told them he was doing publicity for his latest book in the South of France.

"Translation: He's in Saint-Tropez with her," Nadia said to her mother as soon as the girls left the room. But she also knew that he had wanted to be with her, and she wouldn't let him because of her mother's visit. Now, the minute he wasn't with one woman, he was with the other. Nadia was beginning to think he should get his own apartment, but she was afraid that if she suggested it, he would move in with Pascale. But maybe he would now anyway, with a baby on the way. Nadia felt as though she couldn't stop the flow of what was happening to them. He had unleashed a tidal wave of reaction and consequences from his foolishness.

Her mother took them to a nearby pizza restaurant the girls loved for dinner. Normally, she would have invited Nadia and Nicolas to the Voltaire farther down the street where they lived. But Nadia didn't feel up to running into anyone at the fashionable restaurant where designers, fashion photographers, socialites, decorators, and their clients hung out, and she usually knew someone at almost every table. And everyone knew Rose. It was more than Nadia wanted to deal with, so hiding at the pizza restaurant was more her style at the moment, and all she could cope with.

Rose told her granddaughters stories about funny things that had happened to the models at fashion shoots, and they both giggled at stories about when tops fell down, and skirts fell off, a lion cub escaped, and about how at a recent shoot of a bridal gown, they let a flock of doves loose and they pooped all over the photographer and the model in the wedding gown. The girls loved the stories their grandmother told them, and although they knew nothing about fashion, they had a sense that their grandmother was special.

"She always looks so nice," Sylvie said sleepily, after they got home and Nadia kissed her good night and tucked her in. Rose went to pour herself a glass of wine. "I love her bracelets." She often wore interesting bangles, and some unusual ethnic ones she had found in exotic places on her travels for the magazine.

"I like her hair," Laure said softly. "It looks like snow." They were fascinated by her hair, which was the whitest they had ever seen. "She's pretty." Nadia smiled at their comments, turned off the light, and went to find her mother. She was sitting on the couch, admiring the view of Paris in the moonlight, and thinking about her daughter, wishing none of this had happened to her.

"Your fan club had a good time with you today," Nadia said gratefully as her mother handed her the glass of white wine she had poured for her. Nadia noticed in spite of herself that it was Chassagne-Montrachet, Nicolas's favorite.

"They're so well behaved and very sweet. Venetia's boys exhaust me, but I have to admit, India always makes me laugh. She's such a funny child. She told me I should paint my office red, when she came to visit me. That way people could see my hair better when I sit in front of a red wall, and I'd look prettier." They both smiled, and Nadia took a sip of the wine and relaxed. It was nice having her mother there to talk to. She hadn't been as militant about Nicolas as Nadia had expected her to be. She was being surprisingly tolerant of their respective confusion, and Nadia admitted herself that the situation was a mess.

"I love it when you get to spend time with them. I wish we lived in the same city." Nadia missed seeing her mother and sisters regularly. Venetia came to Paris several times a year to buy fabrics or see the couture shows. Athena went to Italy more frequently than she came to Paris, although she did visit Paris about once a year. Olivia never came to Europe. When she had time off, she and her family went to their house in Maine, where they all went sailing on a small sailboat they loved. Her husband didn't like coming to Europe, and Olivia never came alone. Nadia was too busy to go to New York very often, except to shop for her clients.

"I don't blame you for living here. If I ever retire, I might spend a year or two in Paris," Rose said dreamily. "I'm usually on such a tight schedule when I come." At sixty-six, there wasn't the vaguest sign of her retiring. She was still moving at full speed, on top of her game, and the heart and soul of *Mode Magazine*. She was feared and revered by everyone in the fashion industry. She could make or break a designer if she wanted to, and enjoyed helping new young talents just starting out, by what she said about them.

"I always wanted to have a marriage just like you and Daddy. You were so good together and so supportive of each other. And you looked like you had fun," Nadia said wistfully. "I thought we were well on our way to that, and then all this happened. I'd like to think we can recover from it, but I'm not sure we can. I don't know if I can ever forgive Nicolas. That's what I'm trying to figure out."

"Some marriages recover from worse things," Rose said gently. "I don't know if yours will or not. Time will tell. And you're right, your father and I did have fun. I knew he was 'the one' the moment we met. We were in love until the end." She smiled, thinking of her late husband. She thought that in Nadia's life, a lot would depend on what Nicolas did now, and if he stayed with Pascale after she had the baby or made a graceful exit as fast as he said he would. "It's not a good situation, but people sometimes forgive some pretty awful stuff. Or not. I'm sorry you have to go through it." Nadia acknowledged what she said with a nod.

"Me too. Seeing you makes me feel human again. Just going out to dinner with you and the girls makes a difference, and feels normal. I'm so tired of talking to Nicolas about it. It's our only subject of conversation now. Sometimes I feel like I'm on a desert island and can't get away from it."

"What are you doing this summer?" her mother asked her.

"I don't know. Everything is up in the air. We always go to the château for July and August. He says I can go without him if I want to. I suppose he'll be with her somewhere if he's not with us. The girls will be upset if he doesn't come. I can always leave for a while and let him be there with the girls. I don't want to be there with him and pretend that nothing happened. It's all so awkward." Rose nodded. It was more than awkward. It was hideous.

Rose had a small house in Southampton, where she spent weekends in the summer. It was a busy time for her. She sometimes came to the château for a few days if she could get away.

"I wish my sisters would come," Nadia said thoughtfully.

"Why don't you ask them?" Rose suggested, and Nadia liked the idea.

"I think I might." Nadia smiled at her. They talked until after midnight and stayed away from the hot topic. Nadia slept peacefully that night. It seemed odd at her age, but she felt safe just having her mother there.

When Nadia woke up in the morning, she found her mother in the kitchen, having breakfast with the girls. She had made French toast for them, which reminded Nadia of her childhood. Her mother used to make French toast or pancakes for them on Sunday mornings.

They went for a long walk along the Seine after breakfast. Rose loved digging through the bookstalls and finding old books in French. Then they went back to the apartment. She was leaving that night to go back to New York. It had been a short visit but a good one, and had given Nadia relief and perspective. She didn't feel so alone now. She knew her mother had to get back to work, and was grateful Rose had made the effort to come for the weekend.

Sylvie and Laure were sorry to see her leave when she said goodbye to them and promised to come back soon. She was just hugging Nadia when they heard a key in the lock, and Nicolas let himself into the apartment. He looked startled to see them standing there, as though he wanted to back out the moment he saw Rose. She stood looking at him with her piercing blue eyes, as though he were an intruder and didn't belong there.

"Oh . . . I thought you'd be gone by now," he said, which only made it worse. He had assumed she'd leave in the morning to get to New York at a decent hour. But she was taking the latest flight she could, not to lose a moment with her daughter.

"I'm taking a late flight," she said coolly. "Were you trying to avoid me?" she asked, and he felt like a truant schoolboy facing the headmaster. He had never found her frightening, as he did now. They'd had some good times together, but he knew that was impossible under the circumstances. He was The Enemy now.

"I didn't want to intrude on you and Nadia. She said you were leaving today. I just came by to say good night to the girls." He had a deep tan, and it was obvious he'd been in the sun all weekend.

"Do you always let yourself in without ringing the bell now?" Rose said coolly, implying that he no longer lived there. The girls had thrown their arms around him as soon as they saw him, and Nadia looked uncomfortable at the exchange. She was afraid of what her mother would say.

"I live here," he said quietly.

"Really?" Rose responded, as though that was a ridiculous answer. "I think that's very generous of your wife." A muscle tightened in his jaw, but he didn't respond to his mother-in-law. Sylvie and Laure gave their grandmother a last hug and bounded off to their room then.

"I'll come back later," Nicolas said directly to his wife, not wanting to engage with her mother, and assuming he'd be welcome.

"I don't think that's a good idea," Nadia said since the girls were out of earshot. He hesitated for a moment, looked at both women and then nodded.

"New rules now that your mother has been here?" he asked, irritated.

"Reality," Nadia answered.

"I'll call you, then," he said tersely, and was about to leave when Rose's clipped British words stopped him.

"I'm disappointed in you, Nicolas. I thought you were a better man than this. All the gutter nonsense, tabloid press, a young starlet. It reads like a trashy novel, while you trample everyone's heart in your path."

He turned to gaze at her full on then. There was no way he could ignore what she had said, or the look in her eyes that went with it.

"I didn't intend for it to happen this way, or at all actually," he said facing her. His tone was honest, not aggressive.

"It didn't 'happen.' You *did* it. You and that girl created this mess, and now everyone is going to pay the price for it, even your children." He had no answer to that, and he knew she was right, which made it worse. "There are going to be casualties. It's inevitable. There already are," she said, glancing at her daughter, who held her breath watching the exchange and hoping it didn't get worse before it ended. But she didn't try to stop it and her mother hadn't said anything that wasn't true. Rose turned to Nadia then, gave her another hug, and ignored her son-in-law, as though he was no longer worthy of her notice. She would have liked to say much harsher things to him but didn't want to do it in front of her daughter. "I'll talk to you tomorrow," she said to Nadia.

"Thank you again for coming, Mom. It was wonderful," she said. Rose picked up her bag and walked past Nicolas with a last wilting look, opened the door, and left, as he stood there for a moment, shaken by her words. The contempt in her eyes had tied his stomach in a knot.

"I'm sorry. I didn't realize she'd still be here. I want to talk to you about the summer."

"Why didn't you call me? She's right. You shouldn't just show up. Are you planning to stay here tonight?" He shook his head. He had thought of it, but he didn't want to now. And Nadia was looking at him differently than she had before her mother had been there. "Maybe it's time for you to get an apartment," Nadia said in a low voice so the girls didn't hear her. She and Nicolas were still standing in the entrance hall, and she didn't seem as though she wanted him to come in.

"You won't be in town. I can stay here if I need to while you're at the château. And I hope to have things worked out, or at least some kind of plan, by the end of the summer." Nadia didn't comment. She didn't want to argue with him. The baby was due in October. And her mother had almost convinced her to see a lawyer, just to get some advice. "I'm not coming to the château for the first two weeks in July. I'm going to visit friends in the South of France. That will give you some time alone with the girls." He said it as though he were doing her a favor, and she could guess where he would be, and with whom. The paparazzi all over the Riviera would out them quickly anyway.

There were no secrets in that part of the world, not for people as recognizable and well known as he and Pascale were. They were everybody's prime prey now, and favorite topic of conversation.

"Why don't we take turns at the château this summer? That makes more sense than our being there together," Nadia said coldly. She felt braver now since her mother's visit. Rose's strength was contagious. It was just what Nadia needed. Before her mother came, she had felt defeated, now she didn't. Her mother was her strongest ally.

"And how will you explain that to Sylvie and Laure?" Nicolas answered.

"That we're taking a break from each other? Or would you rather tell them about Pascale and the baby and make a clean breast of it?" Nadia said tartly.

"You sound just like your mother," he said with an angry expression. "We can think of something to tell them. They don't need to know the whole story yet."

"You'll have to tell them before the baby comes," she said in a whisper, "or the press will do it for you."

"Not if we're back together," he said with a pleading look, which she ignored. Talking to him made her feel crazy. She felt sane now after her mother's visit and didn't want to spoil it.

"Thank you for letting me know about July. I think you'd better go now," she said, and he slowly walked toward the door, and then turned to look at her, still standing there, watching to make sure he left.

"Don't believe everything you read in the papers, Nadia. A lot of it is just garbage."

"They seem to be writing about you pretty accurately these days.

And my mother's right. It's pure trailer trash. You're not writing a novel. This is real life. Our life." He couldn't think of a response so he walked out the door and closed it quietly behind him. As he rode down in the elevator, he felt faintly schizophrenic, but at least he had told her that he wouldn't be at the château in July. He had promised Pascale he'd tell her. He had just rented a house for the summer in Ramatuelle, with Pascale, so she could be there as much as she wanted, and he would join her off and on. It was close to Saint-Tropez, and the paparazzi wouldn't find them there as quickly. They had rented a secluded villa over the weekend, and Pascale was thrilled. It was what she had wanted, and he gave in to her, to appease her, since he hadn't left Nadia yet. He felt relieved when he drove away, but he was still smarting from Rose's words. She hadn't missed her mark and had struck him to the core with every single one. And worse, he knew she was right. She was always smart and fair and honest, and so was her daughter. He realized that Nadia was being very decent under the circumstances, more than he deserved.

Rose called Nadia from the airport before she boarded her flight to New York.

"What was all that about? He shouldn't come in and out like that as if everything is normal and he still lives there, even if he does spend the night occasionally. He doesn't even call you first?" Rose was incensed by Nicolas's behavior, his entitlement and presumptuousness, and how selfish he was being.

"He told me he wasn't coming to the château for the first two weeks in July. He says he's staying with friends in the South. I assume that means Pascale. But it will give me time to think."

"He couldn't send you an email or a text to tell you that? He had to deliver the message in person?" Rose said, annoyed.

"He probably wanted to spend the night. But I told him to go, after you left. It's just too easy for him like this. He probably went right back to her as soon as he walked out the door. When I don't let him stay, it just drives him right back to her."

"Tell him to act like a man and get an apartment," Rose said firmly.

"I just did. This is all new territory for me, Mom. There are no ground rules here."

"Maybe there should be. That's why you need to see a lawyer."

"I will," Nadia said with a sigh. Like it or not, she knew it was time. Her mother was right. Maybe she'd invite her sisters to visit her in July. She wished her mother a good flight and went to check on the girls. They were playing peacefully in their room, and Nadia went to stand on the terrace. She looked down at the river drifting by, with barges and boats full of tourists. The Eiffel Tower was lit and sparkling. It was odd how it all looked the same, but everything in her life had changed in the last month, and she knew that nothing would ever be the same again. She doubted that her heart and her feelings for Nicolas would ever recover.

Chapter 4

Ironically, the first meeting of the day on Monday—when Rose got to her office punctually, although she had gotten home late and only slept a few hours, worried about Nadia—was about Pascale Solon on the September cover. The decision needed to be made of who was going to style it, which meant working with both the photographer and the subject, being involved in the choice of wardrobe, and everything that went with it, including the hair and makeup. The beauty editor would participate too. They were trying to decide if they wanted to go "soft and romantic" or do something more hard-edged and sexier. Pascale's sensual, sometimes punky look lent itself better to the latter.

"No nudity, please," Rose said firmly. "There's enough going on there, we don't need to be blatant about it, nor should she. We're *Mode*. We don't need to see nipple rings or her Brazilian bikini wax. I want her dressed, and to keep this all about fashion, not her sex life," or Rose's son-in-law's, although she didn't say that. They eventually agreed on which designer's clothes she would wear, and the look they decided to go for was contemporary, youthful, gutsy, bold, without ever being offensive or too sexual. Rose made it clear that she wanted to keep the interview above the waterline too: her recent success, her big movie, the next role she was going to play, her goals for her career. "Let's keep it as professional as possible," Rose said with her work face on.

"Obviously, we're going to mention the affair with Nicolas Bateau in the interview. And the baby?" Charity asked her.

"Let's stay off the baby. Things happen. We don't want to have to pull the interview if something goes wrong with the pregnancy. We're not a maternity magazine either. And let's shoot her now before it shows much." She was five months pregnant, tall, thin, and in great shape. They still had a few more weeks before the pregnancy became apparent. "The interviewer can mention Nicolas, but I want it strictly to be in passing, and no lurid details. Don't open that door," Rose said sternly to the staff writer who had been assigned to write the story and who was only a few years older than Pascale. They thought she would easily relate to Pascale. It was not going to be a deep, intellectual piece.

"We're going to interview him with her for part of the article, aren't we?" Charity pressed the point, feigning innocence, and Rose turned her blue X-ray eyes on her.

"No, we are not. I already vetoed that, and you know it. He's not on the cover with her or part of the interview, except in passing, as I said. If he wants an interview about their affair, he can do it for another magazine. We're *not* interested. May I remind you *again,* Charity, he is a *married* man, still living with his wife and young children.

I'm not going to showcase the affair and turn it into a love story. He cheated on his wife and got a young woman pregnant. We've already heard more about it in the tabloids than any of us wants to know. For our purposes, it stops there. I am *not* interviewing him for *Mode*. I won't allow it. Is that clear?" Her voice rose a notch and everyone in the room fell silent, except Charity, who was fuming. She had won the battle to get Pascale on the cover, now she wanted to make it a clean sweep and interview Nicolas too, which would be much more interesting. He was brilliant, and his novels were hugely successful. He would be a better interview subject and together they'd be on fire. But Rose was not budging. She made it clear that mutiny would not be tolerated. She felt perfectly comfortable holding her ground. They had standards to uphold about what they endorsed and what they didn't. Pascale and Nicolas's illicit liaison was well over that line for her, even if Nadia weren't her daughter.

"I don't find stories about cheaters romantic. And I hope you don't either. You can always write it on spec and freelance it elsewhere, but *not* here. I want this interview clean, strong, and about two subjects: her career and her views on fashion. The rest is off limits." Charity knew when she was beaten, and finally retreated and slumped in her chair like an angry schoolgirl who had been reprimanded by the teacher. And Rose had already been pushed to her limits, and would go no further.

Charity was still stewing about it when she went back to her office and asked her assistant for an Advil and a cup of tea.

"Rough meeting?" her new assistant asked and Charity rolled her eyes.

"The boss wants us to stay off any hot topics with Pascale Solon when we shoot her. And I'm not doing the interview, I'm just styling her. Rose wants her lily pure. She's got the wrong girl for that, and the readers don't expect her to be a virgin or act like one. She's having a baby with a married man, for chrissake, and she does full-on frontal nudity in all her films. Rose has her confused with the Virgin Mary." Charity's assistant, Betty, hesitated for a minute before she went to get the Advil and tea. She seemed as though she wanted to say something but wasn't sure if she should.

"Something up?" Charity asked her, sensing that Betty had more to say.

"I . . . not really . . . this is probably really out of line, and I shouldn't say anything." She looked flustered and nervous, not sure if she'd get in trouble. She hadn't worked for Charity for long and didn't know how she'd react or what she'd do with the information. "My mother is a decorator. She does a lot of jobs in Europe for American clients. She knows Rose's daughter, who lives there. She's an interior designer too. Nadia McCarthy."

"Yeah, I think she's married to some French guy," Charity said, her head pounding.

"She's married to Nicolas Bateau," Betty said softly. Betty was twenty-five years old and scared to death. Charity had a temper and was unpredictable and indiscriminate as to who she would unleash it on. She stared across her desk at her assistant in disbelief.

"Holy shit . . . are you serious? No wonder Rose wants us to go easy on the story, and not make him look like a hero and them like Romeo and Juliet. God . . . what a mess." Even in her initial shock, and with a fearsome headache, she couldn't fault Rose for her ultimate decisions. She had agreed to let them have Pascale on the cover, and to the interview as the main feature, but she didn't want Nicolas in it, or to have *Mode* glamorize them either. But Charity realized now how dicey it was for Rose to be making the decisions she had, and how uncomfortable it must have been for her, with her daughter as the injured wife in the story. She remembered then that Rose had just gone to Paris for the weekend. She had assumed it had something to do with work, since that was all Rose ever did. Her whole life centered around the magazine. Charity had never known another editor to work as hard. "Wow, I have to hand it to her for not saying anything. It's going to be tough on her daughter when the story comes out. I wonder if he's divorcing her to marry Pascale."

"It doesn't sound like it from what I've read in the tabloids," Betty said, blushing. She was fascinated by them, and touched by how in love they were, and now a baby. It was her mother who had mentioned Nadia to her, and who felt sorry for her. She said she was a smart, beautiful, talented woman with two little girls. This put a new spin on it for Betty, and even for Charity, as she thought about it.

"Maybe Rose's daughter is divorcing him. Rose never talks about her personal life. She's famous for it. She wins the prize for this one. Let's keep it between us for now," she said, showing more respect for their boss than Betty had expected. Charity was tough, fought for what she believed in, and had a big mouth, but she admired the editor-in-chief and her decisions, now more than ever. "It must have nearly killed her to agree to put Pascale on the cover, as the feature." She had new respect for her. "Make that two Advil," she said to Betty. "And a martini . . . just kidding about the martini," she added so her assistant didn't think she was a lush. The girl was very literal in her interpretations. "I'm happy I'm not writing the interview." The staff writer who had been chosen to do it was known for her bland, upbeat pieces. She was not out to set the world on fire. She had volunteered and Rose had agreed to let her do it. Charity was now sure Rose must have been relieved by that. "Jesus, life is complicated sometimes, isn't it?"

Charity was forty years old, divorced, and felt like she had to fight to stay on top every day. She loved the dog-eat-dog world of fashion, but underneath it, she wasn't out to hurt anyone, just to get the best shoots she could into the magazine and build her reputation. She was looking forward to working with Pascale. It was going to be a lot more interesting and exciting than styling the First Lady, who was almost seventy years old.

Betty brought the Advil and Charity kept the bottle on her desk. She had a lot to think about. It was daunting to realize that even with something as benign as fashion, people could get hurt. She was suddenly glad the final decision to put Pascale on the cover and run an interview with her hadn't been hers.

There were stacks of fabric samples in bright colors and sketches piled high on Venetia's desk, as she dug through the piles frantically, looking for something. She had her mane of red hair pulled up helter-skelter in clips and three pencils stuck through it. She gave a victorious shout when she found what she was looking for. It was a sketch of a sexy black see-through dress for their resort collection. She went running down the hall with it to their head designer, and showed her where she had gone off course from the original design, while the designer explained to her that the fabric hadn't responded the way they expected, and didn't drape the way they thought it would. The way the dress fell was the whole genius of it, and they sat together for almost half an hour, playing with the fabric and altering Venetia's design subtly until it worked.

"You are a master," the young designer said admiringly.

"No, believe me, I've made plenty of mistakes. As long as we make them pre-production, we're fine." She squinted then, and suggested a dusting of tiny black beads and sequins, just enough to make the dress shimmer, which was Venetia's genius. She knew just what to add and where for a surprising effect. It made every one of her evening gowns feel like a party when women put them on, and her daywear was just plain fun. Venetia was wearing jeans with a sexy red sweater and leopard platform shoes when she ran back down the hall to her office. She wore high heels to work every day, just as she always had. Nothing had changed about the way she dressed when she turned forty, or now at forty-one. She dressed like a twenty-year-old, and had the energy and figure for it. She insisted that her designs weren't for young women, they were for everyone, and she knew that there were grandmothers who wore them, and young girls if they could afford them.

She took her hair out of the clips, and let it cascade down her back. She was wearing no makeup and didn't need any, but her perfume was a mysterious warm aroma that she'd had made specially for her in Paris by Serge Lutens. Everything about Venetia was special, appealing, and sensual, and she worked harder than anyone in her company. Her friends and co-workers knew how much she loved her three kids and husband. She wished she could spend more time with them, she was constantly dashing to some school event, and then came back to the office to work until midnight or one A.M. Her husband, Ben, was used to it. He wanted more time with her, but knew how much her work meant to her, and he respected her enormous talent. The business model he had designed for her was working brilliantly. Her brand, Venetia Wade, was a dazzling success and sound as a bell, as her mother said.

Venetia's cellphone rang as soon as she got back to her desk, and she saw at a glance that it was her sister in Paris. She wondered why Nadia was calling, and hoped that some new horrifying story about Nicolas hadn't surfaced. She knew that Nadia had been through the wringer for the past month, and Venetia couldn't imagine how she was getting through it. She and Ben had never had problems, but she realized that they were unusual and very lucky. She swore that sex three times a week was their secret for success, and her sisters couldn't figure out how she managed it, with a company to run, six collections a year to come up with, three children to raise, one of them on the cusp of becoming a teenager, and a husband who needed her attention too.

"I barely have time to brush my teeth and go to yoga class once a month," Olivia had said, and Athena said that she and Joe were lucky to have sex once a month. Nadia had been discreet about her sex life when the sisters had had a couple of glasses of wine and told all at Christmas. Nadia had their mother's reserve, and they sometimes teased her for being prudish, but she still didn't tell them what the others shared and they wanted to know. Now Nicolas was having sex with someone else. They all felt sorry for her.

"Hi, Squirt, what's up?" Venetia addressed her and Nadia laughed.

Nadia was the shortest of her sisters, and she accused them of being giants. They considered Olivia short too and she was several inches taller and a few pounds heavier than Nadia, the "baby."

"I think Mom and Dad ran out of tall genes when they got to you two," Athena would say to Nadia and Olivia when they got together. Athena and Venetia were even taller than their mother, who was six feet.

"I'm trying to organize a sisters' reunion on the Fourth of July weekend," Nadia said, sounding hesitant. It had been their mother's idea, and Nadia was sure they would all be too busy with their mates and children, and Athena with her dogs and Joe. "What are you doing for the fourth?" Nadia asked her. Venetia stared into space and thought about it for a minute.

"We're going to the Hamptons. I guess Ben could handle it without me. We go to our neighbor's for a big barbecue and picnic every year."

"I'm sure you don't want to miss it," Nadia said shyly and Venetia laughed.

"Actually, I do. The boys will argue about which red, white, and blue flag shirt to wear, India always hates the dress I pick out for her, Ben eats ribs and drinks beer all night and passes out the minute we come home. I gain five pounds eating apple pie with ice cream. I think I'd rather come to France and skip it this year. Why? What do you have in mind?"

"Mom suggested a sisters' weekend, and she might come for the last two days, if she can get away. You can stay as long as you want," Nadia said generously.

"I've got to finish the spring line, but we're getting there. A long weekend in Paris wouldn't kill me," Venetia said, considering it.

"I was thinking about doing it at the château, so we can really relax."

"Great idea," Venetia said enthusiastically. She was always up for an adventure, especially with her sisters. She wanted to be there for Nadia in the crisis. "Count me in. I'll tell Ben he'll have to manage without me this year."

"Will he be pissed?"

"No, he's a good sport about those things, and he loves you. I'll tell him you were crying when you called me and begged."

"Don't make me sound pathetic!" Nadia pleaded.

"He has a soft spot for you." Venetia grinned. "What about the others? Can they do it?"

"I called you first. I'm not sure we can keep Olivia off their sailboat for four whole days, but I'll try. And I'm not sure when Athena's show goes off air for the summer."

"Call them, and tell them they have to come."

"I will," Nadia promised, excited that Venetia was coming. The two of them had always been close. Venetia got along with all of them, and they all got along with each other. Although Venetia didn't say it, this was a sister crisis now, and they all wanted to be there for Nadia. It also sounded like a ton of fun to Venetia. She told Ben about it that night and he agreed to be full-on dad for the whole Fourth of July weekend so she could go to France to see Nadia and all her sisters.

"I knew there was a reason why I love you," she said, as he slipped a hand under her sweater, and she locked the door to their bedroom before the kids could interrupt them. She was going to miss her handsome husband for four days, but it would be that much sweeter when she got home. They were just as attracted to each other now as they had been when they got married sixteen years before.

When Nadia called to invite Olivia to Normandy for the Fourth of July weekend, she caught her during a brief break in court proceedings. She was in her chambers reading a document the defense counsel had just submitted. She was concentrating on it when she heard her cellphone vibrate on her desk, glanced at it, and saw that it was Nadia. She answered in a hurry. She didn't want to let Nadia's call go to voicemail in case something new had happened.

"What's the bastard done now?" she said curtly for openers.

"Nothing. Did I get you at a bad time?" Nadia said, daunted by her sister's tone.

"I'm in trial, but it's okay, I've got a few minutes. I'm in chambers by myself. We just called a recess so I could read something." Decorating and interior design seemed so insignificant to Nadia compared to what Olivia did. She was always slightly intimidated by her next oldest sister, who had the most important career of all of them, or at least the most serious.

"You must have everyone in the courtroom trembling," Nadia said, and Olivia laughed. "You just scared the hell out of me."

"I hope so. That's what the state pays me for," and the chance to use her Yale Law School education. Olivia loved being a judge, much more than she had being a lawyer. She had been a family law attorney, worked for the ACLU for two years in her liberal youth, and had done a lot of pro bono work for the courts. And she had progressively become more conservative over time. It had put her on the fast track and she'd become a superior court judge eight months before. She finally felt that she was in the right place doing what she was supposed to, taking tough positions with criminals.

"Can I help you with something?" Olivia asked. She still had to read the document in front of her, but she was relieved to know that nothing more had happened in the current soap opera that was her sister's life. Olivia had told her mother how she felt about it. She wanted Nadia to divorce Nicolas immediately, to teach him a lesson. But if she did, it was going to be a very long-term lesson for them and their children, like forever. Olivia hoped her sister was strong enough to see it through, and not go easy on him.

Olivia had become a firm believer in accountability and harsh sentences. She had been instructing juries accordingly since she'd been on the bench. She felt that society and the individual could only benefit from tougher consequences for their actions, and that was what the victims were due. She felt that way about her younger sister too, and she wanted Nicolas to really hurt for what he was doing to her. She had expressed it clearly to Nadia, their mother, and her other two sisters. Olivia was a force to be reckoned with. She was no pushover. She was very much afraid that Nadia was too forgiving by nature, and still too much in love with Nicolas to see clearly and make him pay a hefty price for his crimes.

"I'll try to make it quick," Nadia said, sounding flustered. She didn't want to deal with another tirade from her sister about how fast she should get divorced. She hadn't come to that place yet, and was still living their situation day-to-day.

"I know you're busy. I'm trying to get all of us together here for the Fourth of July weekend, just the girls, if you can get away. I don't know if you can leave Harley and Will for the holiday weekend, but I wanted to ask. Venetia said she'll make it for the whole four days. Mom is going to try to come over the weekend, but you know how that is. If there's a crisis with a deadline, she won't make it. I haven't called Athena yet." But their oldest sister was more easygoing than the others. If she didn't have to do her show, she was the most likely to come, and Olivia the least. She planned everything, stuck to her schedule as though it was set in stone, and never left her husband and son for a weekend, or a trip. There was a silence at the other end that lasted so long Nadia thought they had been disconnected. "Hello? . . . Hello? . . . Ollie?" She still called her that, even after all the years since they'd grown up.

"I'm here. I'm thinking. We're going to Maine, and Will is bringing a friend. I'm not sure Harley wants to deal with two fourteen-year-old boys all weekend," but her son was very well behaved, and as serious as his parents. There was no teenage rebellion at their house. It wouldn't have been tolerated by either parent. Nadia liked her brother-in-law, but he was extremely straightlaced and sober at sixty, but so was her sister, who was not quite forty yet. Olivia seemed much older than her years in her behavior, not her appearance. She was a beautiful slim blonde, and looked a lot like their mother, in a smaller version. She and Nadia looked as different as night and day, the one dark, the other fair, and they were so close in age and size that people had always mistaken them for fraternal twins.

"I'd love it if you came," Nadia said gently, "but I understand if you can't. It's short notice, but I'll be alone at the château with the girls for the first two weeks in July and it would be so much fun to be the four of us for the Fourth of July weekend, especially now."

"Where's your shit of a husband going to be then?" Olivia asked harshly.

"In the South with friends for a couple of weeks."

"Has he moved out yet?" Olivia always went straight to the heart of the matter, like their mother, but in a much tougher way.

"Half-assedly," Nadia answered. "We're working on it. I told him he needs to get an apartment, that he can't keep bouncing back and forth between the two of us. I think he's afraid that if he moves out, I'll never let him back in, and it really will be over."

"I certainly hope so," Olivia said in a clipped tone. "It *is* over, Naddie. You just have to get used to that idea. And so does he. I'd say her being pregnant clinches that." Nadia knew that that was not necessarily true, but didn't argue the point with her sister, knowing she wouldn't win. Her sister was as American as the flag, and there were no compromises or turning back with her. As far as she was concerned, they were done. Nadia wasn't quite as sure. She thought it was over, but what if their marriage could be salvaged? It was a living, breathing entity to her, and she wasn't ready to euthanize it yet, even if part of her agreed with her sister and thought she should. Another part of her didn't. Her hope for their marriage was dwindling daily, but the ashes weren't cold yet.

"I'll talk to Harley and Will and see how they feel about it. Can I call you tonight?"

"Of course. I'd love it if you'd come," she said again.

"I'd better get back to work," Olivia said. "I'd love to see you," she said, sounding gentler. "Harley's in a regatta that weekend, I don't know how badly he wants me there. But at least he'll be busy." They hung up a minute later, and Olivia turned her attention to the document on her desk, thinking about Nadia in Paris, and how nice it would be to spend four days with her sisters. They didn't do it often enough, and Nadia's marital disaster gave them an excuse. Olivia was tempted to do it, if her husband didn't object.

Nadia called Athena right after she'd spoken to Olivia. It was still early in California, and Athena had just come off the air. Most of the time, she was preparing food on camera live, usually with perfect results, but now and then it turned out badly. When it did, she would show her viewers how to salvage a dish that had gone wrong. She was creative and funny, and people loved her show. The sales of her vegetarian and vegan cookbooks had gone through the roof since she'd had the show. She was now considered the guru of vegetarian cuisine. Occasionally, she taped the show, but rarely. People loved the fact that it was live. Athena had a strong, happy personality that was like a warm embrace. She sounded delighted the moment she heard her sister's voice.

"How's my baby sister?" she asked, and always sounded as though she really cared and would drop everything to hear Nadia's victories and woes. "Are things any better?" It didn't seem like it from what she'd seen in the press. Normally, the American tabloids didn't care much about foreign stars, but the movie had been such a massive box office hit in the U.S., and the romance between Nicolas and Pascale so titillating, that even the American public was eating it up. Athena was never sure how much of what she read was true. "Is it calming down? How are you, baby?"

"I'm okay. Hanging in. Trying to keep it together. The girls don't know yet, and I'm trying to keep it that way as long as I can. Nicolas comes home for dinner a couple of times a week, and has been spending a night or two here, so they don't figure out he's gone. I tell them he left for work early when he's not there when they get up."

"That can't be easy for you," Athena said gently.

"It's not."

"Are you filing for divorce?"

"Not yet. We'll probably get there eventually. I just don't want to move too quickly and regret it later." It was a sensible position, which was how Nadia did things, in order, with care and caution, and attention to detail. She wasn't given to fast, flighty decisions, which Athena was at times, but somehow her impulses always turned out well. Nadia preferred to move more slowly.

"I'm sure you've heard Olivia's opinions on the subject," Athena said.

"Yeah, the electric chair or the gas chamber. Or a public hanging," Nadia said, and her sister laughed.

"I kind of agreed with her when I heard about it. But that's not real life. People do some really fucked-up things sometimes, even if they love each other. It's really about what the two of you want, and how you feel about it. Personally, I'd probably chop Joe's fingers off, or other parts of him. But who knows? You don't know what you'd do until you're in that position. You're smart to take your time to think about it. Mom always said that good decisions are never made in haste. I kind of think she's right. That's probably why Joe and I have never married after thirteen years together. That looks way too scary to me."

Since Athena had always been sure that she didn't want children, she felt no pressure to marry, and still didn't. At forty-three, she was perfectly content as she was, and so was he. She said she liked other people's children, but didn't want her own, and insisted that her dogs suited her much better. She had six, and it was chaotic in her home. Stanley, the largest, was an enormous white mountain dog of some kind that looked like a crossbreed with a horse, stood as tall as a man, and weighed two hundred pounds. In addition, she had a black Lab, an English bulldog, some kind of dog that looked more like a teddy bear—which she said was some kind of golden doodle, part poodle and part golden retriever, and tried to sit on everyone's lap—and two tiny teacup Chihuahuas, who slept in the arms of the mountain dog and liked to ride around on the doodle's back. Her partner, Joe, successful restaurateur and master chef, put up with all of it and thought that everything Athena did was charming. She was as blond and fair as Olivia, and as their mother had been before her hair turned white. She had a large frame and generous, womanly body.

"I think you're brave to have ever gotten married," Athena said with a sigh. "Braver than I am. Joe and I think it would ruin everything. I feel that not making it legal keeps things fresh. We never commingle money, and the only thing we'd have to fight about if we split up is custody of the dogs." Nadia knew that Joe still had his small house in West Hollywood, where he had lived before he met Athena, but never used it. He used it for storage now. Athena owned the house they lived in, in the Hollywood Hills, with a huge yard for the dogs, and an enormous swimming pool. She called it their Beverly Hillbillies shack. It was full of vintage furniture from the fifties, which was casual, and great looking, and cost a fortune. Her favorite piece was a pink velvet Barbie doll couch that even Nadia thought was amusing and perfect for Athena, Venetia swore she was going to steal it one day, and Ben hoped not. They each had their own style.

"What are you going to do with the girls this summer, with all this crap going on?" Athena asked her. "You can come and stay with us, if you want to get away and hide out. I'd love it."

"Actually, that's why I'm calling. I'm trying to organize a girls' weekend over the Fourth of July at the château. Venetia's in, Olivia is thinking about it, and Mom said she'd try to come for two days, if she can. I'd love for you to come for the long weekend. You can stay as long as you want. It would be nice to be together." Nadia was hungry for time with her family. She needed them more than ever before. Her life had never gone as wrong as it was right now. And being with her sisters was the best medicine there was. "Mom suggested it originally, and I think it's a great idea for all of us to get together at the château. Is your show still on the air then?"

"Actually, we go on hiatus a few days before. I don't know what Joe has planned. He's all wrapped up in looking at a space in Malibu. He wants to open something there. I love the idea of coming to see you in France. Let me check in with him. I'll call you back tomorrow." They functioned as a team after thirteen years together, and were considerate of each other. "He's so busy these days, he won't even notice I'm gone," Athena added. They had a flock of dog sitters and walkers and a housekeeper who could take care of their animals in her absence. Joe insisted on that so they weren't constantly running home to feed and walk them.

Their life ran surprisingly smoothly, despite Athena's haphazard casual nature and disorganized style. She was more efficient than she appeared. She just didn't want to end up like their mother, with nothing in her life but work. All four girls thought Rose paid a high price for it, and worked too hard, especially now, with their father gone. But it was what Rose wanted, and their father had respected her dedicated work ethic. It was only since the kids had grown up and his death that she had eliminated almost everything except the magazine in her life. It filled the void that he had left, so she was happy.

Nadia and Athena talked for a few more minutes, and Athena promised her an answer about July fourth the next day. Nadia was in good spirits thinking about spending four days with them, and hoped that all or most of them could make it. She didn't mention it to Sylvie and Laure at dinner, in case it didn't work out, so she wouldn't disappoint them. They loved their aunts, and their cousins, although Nadia hadn't invited her niece and nephews. It would be easier without them, to just make it a sisters' weekend. They could focus on each other, and talk more freely, when her own children were busy or in the pool at the château. There was lots for them to do there, and the two little girls played well with each other. They noticed their mother's good mood at dinner and were relieved to see it. She had seemed very quiet and sad lately, and Sylvie particularly was concerned about it. It was hard to hide her sorrow from them, although she tried.

Nadia heard from Olivia first, much to her surprise. She and Harley had discussed it over dinner after Nadia's call, and had included Will in the conversation, as they did with all things. It was easier for them having only one child, due to their demanding careers, and they included him in everything and had treated him as an adult since he was old enough to talk. By fourteen, he was used to participating in decisions. Both Will and Harley agreed that they could manage without her for the long weekend. Harley knew how worried she was about her sister, and it was a sacrifice he was willing to make. Since Will was bringing a friend up to their house in Maine, it was fine with him. Although he loved his parents, he was trying to get a little distance from them lately. His father was older than his friends' fathers, and his mother had been even busier since she'd been on the bench. He wanted to hang out with his friends, without being with his parents all the time.

She sent Nadia a text that night, which Nadia found when she woke up in the morning. "Count me in. Arriving Thursday morning, leaving Sunday night. Sisters rule! Love, O."

Athena called Nadia in the morning, which was midnight for Athena in California. She and Joe had discussed it when he came home from the restaurant. He had agreed in four seconds flat.

"Of course. You know I love your sister. She needs you guys right now. You should go. I'm going to work that weekend anyway. We're shorthanded in the kitchen at the restaurant." He was a hands-on owner, and pitched in to help in the kitchen whenever needed. He enjoyed it.

"So I'm in," Athena said, sounding delighted. At her end, Nadia was beaming.

"I can't wait to see you all," Nadia said, relieved. "Wait till I tell the girls!" It was the best thing that had happened to her since the bomb that had exploded in her life after the Cannes Film Festival. She couldn't think of anything better than four days with her sisters. For the first time in a month, she left for work with a smile on her face and a spring in her step. She could hardly wait for the Fourth of July weekend, and she was grateful for their willingness to leave their respective partners and children. She laughed out loud as she drove to the office, knowing that Nicolas would be panicked if he knew about it, because Nadia and her sisters were a force to be reckoned with. If their mother showed up for the weekend, even more so. Watch out, Nicolas Bateau! The McCarthy women were coming! And anything could happen after that.

Chapter 5

Venetia kissed Ben and her children before she left for work on Wednesday. Ben was going to drive them out to Southampton before lunch. Venetia was planning to leave for the airport straight from the office. She was hoping to beat the holiday traffic to Long Island, and catch a flight that would land her in Paris at six A.M. on Thursday. She had a car and driver set to meet her in Paris and drive her on the two-hour trip to the château. By the time she got her luggage and made it to Normandy, she figured she'd be there in time for breakfast. She had tried to pair up with Olivia, who was flying that day too, but Olivia had canceled her court calendar for that afternoon and was taking an earlier flight. Nadia had already gotten to the château two days earlier to get everything ready for her sisters, and the day before they were to arrive, Sylvie and Laure had helped her cut flowers in the garden and put them in their rooms. Athena was planning to arrive at noon, since the L.A. flight arrived later than the ones from New York. It was a ten-hour flight from L.A., as opposed to six from JFK.

"Don't go falling in love with some handsome Frenchman on the flight," Ben whispered to Venetia when he kissed her goodbye. They lingered for a moment, while the children went upstairs to pack their tote bags with favorite toys and treasures to take with them to the Hamptons for the weekend. They were sorry their mother wasn't coming, but Venetia had suggested that maybe they could all go to visit Nadia and the girls for a week in August.

"You're the best-looking, sexiest man I know," Venetia answered as he held her, and she meant it. She was even more in love with him than she had been when they got married. It was a relationship that worked well. They enjoyed doing the same things, liked similar people, and respected each other profoundly. And they were crazy about their kids. "Thank you for letting me go."

He knew how worried she'd been about her sister, and he was planning to have fun with the children at various activities and friends' picnics over the holiday weekend. He loved Nadia too, and was sorry she was going through such a hard time. He had no idea what had gotten into Nicolas. He liked his brother-in-law. They always enjoyed being together, and Ben thought that Nicolas genuinely loved his wife. Ben had never expected him to pull something like this. He'd seen the photos of Pascale in the press, and she was undeniably spectacular looking and very young, but beyond the physical, he couldn't see the attraction. What was he going to do with a twenty-two-year-old actress and a baby, other than destroy his marriage?

"I'll call you when I get to the château," Venetia promised, and rushed out of the house with her suitcase, and a giant white alligator Birkin with clothes to change into on the plane, work she needed to read, and all the little odds and ends she hadn't put in her suitcase. She was wearing white jeans and a T-shirt with a white denim jacket and white ballet flats.

She worked at a frantic pace till lunchtime, and at two o'clock she left her office after signing a bunch of orders and checks in haste, then left for the airport in plenty of time to catch her flight. She was traveling first class, as she always did. She settled into her seat when she boarded and finally relaxed. She texted Nadia when she sat down, "On the plane. Can't wait to see you. Love, V." Olivia was in the air by then, and she knew that Athena would be boarding shortly in L.A., after leaving Joe and their dog walkers a thousand instructions for the special needs of her pets.

Venetia texted her mother too, Rose was still promising to try and come on Friday night, and arrive on Saturday.

Everything was in place for an all-girl family weekend. They had nothing special planned. It wasn't a holiday in France. Nicolas had called the girls and told them he was in Saint-Tropez for the weekend. Nadia tried not to think about it. She didn't want anything to spoil her weekend with her sisters. It had been years since they'd had a girls' weekend like this. It had taken a crisis to inspire her to organize it and make it happen.

Venetia's flight was uneventful, and she had a text from Olivia when they landed, telling her that she had just arrived at the château and they were having breakfast on the terrace in the beautiful weather. The car picked Venetia up on schedule. She had gotten her bag quickly, so there was no delay getting on the road.

Olivia was lying on a lounge chair, sunning herself, when Venetia arrived, and Nadia was in the kitchen, talking to the housekeeper about lunch. Venetia could see her nieces playing with a ball in the distance on the lawn. It was a beautiful old property, which Nicolas took great pride in when his parents left it to him, and he and Nadia had restored and renovated it. Nadia loved it too, and they spent frequent weekends and summers there. It had been in his family for generations. There were well-manicured gardens and well-tended orchards of fruit trees surrounding it. Nicolas and Nadia put in the pool, which everyone loved. It was a wonderful place, and Nadia was trying not to think about the possibility that it might be her last summer there, if they got divorced. It already felt different to her. She felt a little like a guest, but she was grateful that Nicolas was still letting her use it, since they weren't officially separated. It hadn't been tainted yet, since Pascale had never been there. Nicolas had promised that to her. As it was a family property, which he had inherited, Nadia had no shared ownership of it. It belonged entirely to him, and would belong to their daughters one day.

Nadia saw Venetia chatting with Olivia when she came back to the terrace. Venetia was sitting on the end of the lounge chair and jumped up to hug her sister.

"I always forget how beautiful this place is until I see it again." Nadia nodded and hugged her sister.

"How was your flight?" she asked Venetia, as the two girls bounded up to the terrace to see their aunt. They were wearing matching pink shorts and T-shirts, and they looked adorable. They kissed Venetia and then ran off again, Laure tugging at Sylvie's shirt as they went back to the garden. She looked puzzled when she whispered to her sister.

"Why did all our aunts come and not bring our cousins?" They'd never done that before, and Laure had sensed that she shouldn't ask her mother. There seemed to be a lot of secrets these days. Their mother stopped talking on the phone now when they came into the room.

Sylvie measured her words carefully before she answered. "I think Mama and Papa are a little mad at each other, and the aunts came to tell her how not to be mad at him anymore." She had sensed the tension between her parents more than her younger sister had.

"Why is she mad at him? Do you know?" Sylvie shook her head. She'd been trying to figure that out herself.

"My friend Marie-Claire asked me if they're getting divorced, and I said no. People only get divorced if they hate each other, and they're not that mad, they still talk a lot. But Mama is mad at him about something. I think that's why he's in Saint-Tropez a lot these days."

"I thought he was there to write," Laure said pensively, as they sat down on a log to discuss it. They were far down the garden, where the grown-ups couldn't hear them.

"I think he's there to see friends, and until Mama stops being mad. I hope it's soon. I miss him. He's been out a lot lately, and he said he's not coming to the château for two weeks." Laure considered the answer and nodded. It sounded complicated to her.

"I'm glad our aunts came. But I wish they'd brought our cousins. It would be more fun," Laure said wistfully.

"Mama said they might come back in August, with the kids."

"With Papa too?" Laure asked, with huge eyes.

"I don't know," Sylvie said. Most of what she knew she had overheard. Her mother was sharing very little with her these days. But she did know that her mother was angry at her father. She had heard her say it several times to their aunts, and their grandmother. "Grandmama might come this weekend too," Sylvie added, and Laure's eyes grew even bigger.

"Then Mama must be very, very mad at Papa, if it takes so many of them to make her not mad." Sylvie nodded and had nothing more to say.

But they could both see that their mother looked happy when their aunt Athena arrived before lunch. They were all sitting on the terrace of the château, talking and laughing. Their mother poured wine for her sisters and helped herself to a glass. They were all wearing shorts, except Athena, who was wearing a big white dress to cover her size. Laure thought she was pretty anyway. She had a beautiful face and laughed a lot. Laure was disappointed to see that she hadn't brought any of her dogs, not even the two tiny ones, which sometimes traveled with her. She said they hadn't come this time because she wasn't staying long, and it was too big a trip for them.

They had lunch in an outdoor dining room they used in the summer, next to the pool, and after lunch they all went swimming. Then the grown-ups went for a walk, and the housekeeper kept an eye on Sylvie and Laure at a table near the pool.

"Do you think they're talking about how mad she is at Papa?" Laure whispered to Sylvie, as she scribbled in a coloring book, and Sylvie shrugged.

"Don't tell Mama I told you that, or she'll get mad at me," Sylvie told her, wishing that she hadn't, but she knew that Laure was worried too. Their father seemed to be away a lot these days. He never did that except when he was helping to make a movie of one of his books, and he wasn't doing that at the moment. He said he was going to start another book, but he never went anywhere and hardly left the house once he did, so they knew he wasn't writing.

"The girls seem to be doing okay," Venetia commented as the four sisters walked down one of the tree-lined paths on the grounds. There were tall shade trees overhead. The women were relaxed after their lunch and a swim afterwards.

"I think they feel that something is off, they just don't know what it is," Nadia said quietly. "Nicolas is gone most of the time now. I think Sylvie suspects something."

"He should be gone all the time," Olivia said through pursed lips. "He should move out."

"That's a big statement to the kids," Venetia said cautiously. "I think you're right to take it in stages," she said moderately.

"Why? Why drag it out?" Olivia countered, then turned to Nadia. "He's involved with another woman, they're having a baby. He doesn't belong in your home anymore."

"Maybe not for me. But he's still their father. It's going to be a huge change for the girls when he moves out. Laure is only seven, and they worship him. And no matter what he's done now, he's still a wonderful father."

"They'll have to get used to it." Olivia wouldn't temper her position. "They're old enough to understand. They must have friends with divorced parents, even in France."

"I want to make this as easy as I can for them," Nadia said, and Olivia looked at her sharply.

"For them, or for yourself? Are you just trying to leave the door open so he can come back if he breaks up with the girl?"

"He hasn't even left yet," Nadia said quietly.

"That's my point. You should have thrown his ass out after Cannes. What are you waiting for, Nadia? She's having a baby, and it sounds like he's almost living with her."

"I'm just not ready to take such huge steps. I need time to get used to this too."

"Do you want him back?" Athena interrupted both of them. It was probably the most important question of all.

"I haven't decided. He did a stupid thing once years ago. It was just a one-night stand. I was pregnant. I didn't want to end our marriage, and he felt terrible about it. I stayed and he never did it again. This is different. He's up to his neck in it. At first I just thought it was a horrible indiscretion, a moment of madness, and we could recover from it. I'm not so sure of that now. In fact, I'm sure we can't. The whole world knows about it. The baby will tie him to Pascale forever, even if they don't stay together. And even after spending half my life here, I don't think I'm French enough to live with this and pick up where we left off. It's just not possible. I loved him so much. Now I'm not sure what I think, or how I feel. It's like there's too much noise in my head to know what I want."

"You can't love a man who has made a laughingstock of you," Olivia said coldly. "That's pathetic. You should hate him by now."

"I don't," Nadia said honestly. She was a gentle soul, and not given to extreme reactions like her sister.

"I'd leave Harley in a hot minute if he cheated on me." They could see she meant it. Olivia took no shit from anyone. She was a rigid, uncompromising person, even in matters of the heart. She was a colder person than her younger sister.

"I'm not sure what I'd do," Venetia said thoughtfully, as they turned back on the path and headed toward the château. Of all of them, she seemed to have the best marriage, although Nicolas and Nadia had seemed close to it. "I love Ben so much, it would break my heart. I'm not sure I'd go so far as to divorce him, maybe for the kids' sake, but I don't think I'd ever feel the same about him again." She was trying to imagine herself in Nadia's shoes, and had a hard time doing it. At the thought of it, a shiver ran down her spine. She hoped Ben would never cheat on her, and, in spite of all her exuberance and joie de vivre, she thought it would kill her and she'd go dead inside. The idea of losing the life and man she loved was unbearable, just as it was for Nadia now. Nadia still felt dazed and numb. She felt as though she'd been underwater since the Festival in Cannes. "What would you do?" Nadia asked Athena, who had just picked a wild-flower from the side of the path and was twirling it in her hand.

"That's what my carving knives are for. That's why I always keep them with me." She had a professional set in a fancy case that was her prize possession. Her sisters laughed at her response, and then she grew serious.

"I honestly don't know what I'd do if Joe cheated on me and knocked someone up. We're not married, but we might as well be. He's not just my lover, he's my best friend. We're partners in every-thing we do, we give each other advice. We insist that we're separate people because we're not married, but I'm not sure that's true. We're so much in harmony with each other, sometimes we say the same thing at the same time, or come to the same conclusion about a project. Sometimes we even show up dressed alike, which is really weird. We love the same food, same people. It all works. I think if I found out he was cheating on me, it would destroy me. And the bitch of it is I love Nicolas. He's part of our family now. I'd love to sit down with him and ask him what the fuck he's doing. It sounds like he went nuts for a minute, and now he's stuck with the massive consequences of it."

"He feels terrible about it," Nadia said, grateful for Athena's more temperate point of view.

"He should have thought of that before he got into bed with her," Olivia said harshly. Her brief time as a judge hadn't made her any softer. In fact, she had gotten noticeably tougher since she'd been on the bench. Harley was a hardline guy too. He was older and politically conservative. Nadia didn't know what Olivia's excuse was. She definitely made her younger sister feel like a total failure because she wasn't being harder on Nicolas and didn't feel ready to rush into a divorce. Nadia had never been an indecisive person, but this was the biggest decision she had ever had to face, and she wanted to do the right thing for herself and her daughters. Their mother was leaning more in Olivia's direction, Nadia knew, although Rose was more compassionate for all concerned.

The three visitors went to their rooms to relax before dinner, since they were from different time zones and had only arrived that morning. Nadia went for a last swim with her girls, and had fun playing with them in the pool. They were just getting out of the pool when Nadia's cellphone rang. It was Nicolas, asking to talk to Sylvie and

Laure. He tried to talk to Nadia for a minute, but she handed the phone to Sylvie quickly, and walked away while they talked to their father. She was thinking of everything her sisters had said on their walk that afternoon.

They had dinner at the château that night, cooked by Athena, who made some delicious dishes all with vegetables. She even made a pizza for the girls with a crust made of cauliflower. Nadia roasted two chickens to add to the meal. She set a pretty table, with small vases of flowers that Sylvie and Laure had gathered for her. Before dinner, they watched the sunset from the terrace and shared a bottle of excellent Chateau Margaux from Nicolas's wine cellar.

"We'll go to the beach tomorrow," Nadia promised, looking around at her sisters. It felt so good to be together, and however different their lives, their lifestyles, and their opinions, there was a bond that kept them close. They were bound by blood and history, their love for each other and their parents. She realized now how much all of that mattered. Their parents' strong, loving marriage between two kind, intelligent, honorable people had served as a role model for them. Each of them had close, loving marriages and relationships, even Athena without the benefit of paperwork, which seemed insignificant to her. Nicolas's parents had had a long marriage, but he had admitted to Nadia that early disappointments in their union and differences between them had led his father to have several mistresses and many affairs. His mother had turned a blind eye to it, as French women of their generation did, but she had never forgiven him for it. A chilly, polite, well-bred upper-class bitterness had set in. Nicolas said that he could always feel it when he was with them, and his mother hadn't been a happy woman. Now he had created the same scenario, and provided an insurmountable obstacle for them that Nadia didn't feel able to overcome.

"Papa said he misses us," Laure had said when she handed her mother the phone after talking to her father.

"That's nice," Nadia said, forcing herself not to think about him, or who he was with. She didn't want to spoil her four days with her sisters by thinking too much about him.

Their first dinner together turned out to be a festive affair, with Venetia reminding them of some of their most outrageous adventures as young girls. Athena sneaking out of the house to go to parties their parents wouldn't give her permission to attend, so she took matters into her own hands, Venetia getting drunk at senior prom, and the others helping to get her into the house, and running smack into their father in the kitchen at three A.M. He had carried her upstairs and put her to bed. Olivia had accidentally started a fire in her bedroom once, while hiding an ashtray with a cigarette in it under her sheets, and then forgetting it. Nadia dyed her hair blue. They talked about their good and bad boyfriends, their best friends at school, the parties they went to, and the ones they gave when their parents went away for a weekend and left them in the care of their trusted housekeeper, who let them get away with murder and was deaf anyway. They hadn't done anything truly terrible, but had gotten up to plenty of mischief, and were partners in crime.

Things had begun to change when Nadia decided to stay in Paris after junior year. Olivia went to law school then, Venetia had gone to Parsons to study design, got married, and pregnant almost immediately, and Athena moved to L.A. after dropping out of Connecticut College. It had been the slow unraveling of their tight-knit group.

They were known everywhere in school and among their friends as the McCarthy Girls, a united front, the four musketeers. Wherever you found one, you rapidly noticed the others. There had been strength in numbers, and joy and fun, and unforgettable adventures. And even now, whenever they were together, there was that same feeling of allegiance and unity, of being allies and knowing that the others would always be there for them. Their mother had called them the four-headed monster whenever they banded together against her. Later, she admitted that they were a force to be reckoned with. There had always been honor codes between them. They never dated the same boys or stole men from each other. They never betrayed each other's secrets. They never squealed to their parents, or got each other in trouble in school or at home. There had been plenty of papers for school that one of the others had written for them. Olivia had gotten the best English and history grades in high school, Athena had math and science nailed. Venetia was the most creative, and Nadia and Olivia got the best overall grades. If there was a stray dog in the neighborhood, it came home with Athena. She was still doing it. She told Sylvie and Laure all about her latest rescue dogs over dinner, and showed them pictures of the two tiny Chihuahuas, Chiquita and Juanita, riding on the back of Stanley, the mountain dog. The Chihuahuas were wearing little sparkling tutus and looked like dancers on horseback in the circus, which the girls loved.

The girls were sorry that their aunt Venetia hadn't brought her children with her. They always had a wild time with them, playing tag and hide-and-seek and running around outside. Olivia's son acted like the elder statesman in the group, and was very circumspect. He was the same age as Venetia's oldest son, Jack, who climbed trees and gave the younger ones piggyback rides, while Will, Olivia's boy, would sit quietly and read a book. Venetia's second son, Seth, and Will played chess sometimes, but her children preferred more athletic pursuits and contact sports, which Will didn't indulge in. Just as the sisters were different from each other, their children reflected it, and the personalities of the next generation were just as varied. India, Venetia's youngest, had the face of an angel, and took charge and ran them ragged wherever she was. She had her mother's spirit, and her father's irresistible charm. They all agreed that she would be a heartbreaker one day. Sophie and Laure were sweet, well-behaved little girls. And now there would be another child outside the circle, Nadia thought, Nicolas's child with Pascale. She assumed that Sylvie and Laure would be spending time with him or her in the future, and they would be half sisters to a child none of their cousins would be related to or resemble. Until now, there was a family look among all of them. To some degree, they all looked like siblings, and there was a link between each of them, however slight.

Nadia quietly went upstairs to put the girls to bed while the others were drinking coffee. When she returned, they poured themselves more wine. They exchanged more memories, and then Athena asked Olivia how she liked being on the bench.

"I love it!" she said as her face lit up. "I've been jealous of Harley for years. I like it way better than just practicing law. It's so three-dimensional, and I feel like I'm making a difference. It's been really exciting." They knew that Venetia was passionate about her job in fashion, and Athena had fun with her TV show and loved cooking, and Nadia had always loved her interior design work. She had important clients all over Europe, and had done two big apartments in

New York and a spectacular vacation home in the Dominican Republic for one of her French clients recently, before the storm hit.

Each of them had been lucky to find their chosen path early on, just as their mother had. Their father had had a distinguished career in investments and was respected in the financial community. Everyone knew and liked Wallace McCarthy. But none of the girls was drawn to the world of finance. He was the perfect balance to Rose, serious and grounded while she was creative. He had been a devoted father, interested in each of them, encouraging them at the start of their careers. He had died young, four years before, at seventy-two. Orphaned while he was in college, he made his family all-important to him once he married Rose and the girls were born. He was ten years older than their mother, and although old-school and traditional, he wasn't stuffy. He had liked Ben and Nicolas immensely, and eventually got used to Joe and saw his merits, although he was somewhat unorthodox and informal, by their father's standards. He had always worried that Harley was too old for Olivia, particularly since they married when Olivia was still in law school, and Harley was in his forties. Harley was closer to her parents' age than to hers, but the marriage had proven solid, and her father had finally given up his objections, and had a good relationship with Harley. As Rose pointed out to her husband, his concerns about his daughters' choices of men wouldn't change anything anyway. Olivia had always been headstrong and did what she wanted fearlessly. In Harley's case, her instincts had been right. She was still happy with him fifteen years later, more now than ever.

The girls had lived well growing up on the Upper East Side of New York in a brownstone their parents had bought before it cost a fortune to buy one. They didn't live lavishly, but they were more than comfortable and had everything they wanted, went to private schools and the best colleges. They had all gone to Spence, a fancy venerable private girls' school. Venetia had made her debut, after Athena had refused to. Venetia only did it so she could wear a fabulous white dress and have a Cinderella night at the cotillion. Olivia had objected to the whole concept, politically, at eighteen, and refused. Nadia had made her debut because she knew her parents wanted her to. She knew how much it meant to them, which hadn't concerned Athena and Olivia.

Nadia hated disappointing her parents, and tried hard not to. She was the most traditional of all of them. Olivia was extremely liberal politically in her teens, and was influential in women's causes, but grew increasingly conservative with age, and under Harley's influence. Athena had no politics, except where it affected dogs, and animal testing of any kind, and she was against capital punishment. Olivia was in favor of it now. Venetia got the news of the world filtered through the eyes of *Women's Wear Daily,* the influential online trade publication of the fashion world, and the rest she read in *Vogue* and *The Business of Fashion*, also online. Nadia liked to read *The New York Times, Le Figaro,* and *The Wall Street Journal* when she had time to stay abreast of the news in the States. That way, she could talk intelligently with her clients and knew what was going on. Athena wrote articles for culinary magazines, and the readers loved them. She'd had a Q&A column for years in *Gourmet* magazine, but now wrote a blog on her website instead, and she posted beautiful photographs of food on her Instagram every day. They were happy, secure, stable women, who were each on the right path for them.

And they had made good choices as adults, about their men, their careers, and their lives.

"I don't know how you have time for that," Olivia had commented to Athena while she was cutting and chopping things for their dinner that night. She was preparing tiny, delicate *fraises des bois* for dessert, with *crème fraîche,* which looked irresistible, and she photographed them for Instagram.

"Social media is so time-consuming," Nadia complained to her.

"It's an essential tool for communication today," Athena said, and Venetia nodded. She and Athena followed each other's Instagrams. Nadia did less of it. It wasn't quite as popular in France, although she had gotten clients both as a result of her work being photographed frequently in decorating magazines and from her website, which was stylish and well done. Nicolas had helped her with it. He was much more familiar with social media and the internet than she was.

They all went to bed early that night, and were looking forward to a day at the beach the next day. They were up bright and early, and arrived at the kitchen at the same time to make breakfast. Nadia had already fed the girls, who went back upstairs to dress while their aunts sat around eating croissants Athena had made, drinking coffee, and laughing. And then they all got ready to go to the beach.

They felt like kids themselves swimming and playing with their nieces all day. And they had dinner at a fish restaurant in Trouville that night before coming back to the château. They ate bouillabaisse, sea urchins, and other local delicacies from the sea, and were happy and relaxed on the way home.

They got home at eleven o'clock, as Nadia glanced at her watch. Sylvie and Laure went straight up to bed. "Mom must be on the plane by now," Nadia said as she followed her sisters up the stairs. It had been a perfect day, and she hated to think their weekend was already half over. It restored her soul just being with them, and made her feel young and carefree again. They had all talked to their respective partners that day. Ben had taken the children to two barbecues and a picnic for the Fourth of July, and Harley and Will had placed third in the regatta, which was honorable. Joe had dutifully reported that the dogs were doing well.

Nadia knew that the dynamic would change slightly the next day, once their mother was there. Rose was such a powerful, driving force. Even without Rose saying anything, there would be just a little less room for each of them. She didn't mean to take over, and knew how not to overwhelm them, but they were each influenced by her and still wanted to please her. They cared about what she thought, and wanted her approval, which seemed childlike in a way. But she had stepped into the role of matriarch with natural grace while no one was looking, even before she lost her husband. It was the role she had at the magazine too. She was the matriarch of her family and the magazine, the person on whom all the decisions and responsibilities rested. In a sense, she wore a crown that no one could see but everyone knew was there. Along with it went the burdens. She never complained about what the role entailed or shirked her responsibilities. She was a living legend and had served as an example to all of them, each in a different way, according to their needs and perception of her. They had emulated her work ethic without hesitating for an instant, and for each, in their own field, success was a given, although hard earned, and richly deserved.

* * *

Nadia heard the car pull up to the house on the gravel driveway early Saturday morning and went downstairs to greet her. Rose looked as immaculately put together as always, in white slacks, a crisp white shirt, a trim navy linen blazer, and a straw hat, with the familiar black alligator travel bag. They spoke softly so as not to wake the others. Sylvie and Laure appeared in their nightgowns and threw their arms around her. They walked her to the largest bedroom, which Nadia had saved for her, with its own dressing room and pink marble bathroom. Rose loved coming to the château, and appreciated how simply and elegantly Nadia had helped Nicolas renovate and redecorate it when he had inherited it. It remained true to its original look, with beautiful antique parquet floors, wood paneling and moldings throughout, and she had added just a touch of modern, in order to make it comfortable but not look incongruous. It was a perfect example of a three-hundred-year-old home smoothly brought into the present. It was the ideal showcase for Nadia's decorating talent.

"I'll just take a quick shower and change into jeans," Rose said, and they left her after she and Nadia hugged again. By the time she joined them in the kitchen in white jeans and a T-shirt and white Hermès sandals, the others were chatting animatedly and having breakfast. She sat down and entered the conversation with a smile, after she hugged each of them, delighted to see her daughters all in one place for a change. The long weekend together had been a great idea and was going well. After their initial discussions about him, Nicolas hadn't been mentioned again and Nadia was relieved. She wasn't going to be making any big decisions over the weekend. It was a family reunion, and a vacation, for all of them, Rose as well. She didn't even mention the September issue, which was a sensitive subject. This was family time, a sacred time for all of them.

They spent the day at the pool, reading magazines and dozing, exchanging sun creams and sunscreens, while Rose sat under an umbrella on a lounge chair. Athena made a big, healthy salad for lunch, which was perfect, and at the end of the day, they all compared how tan they were, except Venetia, who, with her fair skin, had been happy to lie in the shade under the enormous umbrella with her mother.

Dinner that night was going to be their last big meal together, and their mother's only evening meal with them. The others were flying home the next day, and Rose was going to Paris for a day of work and meetings before she went back on Monday night. She made use of the time while she was there. Nadia had gone all out and ordered lobsters and écrevisse for all of them. There was a tin of caviar on the table. Nadia had chilled some of their best white wine and champagne, Athena made another very creative salad, and after the meal they put three flavors of gelato on the table: peach, lemon, and chocolate. The combination of flavors was exquisite after a sumptuous meal. They sat back in their chairs, happy and sated, as Athena poured another round of champagne.

"Oh God, I'm going to get drunk in front of Mom," Olivia said, and they all laughed, including Rose.

"I'll be asleep on the table before you can do anything outrageous," Rose assured her, and accepted another glass of Cristal herself. Every aspect of the meal had been perfect. The girls went to bed on their own, tired from a day in the sun and the pool.

As they relaxed, the conversation turned to their children, what their talents were likely to be, and what their hopes were for them.

"Will is going to be just like Harley and you," Venetia said, smiling at her sister, "serious, hardworking, ethical, successful."

Olivia looked at her for a minute, and with the benefit of the champagne, she looked pensive. "He won't be like Harley," she said, sounding certain.

"Why shouldn't he? You both have the same values," Venetia proceeded innocently, and sipped the champagne.

"He's not Harley's." The words fell into their midst like an unexploded bomb that lay on the table, ticking loudly.

"What do you mean?" Athena questioned her, confused by what she'd said.

"Will is not Harley's," Olivia repeated, as her sisters and mother stared at her. "I made a terrible mistake right after we were married. I was in my first job after I'd passed the bar. I got sent as low man on the totem pole on a big case. We had associated with a firm in San Francisco. The case settled, and we all got drunk to celebrate. The associate they had me working with looked like some kind of god. We had fun working together, and I don't know how it happened or how I could have been so stupid, but we wound up in bed on the last night. I tried to forget about it afterwards, to just erase it from my mind, I felt so guilty about Harley. I wasn't in love with the guy. We just got drunk and went crazy for a night. Then I found out I was pregnant, and I didn't know if it was Harley's or the associate's. Bernie, his name was Bernie. I didn't want to have an abortion in case it was Harley's. I told Harley there was a problem, and I needed an amnio, and had them do a DNA test. I was five months pregnant when I got the results, and found out he wasn't Harley's. I really didn't want an abortion by then. I never told Harley. I did tell Bernie, who had left the firm by then. He signed away any rights and didn't want any part of it anyway. I've never heard from him again. I didn't tell Harley then and I never will. It would break his heart that his only son, whom he adores, isn't really his. I've got the relinquishment paper in a safe deposit box. I should probably destroy it when Will turns eighteen. And that, my beloved sisters, is my one dark secret. So now you know. Will is not my husband's son." There was total silence at the table for several minutes as Olivia's mother and sisters stared at her in astonishment. She was the last person on earth any of them would have expected that from.

"Do you think you'd ever tell Harley?" Venetia tried not to look as shocked as she was.

"Never. Just as I said. It would kill him. He thinks I'm some kind of modern-day saint, ultra-moral woman. He always tells me that my integrity is what he loves most about me. How can I tell him I've been lying to him about something as important as that for fifteen years? He'd never trust me again. I've never cheated on him except that one night. I felt so guilty that I had robbed him of the opportunity of having a child of his own that even though we had only wanted one child, I talked him into having a second one. We tried to have another baby and we never did. He thought maybe he'd gotten too old, but maybe he never could have children. I didn't want to get tested to find out. Then he'd know I lied to him, so I said that Will was enough for me. And he is. He's such a great kid." The ramifications of what she'd done were so far-reaching and seemed so enormous to all of them that none of them knew what else to say for a few minutes. It wasn't lost on Nadia that Olivia was the first and the loudest to condemn Nicolas for what he'd done with Pascale, and yet she had done something just as bad, or maybe even worse, lying to her husband about their son's paternity. Nicolas hadn't lied about it, Olivia had, and she was pressing her sister to divorce Nicolas. The hypocrisy of her position left Nadia stunned.

"Well, I think we'd all better forget that immediately and make a pact to bury it now and never discuss it again," Rose said quietly. "Too many people could get badly hurt if that ever comes out. Olivia, thank you for your faith in us, trusting us with information like that. We can't ever, ever mention it again." She looked around the room at all four of her daughters. She passed no judgment on Olivia, and felt sorry for her for the burden she had carried for so long, alone. The wine had loosened her tongue, and she looked both frightened and relieved as she nodded at her mother. "I don't think Will should ever know, even after his father is gone. They love each other. It wouldn't be right to interfere with that now. Harley's a wonderful father, and always has been. That's all Will ever needs to know."

"Thank you, Mom," Olivia said, grateful that none of them had jumped up and called her a lying whore. For years, she had been afraid she would blurt it out one day. She had taken no drugs when she gave birth, for fear of what she'd say. The agony she'd experienced delivering her ten-pound son naturally had seemed like adequate punishment, and a price she was willing to pay.

"We all have our secrets, I suppose," Rose said calmly. The others hadn't quite recovered yet.

"I don't." Nadia spoke up. "I can't believe you've been so harsh about Nicolas, when you did something even worse yourself," she said to Olivia, with an edge to her voice.

"I didn't make an ass of Harley, or drag some other guy around with me, all over the press. I made a terrible mistake, but I hate what he's put you through, Naddie. He should be made accountable for it," Olivia said emotionally.

"Are you accountable for what you did?" her younger sister asked, looking straight at her. It was a moment of truth between them like no other they had experienced, or probably would again. Olivia had laid her heart bare to them, and Nadia's was raw. It felt good to Olivia to finally get it off her chest and share it with them. She had regretted it for fifteen years.

"I feel guilty about it every single day," she answered. "Every time I look at Will, I remember what I did."

"I slept with a married professor when I was in college," Athena offered to provide some distraction. "I didn't really feel that guilty. He was kind of a jerk and was sleeping with half the girls in the class." The others laughed.

"I have a confession," their mother said and surprised them all. She was so honest and upstanding, none of them could imagine she had done anything too shocking. "I always thought you should know. Your father didn't agree with me, and didn't want me to tell you, so I never did, out of respect for him. I was married once before I met your father, when I was a student at Oxford. He was a very sweet English boy. His parents were horrified, and mine weren't happy about it either. We snuck off and eloped, and regretted it after. We were completely unprepared for marriage. We were more like two children than adults, we were both nineteen. We got divorced after a year, which was why I left Oxford after only two years and transferred to the Sorbonne. And then I met your father, shortly after I got there, and it didn't really matter that I was divorced. My life began with Wallace. Nothing that came before mattered to me after that. We started fresh, with a clean slate, and I moved to New York for him when he went back. And we got married very quickly without any fanfare, since I'd been married before. I just thought you should know. My father knew my first husband's family. He married an Irish girl after the divorce, I think she was his cousin, and they had six kids. I saw him once years later, on the street in Dublin, when I was there for work. He had gotten fat and bald. He didn't recognize me and I hardly recognized him. Neither of us said hello." What she shared with them didn't really shock them, but it was touching somehow, to think of their mother with a past. She had shared it to take the heat off Olivia, and Rose had had a little too much champagne herself.

"Where did you live with him, Mom?" Athena asked, curious.

"At Oxford, where we were both studying. We were really like two children. He was studying to be an architect." There was nothing racy about it. It just sounded like a harmless teenage romance.

"I think Olivia still wins the prize," Venetia said with a wry look, and the others laughed. "That was quite an announcement, Ollie. Now you're going to have me worrying about making a slip if I get drunk at Christmas Eve dinner. Poor Harley."

"He doesn't ever need to know," Rose said, meeting their eyes, and they nodded. It was an enormous piece of information for Olivia to have shared with them, and it could damage her marriage irreparably and upset her son profoundly if it came out. It was a measure of her trust that she had told them.

"I feel like I should go out and have an affair, or steal a car or something to stay in the running," Athena said, and the others laughed. "Actually, I got arrested in college for being drunk and disorderly after a protest about animal testing. I drank so much wine with my buddies, I couldn't remember what the protest was about. All things considered, I think we've all been pretty well behaved. And so has Olivia. That's a hell of a lesson to have learned," she said sympathetically.

"I've never looked at another man again, only Harley." She seemed humbled by her confession, and not quite so bold.

"I'll bet you didn't," Venetia commented.

"Maybe now you'll stay off my back about what I'm going to do about my marriage, and let me figure it out for myself," Nadia said, still somewhat bothered. Olivia had been so harsh with her advice till then.

"I'm sorry, Naddie," Olivia said softly, genuinely contrite. "I've always had strong feelings about cheaters because of what I did myself."

"I don't like them much either." Nadia smiled at her. "But I love you anyway. It was a long time ago. Maybe it's time you forgave yourself."

Olivia shook her head in answer. "I don't think I'll ever forgive myself."

"I'm sure Harley would have if he'd known, but he doesn't need to," Venetia said sensibly.

"I'm not so sure he would," Olivia said. "He's the most moral person I know. I don't think he would have understood, and he'd never forgive me for lying to him. Sometimes I think I should tell him one day, just so we have a clean slate, but I don't want to hurt him, or cheat him and Will of the relationship they share."

"It's best to let sleeping dogs lie," Rose said. "I'm disappointed that none of you are impressed with my racy youth." She smiled at them and Venetia laughed.

"You married the guy, Mom. That's not racy. And an early marriage doesn't exactly qualify you for the Scarlet Letter."

"I guess not. We felt like Romeo and Juliet because our parents were so unhappy about it, but they didn't stop us, and we figured out very quickly that we'd made a terrible mistake. I was enormously relieved when we separated. I left for Paris to study at the Sorbonne, and I could put it behind me. And then I left for the States, after I met your father."

"I can think of several older people who had early marriages no one ever knew about. And they never talk about them. You pretty much had to get married to have sex in those days, and divorce was considered a disgrace." Rose nodded when Venetia said it.

"Actually, I was a virgin when I met him. It feels like several lifetimes ago, as though it happened to someone else. Your father used to tease me once in a while, and said he loved me more because I was a woman with a past. I was such a baby then, even when we married. It always stuns me how fast the time goes. You don't realize that when you're young," she said wistfully. "You think you'll be young forever, and then suddenly you're not, and the best part is over." The wine was starting to make her morose, and they all realized how much she missed their father. She was widowed so early, and hopefully still had many full, creative years ahead of her. But she had not looked at another man since he'd died. She filled the void his absence left with work, and time with her girls.

They sat and chatted for another hour, and no one else came forward with shocking revelations. They all gave Olivia a warm hug when they said good night, and Olivia clung to each of them for a moment, grateful that whatever any of them did, the others accepted it. They were all determined never to raise the issue of Will's paternity again. It simply didn't matter. And Nadia hoped that her somewhat harsh, judgmental older sister would be a little more compassionate in future about her situation. If anyone was going to get tough with Nicolas, it had to be Nadia herself, and not because Olivia was prodding her. She was angrier at him now than she wanted to admit to her mother or sisters. She wanted to scream every time she thought of him with Pascale. He had been such a damn fool and had ruined everything. She was furious with him, but she didn't quite hate him yet. She was discovering that it took longer than she thought for love to turn to hate. And even longer for love to die. But she knew she'd get there in the end.

She felt sorry for Olivia when she went to bed that night. Then the wine they'd drunk caught up with her too, and she fell asleep and dreamed of Nicolas holding a baby. She couldn't remember if the baby was hers or not, but a beautiful young woman was standing near, watching her and laughing. She could see clearly that the woman was Pascale. And then, Nicolas and Pascale walked away with the baby and left her. She woke up in tears. She tried not to think about the symbolism of the dream and didn't want to know. But it was obvious to her anyway. Pascale and Nicolas were together, with their baby, and she wound up alone.

Chapter 6

The next morning at breakfast, none of them mentioned Harley or Will. Out of the blue, Venetia commented that she wanted to have another baby. She had loved growing up as one of four girls. It pleased Rose to hear that.

"I'd actually love to have five or six," Venetia said with a mischievous smile, "but Ben would probably kill me. Our life is chaotic as it is. Big families always seem so cozy to me."

"I wanted another one too. We wanted to wait till next year," Nadia said wistfully. "Now that's not going to happen. I'm happy with my girls." With the current state of her marriage, whatever happened, she couldn't see herself having another child. Only if she divorced Nicolas and married someone else. She would never trust him enough again to have another baby with him.

"My dogs are more than enough for me," Athena said, content as always.

"Your father loved having four daughters." Rose smiled at them. "He was so proud of all of you."

They lay at the pool after breakfast, enjoying their last few hours together before they had to leave. The weekend had gone too quickly, but it felt like they had been there for longer than four days.

"Why don't you and Sylvie and Laure come to California this summer?" Athena suggested to Nadia as they lay there. "I'll still be on hiatus, and it would be fun for them. We can take them to Universal Studios and Disneyland." The idea appealed to Nadia, but Nicolas hadn't told her his plans yet.

"I'm not sure when he wants to see them. But I'd like to come out. I assume he's going to want to use the château at some point," presumably with Pascale. The thought of it felt like an open wound and almost made her wince. California, visiting her sister, would be a pleasant escape. "I'll figure it out and let you know."

"You can come to Southampton too. I take three-day weekends in August, and stay out for a couple of weeks, and so does Ben. We'd love to have you," Venetia spoke up. And their mother would be at her own small house there on weekends.

"Will you be in the Hamptons this summer, Mom?" Venetia asked her. Rose's house was like a dollhouse, but she enjoyed it.

"If I'm not too busy working on October and November." Rose never stopped, year round. Her life was a constant merry-go-round of perfecting the next issue. Venetia knew that Olivia would be in Maine with Will and Harley, spending as much time as they could on their sailboat. Athena would be happily at home in California, trying out new recipes for the show for after the hiatus. Nadia was usually at the château all summer, but this year, she was grateful for their invitations. It would be nice to leave France for a while and get away from the furor over Nicolas and Pascale. She was sure Nicolas would want to use the château part of the time. And she had nowhere else to go with the girls.

They ate a light lunch at the pool, and then Rose and Nadia's sisters went to their rooms to pack. Olivia and Venetia were flying back to New York together that night. Athena was going to the airport with them and catching the L.A. flight.

The van Nadia had hired for them came to pick them up, and the five women hugged, and almost cried as they said goodbye to Nadia, while Laure and Sylvie watched. It had been a perfect weekend, full of good moments, happy times, and startling revelations. Venetia had confessed to Nadia privately that she was finding it hard to put out of her mind what Olivia had shared with them.

"Every time I see Will or Harley, I'm going to think of it. I almost wish she hadn't told us." Nadia admitted she felt the same way about it.

"I don't know how she has lived with a secret like that for all these years."

"Maybe that's why she's so hard on everyone else," Venetia ventured.

"You'd think it would make her more forgiving and compassionate," Nadia said.

"Maybe it will now."

She and the girls stood waving as the van pulled away. Rose went with them, since she had meetings the next day and was flying back to New York on Monday night. She was spending the night at the Ritz. The van was going to drop her off after they dropped the others at the airport.

Nadia knew that the time they had just spent together would provide warm memories for a long time.

"I hope that one day you two love each other the way I love my sisters. A sister is a very special thing," she reminded them, as Sylvie rolled her eyes, and Laure stuck out her tongue at her sister. They had dinner in the kitchen that night and Nadia missed her mother and sisters.

"When is Papa coming home?" Sylvie asked. She was eager to see him. He had been away so much lately. She missed him.

"I don't know. You talked to him. What did he say?" Nadia said noncommittally.

"He said he'd be back tomorrow."

"I have to go to London on Tuesday, so he can stay with you then." The girls liked the sound of that, though Sylvie had noticed and already commented that they were getting to be like their friends whose divorced parents alternated being with them, and were never there at the same time. Nadia didn't respond. She knew that the girls would figure something out sooner or later. They couldn't fool them for much longer. She was working less during the summer, but still trying to keep her clients happy, despite the upheaval in her private life.

Nicolas called them that night before bedtime. Nadia knew that her sisters would be on their flights by then, she was thinking of them. Then Sylvie handed the phone to her mother. Nadia didn't want to talk to him, but took it anyway, so as not to arouse any more suspicion in her children. She had to play the game for them, as though they were still truly married.

"How was the weekend?" he asked her.

"Really nice. It was lovely being together. How was yours?" she inquired with an edge to her voice.

"Hot. There's a heat wave in the South, and it was jammed." She didn't ask who he'd been staying with and didn't want to know which of their friends had welcomed the famous movie star with open arms. She knew many had, and she didn't consider them friends anymore. She told him about her trip to London, to see a new client, and he sounded delighted to have the excuse to stay with the girls. Then Nadia got off the phone. She didn't want to spoil the warm glow of the weekend by getting upset with him.

Nadia and the girls drove back to Paris the next morning, and when she saw the newspapers, she was angry all over again. There was a brief mention that he and Pascale had rented a house in Ramatuelle, near Saint-Tropez, for the summer, and there was a paparazzi photo of Pascale looking ravishing in a bikini, with her round six-month belly showing, and Nicolas looking blissful beside her. Nadia threw the paper away before the girls saw it.

She dropped the girls off with friends for the day, and went to her office, and when the girls got home that night, Nicolas showed up minutes later. He had a deep tan, which made his fair hair look even blonder, and his green eyes seem even greener. When the girls left them for a few minutes, Nadia spoke to him in an angry undertone.

"We have to say something to the girls soon. Someone else is going to tell them. For God's sake, you're having a baby in three months, and you were in the newspaper again."

"It's a boy," he said, trying not to look as elated as he was, but he was happy to see Nadia and his daughters too. His heart seemed to have expanded to include all of them, which was impossible to explain to her. "I agree, we have to tell them something. But after the baby comes, I want to come home and try to put our marriage back together. I love you, Nadia. I've been a fool for the past few months, but that hasn't changed." He looked serious as he said it, and she wanted to hit him. These days, he brought out the worst in her. Her nerves were stretched to the limit whenever she saw him, or even thought about him. What he wanted was just too unreal.

"How can you say that? You're living with another woman half the time. You use our home like a hotel, and you expect me to be the innkeeper, and just sit here patiently waiting for you. Why don't you make a clean break, and at least try and do it right with her?" She was tired of his hanging on to both of them.

"She's twenty-two years old. She knows she's too young and immature to be married, and she's right. She wants me around, at least until the baby, but she's not looking to the future. This is all about now for her. And it has been for me too. Nadia, we're adults. We have a life, a history, a future. This is some kind of aberration I've fallen into. I know it sounds terrible, but can't you give me time to work this out as decently as I can and then come back to you?" His eyes pleaded with her, and she had a knot in her stomach looking at him. Not a knot of longing, just a knot of frustration and fury. What he wanted from her sounded impossible and wasn't fair to her.

"And then what? Wait until you do it again? Life doesn't work like that, Nicolas. I'm not going to forget these months of hell you've put me through." He had tears in his eyes when she said it. But this time, she didn't.

"I swear to you, I'll make it up to you every way I can for the rest of our lives. Just give me these few months." She shook her head, speechless at what he was asking for, and determined not to give in to him.

"You're as much of a child as she is if you think you can walk in and out of marriage, take a break, have a baby with someone else, and come back and pick up where you left off. You're crazy." Her eyes blazed at him.

"I probably am crazy, but I'm also still very much in love with you." He wanted her to know.

"Then you're a selfish asshole on top of everything else, and a damn fool," she said, as Sylvie walked into the kitchen. She could see that her mother was angry, and had heard her father's pleading tone, although she couldn't make out the words, since they were whispering. She wanted them to stop fighting. They had been arguing almost constantly for the past two months, and it frightened her. Laure didn't understand it, but she was upset too.

Nicolas turned to Sylvie then, gave her a big hug, and promised to watch a movie with her the next day when their mother went to London.

"We'll stay up late, just don't tell her," he said in a stage whisper Nadia could hear, and Sylvie grinned. Then Laure came bounding in and begged her father to sit down to dinner with them. Nadia didn't stop him, and he sat down looking embarrassed, but she couldn't eat. The weekend with her sisters had done her so much good to restore her strength and self-confidence, and he was rapidly undoing it.

"Are you going to use the château at all this summer?" she asked him after the meal, once the girls had gone to their rooms. She had been silent all through dinner. She had nothing to say to him.

"I'd like to be there in August, with you and the girls," he said cautiously, not wanting to infuriate her. He hadn't told Pascale yet, but he wanted vacation time with his children, and Nadia if she was willing. Pascale had plenty of friends to keep her busy in Saint-Tropez, and several who owned boats or chartered them. She moved in a very jet-set crowd, and he was enjoying it, but he wanted to use his ancestral home too. And she would only be seven months pregnant in August, so he felt it wasn't urgent that he be with her. She wouldn't be about to give birth then. And she was still busy, going to parties, and wanted to have fun with her friends.

"I'm going to take the girls to visit Athena and Venetia, in L.A. and the Hamptons, probably for a few weeks in all," Nadia said coolly. He nodded, feeling he didn't have the right to argue with her, or make demands, given what he was putting her through, and doing himself.

"I thought I'd spend the Fourteenth of July weekend with you, if that's all right," he said cautiously. "We can go to see the fireworks in Deauville." He knew how much their girls loved fireworks, and Nadia didn't want to disappoint them or argue with him. She had wanted to be with the girls and not with him. But she knew the girls would prefer them together. She wondered what he was planning to do with Pascale then. Leave her in their rented house in Ramatuelle apparently. She wondered why Pascale was willing to put up with it, or what he'd tell her to explain it. Nadia didn't understand their seemingly open relationship. But she was fourteen years younger than Nadia, a child in many ways, and wanted a considerable amount of freedom herself. Nadia didn't want to share her summer with Nicolas, as long as he was involved with Pascale. But she also didn't want to upset her kids.

Nicolas left the kitchen to see the girls while she put the dishes in the dishwasher, and she realized that if she didn't refuse, she would now be stuck with a family Bastille Day weekend, to accommodate him and their daughters. It was untenable, and she felt torn between trying not to upset her children and wanting breathing room and space from Nicolas herself. It felt like it was time to see a lawyer to set down some rules for visitation, and a plan for how to get through this awkward time. She went straight to her room after that and closed the door. She knew that Nicolas wouldn't dare to come in. He would stay with the girls until bedtime, and then take refuge in the guest room where they didn't know he was sleeping. He would remove all trace of himself in the morning before he left. Nadia was relieved that she didn't see him again that night. She didn't want to.

Her mother called her from the airport before she flew back to New York. She was rushing for the plane but wanted to give her a kiss before she left.

"Are you okay? You sound upset," Rose asked her.

"He's here, driving me crazy," Nadia responded.

"I saw the papers today," Rose said seriously.

"So did I," Nadia said. "And the photo of Pascale with him in Saint Tropez."

"I'll call you from New York. I love you," Rose said, and they hung up.

After her mother's call, Nadia lay on her bed thinking of something Venetia had said to her that weekend, that Nadia should get pregnant too, and then his loyalties would be to her, and not Pascale.

She had history on her side. But Nadia couldn't imagine doing something like that. The war of the babies. And he had absolutely glowed when he had told her the baby was a boy. The whole situation seemed disgusting to her. She was relieved that he would be gone the next morning, before they all got up and she left for London. His presence in the apartment made it feel toxic to her.

"Why does Papa go to work so early now?" Laure asked her at breakfast. Nadia fumbled for an answer and burned the toast.

"He has a lot to do," was all she could come up with. As soon as they left for the day with their regular babysitter, Nadia made two phone calls. One to the airline to book her flights for their visits to Athena in L.A. and Venetia in the Hamptons, and the second to the lawyer whose name her mother had given her. Rose had gotten it from someone in their Paris office, whose discretion she trusted. The lawyer was out of the office, and Nadia left him a message. She booked the flights for right after the Bastille Day weekend. She was willing to sacrifice herself for a weekend with him and the girls. After the weekend, he could enjoy his château alone, or with whomever he chose to invite, but not with her. She had to draw the line somewhere.

It was going to be a relief to spend the day and the night in London with a client and get the whole mess out of her head. And she couldn't wait to go to the States to visit her sisters and her mother.

"Why do you have to spend the holiday with them?" Pascale asked Nicolas, looking petulant, when he told her his plans to be at the château with Nadia and the girls for the Bastille Day weekend.

"That's ridiculous. And we're invited to a wedding at the Hotel du Cap. I booked a room for the weekend."

"You can go without me," he said gently. There was nothing shy or reclusive about Pascale, and he knew she would shine at the wedding, and probably upstage the bride. "I need to spend some time with my daughters."

"Fine. Then bring them to Ramatuelle some other weekend. Or we can go to the château with them."

"They don't know about you yet," he reminded her.

"When are you going to tell them? When our son goes to college, so they can attend his graduation? You should tell them. They'll be excited to have a baby brother," she said naively.

"It's not as simple as that, and you know it." He had explained it to her before. He had unlimited patience with her, almost as though she were a child too, which she was to him, or it seemed that way at times. He was twenty years older. He found her childish side charming most of the time, but not always. "We were premature with the baby, before they even met you. And I'm still married to their mother. It makes introducing them to you now difficult. They don't have time to get used to the idea of us." She was suddenly very visibly pregnant in the last two weeks. "This isn't the example I want to set for them. And it will be hard for them to understand. Everything has happened so fast." They had no plans to marry. Pascale didn't believe in marriage, like much of her generation, and her own parents hadn't been married. She didn't see marriage as a necessity, or even desirable. And she saw nothing wrong with having a baby out of wedlock, which was not what he wanted to teach his children. But it was a fact of his life now, and it would be difficult to explain to them.

"For your age, you act like we live in the Middle Ages. People don't get married to have babies anymore. No one I know does," she said blithely.

"Some people still do. Their mother and I did. At their ages now, I'm not happy to demonstrate alternate lifestyles to them. I don't want them doing this one day. And they'll be upset for their mother."

"Don't be such a prude," she said, smiling at him, and slowly unzipping his trousers. The languid sensual way she did it, and slipped her hand inside them, drove him insane, which was how it had all started. He was a gentleman and wouldn't have accused her of it, but she had seduced him while they were working on the film together. She had flirted with him shamelessly until he could no longer resist her, although he had tried at first. She wanted him, and he had found her naked in his bed one night, waiting for him. It was beyond his abilities to refuse her, and he thought it would just be a lark while they were on location. Their passion had overcome reason, and a few times, they had been careless about protection. And the lark had turned serious when she got pregnant. Then he had lost his mind in Cannes, and momentarily forgot he was married. But the baby would have outed them anyway. It didn't bother Pascale at all to be having a baby, unmarried. What bothered her was that he was still halfway living with Nadia, and was still emotionally attached to her, which he had told Pascale. He wasn't willing to drop everything for a girl who took relationships as lightly as she did, even if they were having a baby. He had risked enough. And he was sure that she had no idea what she was getting into, or the ramifications of it. Her life was about to change forever, even if her mother was going to take care of the baby and keep it in Brittany with her. Pascale would be as free as before, but she still had a responsibility to her child, she couldn't totally ignore it. She was planning to do exactly what her mother had with her.

His life had already changed far more than hers. And he had far more at risk.

Pascale was still hanging out with her friends, going to parties, smiling for the press, showing off her round belly. Her mother had been an actress of little note, her father had disappeared when she was born and she'd never met him. She had had a very loose upbringing among her mother's boyfriends, and had been brought up by her grandmother most of the time. She had lost her virginity at fourteen. And it wasn't lost on him that in being with him, she was sleeping with one of the producers of the movie, which was a good career move for her. Pascale kept her eye on her career, and knew how to get where she wanted. It had worked well for her so far, and luckily for her, she had talent and was a major star now at twenty-two. He couldn't imagine her settling down for many, many years. Pascale was not planning to alter her life significantly after the baby. But she wanted Nicolas at her side, as much as possible, for as long as they wanted to be together, however long or short that was. She wanted Nicolas with her, not to care for her during the pregnancy, but to have a good time. And she'd had an easy pregnancy so far.

For the first few weeks of their affair, he thought it was just a fling, and then he believed he was in love with her when she told him about the baby. He was attached to her, but he was even more so to his wife and family. He was sexually addicted to Pascale, and he knew the difference now. He was giving himself three months to get over her, by the time the baby was born, but he wasn't ready to leave her yet. It was awkward that their affair had become so public. He had no idea if Nadia would ever take him back and be willing to continue their marriage. It didn't look that way at the moment, and with every passing day it seemed less likely, which had begun to panic him. The press continued to add insult to injury. He didn't want to let Pascale add to that. He doubted that she really loved him. He was the father of her child, and her lover, but that was as far as it went for her. Like most of the actresses Nicolas knew, she was only interested in herself, and oblivious to the impact and the consequences for him. Nadia was a woman of integrity and courage. Pascale was an entirely different breed. She was narcissistic and amoral, and even now, her appeal for him was mostly physical. She was the sexiest woman he'd ever met. He had lost his mind temporarily, but he was certain now he didn't want to lose his marriage because of their affair.

"I want to be in Saint Tropez with you in August, when it's fun. We can go to your château in September," Pascale insisted, it sounded dull to her, with no social life in the area and nothing to do. She wasn't anxious to spend much time at the château and miss time in Saint-Tropez. And in September, she couldn't go far anyway, a month before her due date. The people he knew who lived near his château, in lives similar to his family life, sounded deadly boring to her. She wanted the fast lane, just as she was living it now in Saint-Tropez, and had been for the past few years. That was the excitement and one of the benefits of fame for her.

"Nadia is taking the girls to America for a few weeks in July and early August. We can go to the château then. It's beautiful there in summer," he said to Pascale, as she freed him from his underwear and closed her mouth around him. He forgot everything else when she did. The discussion ended there about where they were going to spend July or August or weekends, or his being with Nadia for Bastille Day. He could think about that later. Like everything else he didn't want to face now. Even the baby faded from his mind when Pascale worked her magic on him.

When Rose got back to her office after the Fourth of July weekend at the château with her daughters, two of the senior editors were lying in wait for her. They had discussed it the previous Friday, after Rose left, and they strongly felt that Nicolas Bateau needed to be part of the interview that was going to be their feature story in September.

"He's too big a part of her stardom right now, because of the movie. If he were just an ordinary guy, or only her boyfriend, we could leave him out of it. As it is, the interview will be hollow without him. And let's face it, he's the more interesting subject. She has nothing to say. She's a decent actress, and a gorgeous girl, but we're not going to get much out of the interview. We need him."

Rose argued the point with them as intelligently as she could, but editorially, she knew they were right, and with a terrible tug in her heart, she was tempted to concede for the sake of the magazine. She hated the idea of Nicolas being part of the interview and in the photographs that would be taken of them together as a couple, and what it would do to Nadia when the magazine came out. She promised the editors to think about it and called Nadia as soon as they left her office. She had promised them a definite answer by the next day. She reached Nadia at Heathrow, waiting to catch her plane back to Paris.

"I really want to keep him out of it," Rose said after explaining the situation to Nadia. She had tears in her eyes that her daughter couldn't see. "I'm under a lot of pressure about it. But I don't want you hurt."

Nadia was characteristically gracious about it, and appreciated that her mother wanted to protect her. She sounded sad and defeated with a quiet sigh. She'd had a good day with her client, and hated to face the nightmare again.

"I'm not sure it matters. Everyone knows about the affair and the baby anyway," Nadia said wearily.

"He's made a total ass of himself with this girl, ever since Cannes," Rose said angrily, "and she isn't worth a damn, baby or no baby. I think the baby is just an accessory to her. I feel terrible letting him be part of the interview. The editors feel they need him in the piece. She has nothing to say that anyone wants to hear. But you're what matters most to me." Rose sounded emotional about it.

"Don't worry about it, Mom. I can live with it," Nadia said, dignified. She was determined to rise above it, and not let Pascale and Nicolas ruin her life. It was a major challenge.

"At least we have a writer who isn't going to dig for dirt," Rose said quietly. "I'll do everything I can to keep your name out of it and to make sure the interview isn't shocking and doesn't romanticize them, if I let them do it."

"You can't keep me out of it, Mom," Nadia said realistically. "I'm his wife, the woman he dumped for her." But the problem was that he hadn't dumped her. He wanted both of them, and to eventually come home to her after the affair ended, when the baby was born or when Pascale moved on to her next film and her next man. So far, Pascale had gotten involved with every leading man she acted with, and this time, with the producer/director. "Don't worry about me, Mom. I'll be fine, even if he's in the interview. Thank you for asking me. You have to do your job, and I'm sure it will be a respectable piece. I love you, it's okay."

Rose still hated to let the editors have their way, and thanked Nadia for her understanding. After she hung up, Rose was in a bad mood for the rest of the day, which was rare for her. She was sick and tired of the Nicolas Bateau/Pascale Solon story. She couldn't wait for it to be over, and dreaded what they'd say in the interview. Nicolas had put them all in a terrible position, even Rose.

Nadia knew it was just another form of the torture she was living through. She could hardly wait to leave for the States. She was starting their trip in L.A., at Athena's. And all she had to get through before that was the Bastille Day weekend, with Nicolas at the château with them. It was hurdle after hurdle after hurdle these days. But she was determined to clear them as gracefully as she could, and survive it. She was facing it with courage and dignity. No one could take that from her, no matter what he did.

Rose sent her senior features editors an email at the end of the day, giving them permission to include Nicolas in the interview, but she informed them in no uncertain terms that she would do the final edit of the piece herself, which was nonnegotiable if they wanted him in it. They didn't argue with her about it. They knew better. Rose's word was law at *Mode,* and no one was going to cross her on this. Having Nicolas in the interview was victory enough for them.

Chapter 7

The Bastille Day weekend at the château had a surreal quality to it. Nicolas made a huge effort to act as though nothing had changed, and put on a show for their children. He was attentive to Nadia and adorable to the girls. Nadia tried to keep to herself, and leave the girls alone with him, while Nicolas insisted on including her in everything. They took the girls to the beach and collected seashells, wandered through the little shops in Deauville, went to their favorite restaurant, and the rest of the time, stayed in the pool at the château. Nicolas taught Laure how to dive off the diving board, and had endless patience with them. He seemed to be loving every minute of it, which Nadia wasn't. She felt crazy halfway through the weekend. It was as though Pascale had never happened, he wasn't in love with her, and she wasn't carrying his baby. To anyone who didn't know them, they looked like a normal family having a terrific weekend.

"What are you doing?" she said to him in a harsh whisper when the girls finally left the pool to change for dinner. She was about to follow them, to oversee their baths and wash their hair, but stayed to talk to him. "Are you insane? What are you doing here? Or what am I doing here? How do you think the girls are going to feel after a weekend like this when we tell them we're separated? We've been lying to them for two months. And you're having a baby with another woman."

"They deserve to have some happy times with the two of us. And it's not over between us yet, Nadia. I still love you."

"Stop saying that, for God's sake!" Nadia looked furious and had tears of rage and sorrow in her eyes. "You have a mistress, you're having a baby with her. Why do you want to confuse everything? Our girls will never trust us again." He was breaking her heart. She was trying to let go of him, in her heart and in her mind, and a weekend like this just reminded her of how it used to be, and could never be again.

"Why won't you leave things open for a while?" He looked like a schoolboy who had been scolded and truly didn't understand the harsh punishment he felt she was meting out to him.

"I'm not a car you can just park somewhere, and our daughters aren't toys for you to play with whenever you want. My mother tells me you're doing an interview for *Mode* with Pascale. The whole damn world knows about your affair, or will shortly. Meanwhile, you're lying to our daughters and confusing the hell out of me. This isn't a game, Nicolas, it's our life. Or it was. It's nothing now, except a joke you're playing on us and a nightmare."

"I'm not joking. I love you, Nadia," he said with tears in his eyes too. The moment was intense. "I don't know what happened. I went crazy, I'm still crazy. I care about Pascale, but I love you. She's fireworks on the Fourth of July. You and I are real. We're forever."

"No, we're *not,*" she shouted at him, since the girls weren't around. "Nothing is forever, and certainly not our marriage, not now. I saw a lawyer last week," she added, lowering her voice.

"So did I," he responded, and she looked shocked. He hadn't mentioned it to her before. Nor had she.

"Are you filing for divorce?" she asked him.

"No. I just don't want to do anything dumber than I already have," he said. "He told me that as long as I have not abandoned our family residence, we're not separated and you don't have grounds for divorce." She realized then that he wasn't as crazy as he looked at the moment. "I have not moved out. I'm not going to. I want to see this through with Pascale until October, and then come back to you. I'll do whatever you want. I'll stay with her until the baby, and then I swear, I will never do anything like this again."

"I don't believe you," Nadia said angrily. "And I'm supposed to sit around quietly for the next few months while the two of you show off and give interviews? You *are* insane." She looked as though she hated him for a minute. "Why is everything always about you? And we're the wreckage you leave in your wake. Stop it, Nicolas. This is not a game. It's my life." She got up and left the pool area then, and hurried back to the house, while he sat staring into space in the deck chair for a long time. He was terrified to lose Nadia and the girls, but he felt he had to see it through with Pascale until after the baby. He couldn't leave her pregnant, and the baby was his child too. Pascale called him at that exact moment, as though she was psychic and had picked up his vibes. He didn't want to talk to her but took the call anyway. He felt torn in half.

"How's it going?" she asked, sounding relaxed.

"Okay, most of the time. It's a little tense," he said with a sigh. He didn't want to explain it to her. She thought he should just walk away from Nadia and not look back. The way she would have.

"You should have come to Ramatuelle with me. The house is full, the weather is gorgeous, and the fireworks will be fabulous tonight." There were plenty of fireworks between him and Nadia at the moment. He understood why she was upset, and he felt pulled between the two of them. "I miss you," Pascale said, sounding instantly sexual and he forced himself not to think about it. Not here. "The two of you fighting all the time is why I never want to get married. It doesn't seem like fun to me." She laughed when she said it, but Nicolas was in a serious mood, after being with his family all weekend and seeing Nadia's suffering at close range. And he could see her fury too.

"This is incredibly difficult for her," he said sympathetically, well aware of what he was putting her through and deeply sorry about it. Pascale had no empathy for her, or even for him and the guilt he felt because of her.

"Don't forget we have the interview with *Mode* next week," she reminded him, and changed the subject back to herself. "I just bought a new dress for it, see-through white lace, I can wear it over a bathing suit. I look like a madonna in it." She was conscious of her striking, sensual beauty and used it to her advantage whenever possible. It was her secret weapon and so far always worked on him. But not tonight. He was upset about Nadia, and what he was doing to her.

"You're too sexy to be a madonna." He was surprised they were including him in the interview, with his mother-in-law as editor-in-chief, but he was a big name. They were assigning one of their most important photographers and had begged Nicolas to participate. They wanted to do it at the rented house in Ramatuelle, and Pascale had agreed without consulting him. They wanted photographs of them together. "I'll come down on Monday, the day before the interview. I'll give them a few minutes, but I won't do the whole interview with you." He couldn't do that to Nadia, and he didn't want to. "I need to do some work this week," he said, sounding stressed. He had hardly written a word in the last two months. His new novel was half finished, sitting on a shelf. He couldn't concentrate on anything these days except Pascale and Nadia. "Nadia and the girls are leaving for L.A. in a few days, so I can stay down South with you for the next few weeks." He felt like a bouncing ball.

She reminded him that she was going to the wedding at the Hotel du Cap the next day, hoping to make him jealous, but he wasn't.

They hung up and he went back into the house then, feeling depressed about the situation. They had bought sausages, fruit, and salad for a simple country dinner. Nadia and the girls were in their rooms when he walked in. He was staying in a small study off the main bedroom, but the girls had no idea he wasn't sleeping in the master bedroom. He wondered if Nadia was right, and it wasn't fair to keep things hidden from them. He kept hoping there would be some kind of resolution, but there wasn't. It unnerved him that Nadia had seen an attorney. This was the first he had heard of it. He had gone to a lawyer to make sure he didn't make any glaring legal mistakes that would deal a final death blow to their marriage. Nadia had gone to see a lawyer to find out what those mistakes were and what grounds she had to end the marriage. Their goals were no longer the same. They were in direct conflict, like everything about their life.

Nadia and Nicolas were quiet at dinner, and the girls chattered on. Laure wanted to decorate a shoebox with the seashells she'd collected, to make it a jewelry box for her mother. And Sylvie wanted to know how soon they would go to Disneyland after they got to L.A. They provided some distraction during the meal. Their father took them outside to throw a ball with them afterwards, and Nadia went to her room. She called Venetia in Southampton, who said it was blistering hot there, wished Nadia a happy Bastille Day, and asked how things were going with Nicolas there for the weekend.

"He's making me crazy. He still acts like we're a happy family and tells me he loves me every five minutes. I don't want to hear it, and I don't think this is good for the girls." Or for her either. And Nicolas seemed nervous too. It was putting pressure on both of them, and the tension was palpable. Nadia was worried that the girls were sensing it too.

"He probably does love you," Venetia said simply. "He just wants to have both of you for now. He can't do that forever, and sooner or later it's going to blow up in his face. She may walk out on him before you do. By the way, Ben and I talked about it last night. We can come for a week in August if you really want us. Three jet-propelled kids does not make for a restful week," she reminded her sister, and Nadia smiled.

"I'd love it. And so will the girls." The cousins loved being together. Venetia and Olivia tried to get their children together as often as possible, and Nadia made sure that her daughters saw their cousins every summer. They wanted the next generation to be as close as the four sisters were.

"When do you go back to Paris?" Venetia asked her.

"Tomorrow night, at the end of the weekend. I can't wait. I'm fed up with playing this game of happy family when our life is in shambles at our feet. We leave for L.A. on Tuesday. I'm looking forward to that." They had planned a week after that in the Hamptons. And they were going to visit Rose at the magazine. Olivia and her family were in Maine for two months, so they wouldn't see them. It was too long a trip for Nadia and the girls, a six-hour drive from New York.

After the call to Venetia, the girls came in and Nadia put them to bed. They were happy after the day with their parents and they loved being at the château. They had freedom there and could run around, and they were enjoying the time with their father.

After she put them to bed, Nadia went for a walk by herself and ran into Nicolas when she got back. He looked sad, as though he'd been crying.

"I'm sorry I've made such a mess of everything," he said in a low, raw voice, and she could see he was, but she didn't want to fall prey to his charms. He was the only man she had ever loved and she wanted to forget that. "I want to fix it, but it's like finding my way out of a maze right now." She nodded but didn't know what to say to him.

"I think we need to be away from each other, until we figure it out, and decide what to do," she said softly.

"I don't want to lose you, Nadia. Whatever it takes, I want to come back." In truth he had never left, not fully. But he was afraid he had lost her anyway. There was something dead in her eyes when she looked at him, and he couldn't blame her, after what he had done. He felt deep remorse about it, but he wasn't sure that would ever be enough. "Please don't make any big decisions while you're gone. Give me a little more time." She didn't answer him, and a minute later, she went upstairs to her room and closed the door. She didn't want to make him any promises she couldn't keep.

Nicolas spent Sunday night with them at their apartment when they got back to Paris. They were both subdued after the weekend. It had reminded him of everything he had risked and was about to lose. And Nadia didn't want to talk to him about it again.

First thing Monday morning, he took a commuter flight to the South of France from Orly. And it was no secret to either of them where he was going. Pascale was waiting for him in Ramatuelle, and the *Mode* interview was the next day.

Nadia had to go to her office, and left the girls with their babysitter, and that night they showed her all the things they wanted to take with them to L.A., their favorite shorts and T-shirts, Laure's light-up sneakers, and Sylvie's sneakers that she said were "cool." Nadia packed for all three of them and the girls were excited about the trip.

Nicolas called them the next morning. Nadia was too busy to talk to him, and he wished the girls a wonderful time in the States. They promised to FaceTime with him while they were away, a miracle of modern technology which allowed them to show him everything and see each other while they talked. He was disappointed not to speak to Nadia before they left. Their weekend together had made him miss her more, and he'd been irritable with Pascale when he got back, but was really only angry with himself. He had created the hell he and Nadia were living in.

Nadia and the girls left for the airport in a flurry of activity, and were right on time. Nadia sat back in the van, trying to figure out if she had forgotten to pack anything, although it was too late now. But everything was in order and she had made careful lists. She put an arm around each of her daughters with a smile.

"We're off to our big adventure. Aunt Athena says she can't wait to see us," Nadia said, feeling liberated to finally be free of Nicolas lurking around them like a ghost. He had looked miserable when he left them the day before, and she didn't want to think about it. This was her time with the girls, and she didn't want anything to spoil it.

"I can't wait to see Aunt Athena's dogs," Laure said happily. "I love Hugo . . . and Juanita and Chiquita, and Stanley." She went down the list of dogs, while Sylvie sent another text to her father and told him how much she wished he was there with them. He responded immediately.

"Me too." He had told her he had to get back to work on his new book. Sylvie thought it was too bad that he couldn't take a vacation with them, but at least they'd had the Bastille Day weekend with him. It had been perfect, from her point of view, with her mother and father together. They were both nervous and in bad moods lately, but probably things would be better when they got back. She hoped so anyway. She had asked her father about it, and he had promised they would never get divorced. And she knew he never lied to them.

"You look incredible," Nicolas said, standing in the doorway of their bedroom in the rented house in Ramatuelle. It was tropical and luxurious, with lovely gardens and an enormous pool. Pascale was wearing the white lace dress she had bought for the interview. You could see her belly clearly through it. She was wearing her bikini bottom but not the top under it. Her breasts were huge and full from the pregnancy. Her arms and legs were slim, her face was lovelier than ever, and her long white-blond curls looked like a halo that framed her face, with the rest of her hair piled on her head. She looked more womanly and less like a young girl with her pregnant belly, and she was every bit as sexy as he said, definitely not like a madonna, as she stretched her long legs out on a chaise longue under a large beach umbrella next to the pool. A waiter with a starched white jacket who had come with the house served her a tall glass of lemonade. There was a splash of gin in it, which Nicolas didn't know.

He was wearing shorts, Hermès sandals, and a white linen shirt. They looked like some kind of ad for yacht owners, or people who had tons of money. They appeared to have it all. Nicolas was less nervous than he'd been the day before, when he'd arrived, and had settled down. Pascale had sensed his dark mood as soon as he walked in, had lured him into bed, and cheered him up considerably. He said she had magic powers over him. She bewitched him.

A few minutes after Pascale installed herself on the chaise longue, the house man escorted two people out to the pool, a small woman in jeans and a T-shirt, with dark hair in a braid down her back, holding a large notebook, and a man also wearing jeans, but with a Mexican embroidered shirt. They were the writer and photographer who had come to do the article. They were young and looked somewhat awestruck in the presence of such luxury and beauty, and two very famous people. Nicolas stood up and shook hands with them, and Pascale remained reclining, not wanting to disturb her "look." She was wearing high-heeled white sandals, which laced up her legs to the knee, and were very sexy too. She was so appealing and sensual one almost forgot she was pregnant. She wasn't ready to be the poster child for motherhood yet. There was a white Hermès Birkin bag on the ground next to her, which Nicolas had bought her.

Nicolas asked if they'd eaten and offered them lunch as soon as they arrived. They said they'd eaten at the Gorilla Bar in Saint-Tropez, and weren't hungry. But they both accepted wine, and the photographer set up his cameras while Barbara Jaffe, the writer they'd flown out from New York, sat down and chatted informally with them. Pascale was playing the star, which Nicolas didn't mind. It suited her, and kept the attention off him. He didn't want to be the focus of the interview and wasn't planning to stay long.

The photographer suggested a few casual photographs before they started, and Nicolas sat on the arm of her chair, feeling awkward at first, and then slowly relaxed as Pascale leaned toward him. They stood up near the pool then, and the photographer positioned her so they got a good view of her profile to show off the baby. Then in a more relaxed moment between shots, she sat on Nicolas's lap while they were laughing, and kissed him. It was a perfect moment of tenderness and humor, and the photographer snapped it instantly, knowing the shot was pure gold. Then the interview began.

Barbara had a full list of questions in her notebook, about how and where they had met, what they had thought when they first laid eyes on each other, was it love at first sight? What had it been like working on the film together? How had their relationship developed? How did they like to spend their time? Where were they living? How did they envision their life together now as parents? She asked about their views of the future and how their relationship would affect their work. She wanted to know if they planned to work together again and how they thought the baby would impact their careers, and their life together. It was the full-court press about everything people wanted to know, both their fans and their detractors. And the answers the writer culled from them were everything Nicolas hadn't wanted to tell them and promised himself he wouldn't, but she was artful and adept and got what she wanted, although most of it wasn't true. Pascale was much more relaxed than he was, and willing to tell Barbara anything. Nicolas was less accustomed to giving interviews, which he seldom did. Barbara never asked him directly about Nadia and their marriage, but her existence was implied in several of the questions.

Nicolas successfully deflected some of it, and whenever he did, Pascale leapt into the breach and supplied everything they wanted to know. Nicolas cringed a few times as he listened, and tried to temper what she said, but Pascale would not be curbed. She wasn't afraid to voice her opinion that she thought marriage was a ridiculous, antiquated tradition, which no longer served any purpose in today's fast-moving, ever-changing world. She said that people needed to be free in order to grow, and no relationship was meant to last forever. That was a fairy tale, not reality. She said she thought that having babies was a natural part of life, and you didn't have to be married or even be with the same partner to give a child a happy life. She used the example of native tribes in different cultures where the tribe raised the child, and not the mother or father. She said she'd been raised by her grandmother when her mother was working, and she had benefited from it. And their child was going to spend time with her mother when she was busy. Her answer inspired Barbara to ask her if she intended to bring up her baby and care for it herself at all.

"I hope not," she said, laughing, and explained that she was going to leave him with her mother most of the time, while she pursued her career. She said she was too young to be tied down changing diapers, and Barbara asked Nicolas how he felt about that. He said, in his charming French accent, that Pascale's point of view was very different from his. He said he had grown up with a traditional mother and father and a stable family life. He mentioned too that he had two daughters who were also being brought up in his more traditional style.

"And how do they feel about the baby?" Barbara asked him. She was inching up on his marriage, but he saw her coming and sidestepped her. But he had walked right into her trap about his daughters.

"I'm sure they will be delighted," he said smoothly, without saying that they knew nothing about it.

"And your wife?" Barbara lobbed a potential bomb at him, and he sent it right back to her with a smile.

"She's not part of this interview, Miss Jaffe. She's not here to speak for herself."

"Thank God," Pascale said, and laughed, and Nicolas shot her a warning look, then realized he had stayed far too long, and waited for an opportune moment to leave.

"Has the transition from one woman to the next been difficult for you?" the interviewer asked him. He smiled and didn't answer. She had been warned not to go there, but couldn't help trying, and she got nothing from him. Instead, he thanked her for her time, kissed Pascale on her forehead, and quietly disappeared. But despite his elusive exit, which took the writer by surprise, he knew that he had said more than he should have and was worried about how his answers would look in print, especially to Nadia if she read it, and he feared she would.

They took more photographs of Pascale then, nearly naked in her bikini bottom, without the lace dress, getting into the pool. She had a body that every woman would have died for, pregnant or not. They wanted some of her in the pool with Nicolas, but he said he was busy and did not reappear.

When Pascale told him the interview was over, Nicolas returned to thank them and say goodbye. The two emissaries from *Mode* left a few minutes later, and Pascale lay dripping wet on a deck chair and smiled at him.

"I thought that went great, didn't you?" He wasn't so sure.

"They asked quite a lot of questions they weren't supposed to." He was worried about some of Pascale's answers, and his own, which gave them too much information they could use that he hadn't wanted to reveal. Pascale was naïve and assumed they'd be kind, and said she didn't care what they said about her. But he did. He didn't want them making his situation with Nadia even worse than it was, or wounding her even more than she already had been. The fact that Pascale was in his life was enough. Her words were dangerous. She had supplied all the ammunition they wanted, gift-wrapped, and handed it to them. And even worse, he feared he might have too.

* * *

When Rose saw the first draft of the interview, she sat at her desk and groaned out loud. Barbara Jaffe had quoted Pascale on every subject, and her answers made her sound stupid, narcissistic, amoral, irresponsible, and hard, all of which was probably true. Nicolas seemed like a besotted fool who had thrown his life out the window for a girl with a sensational body, little brain, and no heart.

"I'd like to trim this down," Rose said through pursed lips when Barbara came to her office a few days later. "I think you have more than you need. We don't have to drive the point home."

"She said all of it, and so did he," the writer said innocently, disappointed that Rose wanted to cut it down. "It doesn't run too long. I counted the words." But Rose had final say.

"True, but she repeats herself quite a lot. It's obvious that she's a young woman with loose morals, who isn't looking to a future with him, and has very little interest in her child. We always have to keep our eye on the periphery. Who is standing just out of sight who is going to be hurt by this? His wife, his two daughters. I'd like to keep the piece as clean as possible. It slides too easily into the tawdry with what she says. It's obviously a story about lust and not love, and the baby was an unfortunate accident. I want to keep it simple. She's a movie star, people will forgive her some of it. But let's not go too far." She had used a red pencil to indicate where she wanted it cut. The writer looked disappointed but knew better than to argue with her. That wouldn't have been a smart move, and Barbara Jaffe was ambitious. This was a big break for her. And her enthusiasm had caused her to cross some boundaries that she normally wouldn't have. She also knew from the grapevine that Nicolas was Rose's son-in-law, so it didn't totally surprise her that she was protecting both of them and wanted to trim the piece.

They went over the photographs together then, and Rose couldn't help noticing Pascale's flawless body. She circled the friendlier, more casual shots to include in the piece, eliminated the naked ones with a red "X," and tried not to focus too much on her belly. Nicolas was sitting close to her in several of the shots. They selected one where she was dressed and you couldn't see her belly at all. They were the most benign, least suggestive shots of the shoot, all in good taste.

The photos she chose would illustrate the story well, but didn't have the tabloid feel Rose wanted to avoid. She was thinking of both her daughter's and the magazine's best interests. She initialed what she had approved and felt sorry for her daughter to have her husband's affair so blatantly exposed. Rose hoped she would be rid of him soon. The embarrassment and the pain had gone on long enough, and too many people were going to suffer. It had been mentioned in the interview, though, that Nicolas was still very close to his wife and daughters, and planned to stay that way. So he hadn't betrayed her entirely. All she could hope now was that Nadia would divorce him in the near future. He might not be an evil man, plotting to destroy her with heartless cruelty and premeditated motives, but at best, he was certainly a fool.

Chapter 8

Joe went with Athena in their SUV to pick up Nadia and the girls at LAX when they arrived. He was a big, burly teddy bear of a man, and loved kids. He was the perfect partner for Athena. They looked just right together. Both were tall, heavyset, warm, jovial people who always had a smile on their lips and laughter in their eyes. He knew some of what had been happening to Nadia, but not all of it. Athena didn't want to give away all of her sister's secrets and confidences, but he knew enough to strongly disapprove of the mess Nicolas had gotten himself into. Joe had come into the family after Nadia had met Nicolas and was dating him. She had already been living in France for three years. He had been an usher in their wedding, and had always enjoyed being with them. Although he and Athena weren't legally married, and didn't want to be, they acted as though they were, and after so many years, Joe had a respected position in the family as her mate. He was five years younger than Athena, and was thirty-eight, four years younger than Nicolas but wiser about life. He'd never been married and had no children. He would have liked to have children, but Athena had been clear from the beginning that it wasn't what she wanted, and he accepted that. He had enough nephews and nieces and friends' children to satisfy him, and they had their dogs.

Nicolas was from an aristocratic family, and an only child. He had gone to the best schools in Paris, studied political science at a prestigious university, and had a master's degree and the means and encouragement to pursue a career as a writer from a young age. He had never had to worry about how he would support himself.

Joe's origins had been simpler and rougher, and more real. He was one of four siblings. His father had died when he was young. He had grown up in Michigan, had put himself through college, and worked from the time he was a teenager, at rugged jobs since he was big and strong. He had been a lumberjack, a stevedore, drove a truck while he was in college, and had discovered how much he loved to cook. He had gotten a job as a fireman, and was assigned cooking the meals at the firehouse when he was on duty, so he had a chance to hone his skills. He took several cooking classes, saved his money, quit his job, and went to Europe to work in restaurants in Italy and France, and finally became a master chef. He then moved to L.A. and started his own restaurant. He had met Athena on a cooking show, and they got along famously. They each felt as though they had found their other half. Athena had gone on to have her own successful TV show, while Joe preferred running his restaurant and having direct contact with clients. He also helped her run her vegetarian and vegan restaurants, which were popular lunch places, and much smaller operations than his. He was a smart businessman, a hard worker, and a warm, down-to-earth person. He had a natural instinct to protect people he cared about, so he hated to hear what Nicolas was putting Nadia through. Nicolas sounded like a spoiled boy to him, although he hadn't thought of him that way before. He wanted to do everything he could to make Nadia and her daughters' visit to L.A. as much fun as possible.

He had bought tickets to take them to a Dodgers game himself, and was hoping to have time to join them at Universal Studios. He knew Athena was taking them to Disneyland. It wasn't going to compensate for their currently stressful home life, but he hoped that it would take some of the burden off Nadia, whom he liked a lot, and give them a chance to have some fun after two very tough months. He was aware that the girls didn't know that their parents' marriage was at risk. Athena had warned him, but he was sure that they sensed something, which was frightening for them too. He felt sorry for Nadia, and her kids.

He and Athena were both waiting as Nadia and the girls came through customs at LAX. He found a porter for them and folded them all into a big hug. He thought Nadia looked tired and stressed after the long plane ride from Paris, but the girls were happy and excited to be there, and Nadia smiled gratefully at him and her sister.

He took them out to dinner that night, at a restaurant with great burgers for the kids, and very good fare for the adults. They had several vegetarian options for Athena, and Joe ordered a steak.

"So how are my favorite French girls?" Joe asked all three of them. Nadia had lived there for so long that the whole family considered her more French than American now, and she did too.

"We are very good, and very happy to be here," Sylvie said, pronouncing the words carefully with her French accent.

"And your English has gotten better," he commended her and she grinned. "What about you?" He turned to Laure as she wrestled with an enormous burger with all the trimmings. She had ketchup all over her face.

"I want to see your dogs," she enunciated carefully with a grin. She had recently lost her two front teeth.

"They're excited about seeing you too. Especially Juanita and Chiquita. Your aunt Athena just bought them new ballet tutus." He gave Athena a wry look and she laughed. "Hugo and Stanley are my guys," the Lab and the mountain dog. "We go hunting together." The weather was so warm that they swam in the pool after dinner at Athena's sprawling ranch-style house in the hills above L.A.

Joe had his own small house he referred to as a "shack" in West Hollywood, but he hadn't stayed there in years. He called it his "insurance policy" in case Athena ever threw him out. But Athena said they got along better than any of the married people she knew. "Why spoil a good thing?" she always said to her mother, when Rose suggested they get married. She'd finally stopped mentioning it. At forty-three, Athena knew what she wanted, and how she wanted to live. Since children weren't on her wish list, getting married made no sense to her.

Athena had arranged a whole program for them in L.A. Since she wasn't back on her show yet and was still on vacation, she had time to spend with them, and thoroughly enjoyed it. She took them to museums, Universal Studios, and Joe came with them as promised.

Disneyland was the main event. Nadia and Athena walked all over with Sylvie and Laure, and they saw everything they wanted. Both girls fell asleep, exhausted, after the parade, on their way back to Athena's house. They had stocked up on Disney pajamas, T-shirts, costumes, magic wands, and Minnie Mouse ears.

"That was really fun," Nadia said to her sister. "I loved it."

"Me too." Athena smiled at her. Nadia was starting to look like herself again and had relaxed in the few days since she'd arrived. After they got the girls to bed, and went to sit in Athena's modern, professional kitchen, Nadia told her sister her plan.

"I'm going to start the divorce when I get home. I don't want to sit around and wait anymore for what's going to happen, and for him to figure out what he wants to do. I can see the handwriting on the wall. Pascale is not a solid bet for the future, and he's a fool if he thinks she is. He says he'll end it with her in October after the baby is born, but I don't think he'll do it. She'll probably stick around for a year or two, until the novelty of the baby wears off. I don't want to waste my life waiting for him. I'm going to tell him I'm starting divorce proceedings when I get home."

"Are you sure that's what *you* want, and not what someone else thinks you should do? Like Mom or Olivia? I know they've both taken a hard line about it. But it's your life, your marriage, and even if he's a jerk, he's your jerk, and if you love him, it's really up to you what you want to do."

"Thank you," Nadia said softly and smiled at her. "You're a great big sister. You should have been a mom. You'd be good at it."

"No, I wouldn't. Kids stress me out. Too much responsibility, and

I'd be terrified to do the wrong thing and screw them up forever. I don't know how you handle it, or Venetia, or Olivia."

"You grow into it. Marriage is kind of like that too. Or I used to think so. Now I don't know what I believe."

"Do you think you'd ever come back to the States to live?" Nadia thought about it for a minute and shook her head.

"I have a business in Paris, I love our apartment. My kids are French and they should be close to their father, in the same city. I know it sounds weird since I grew up in New York, but I'm not comfortable there anymore. I've lived in Paris for so long that I feel like a foreigner when I'm here. It's just easier in France. Sometimes I feel more French than American."

"Maybe that's why you didn't file for divorce immediately. A lot of American women would have," Athena said.

"Divorce is easier here. I don't even feel ready for it now. But cheating is not okay, and I'm going to lose all respect for myself if I don't do something about it."

"Just make sure it's what you want. Not what someone else tells you that you should want, or should do."

"I don't know if you're ever sure if you walk away from someone you love. There are always things you love about them. I still love him. I probably will for a long time. But he's not letting go of Pascale, and the baby complicates everything. He probably loves me too, just not enough to do the right thing."

"You're young, Naddie, and beautiful. You'll find a good guy," Athena said gently.

"Maybe." Nadia didn't look sure. "I think it's going to be hard to trust anyone again. I thought we had it all sewed up forever, and we were a sure thing. I was wrong."

Joe came home from the restaurant then. He was at his restaurant every night. And he checked on Athena's restaurants in Santa Monica at lunchtime. She owned them but rarely went herself. She had managers run them for her, with Joe supervising. Joe was more hands-on at his own restaurant, and catered to an elite clientele who expected him to be there. The success of his restaurant was because he was there himself, watching every detail.

Their week with Joe and Athena flew by, and they were sorry to leave. Both girls were wearing their Minnie Mouse ears from Disneyland when they left, and Laure had a little pink rolling traveling bag with Minnie on it that Athena had bought for her. She was pulling it along behind her with all her treasures in it. Nadia's eyes were damp when she hugged her sister and thanked her. Then they went through security, waved, and boarded the plane for New York. They were planning to stay with Rose in the city for three days, and then head to Southampton for a week to stay with Venetia and Ben and their children.

Rose was waiting for them when they arrived. Sylvie and Laure told her all about their adventures with Athena, and Rose took them to the office with her the next day. She showed Sylvie and Laure around, explained to them about layouts and photographs, and how they picked the photos to go with a story.

At the end of the tour, Sylvie announced that she wanted to work at a magazine one day, and Laure said she wanted to be a dog doctor, which made them smile. She'd had a ball with Athena's menagerie.

Rose took the afternoon off and they went to the Statue of Liberty and the top of the Empire State Building. It was turning into a fun summer for them. Their week in the Hamptons with Venetia and Ben's family was even better. Running on the beach, building sand-castles, wading in the ocean, swimming at their beach club. It was a real vacation. Sylvie and Laure couldn't keep up with Venetia's sons. They were too big and rough, but they had fun playing with India, who worshiped them.

Nadia and Venetia took long walks on the beach, talking about life, their businesses, children, and marriages. Venetia was always easy to get along with, and she was protective of her younger sister and smart about many things. She had a good head for business. But what Nadia noticed most was how happy she and Ben were together. They seemed in harmony most of the time and did a lot to help each other. Ben walked on the beach with Nadia too, and told her how sorry he was that Nicolas had behaved so badly and made such a mess of things.

"He has a lot of growing up to do," he commented. But he doubted that Nicolas would achieve it soon enough for Nadia. He thought she needed someone to share her life with, not someone who put every-thing on the line, risked all, and created a public scandal. She didn't disagree with him.

They had agreed to come to the château for the last week of sum-mer vacation, and Olivia said she might come too. Nadia had seen more of her sisters that summer than she had in a long time, and was grateful for it. And she saw her mother in the Hamptons on the weekend, when she came to Venetia's house for dinner.

They flew back to Paris with their souvenirs and memories. Nadia knew it was a summer she'd never forget, and her family was getting her through it. She was eager to get back to work when she got home. She had an appointment with her lawyer. She was going to try and cut her losses with Nicolas. It had taken her two and a half months to make the decision. But she was ready now. At least she hoped so.

Nicolas came to see the girls the first night they were back, and Nadia left him alone with them. He hadn't seen them in nearly three weeks, and she didn't want to interfere. They were tired from the trip and went to bed early. After they did, Nicolas came to see her in her little office. She was going through all the mail that had piled up while she was gone. All of France took vacation in summer, so she knew that nothing important would happen in her absence, and her office kept her informed whenever her clients called.

"It sounds like you had a good trip." He smiled at her and sat down in a chair across from her desk. He had been in the South the whole time they were gone and had a dark golden tan.

"We did. I'm seeing my lawyer tomorrow," she said calmly, and he looked surprised.

"Why now?"

"I think it's time. You're doing what you're doing, and I want to get on with my life. I feel like an idiot while you have a whole other life with Pascale."

"I want to try and put things back together with you after the baby comes," he said, looking distressed by what she'd said.

"That's over two months away, and who knows how you'll feel

then. This doesn't work for me. We're lying to the girls. It's not healthy for anyone. It isn't for you either. You say you want to come back 'later,' so you're not fully engaged with Pascale, even though you're having a child. You're trying to hedge your bets with me, in case it doesn't work out with her. That's not who I want to be, in your life, mine, or anyone else's."

"You're starting the divorce?" He looked like he was going to cry, and she wanted to, but she was trying to keep the conversation matter-of-fact and as unemotional as she could.

"I want you to move out and get your own apartment." She didn't "want" him to, but she thought it was best if he did. She wanted Pascale to never have happened, but they couldn't turn the clock back, and she was real, and her baby too. "I want to be legally separated from you. The girls need to know the truth. You pretend to live here but you don't. It's confusing all of us." He nodded. He understood what she was saying. Their life had been a disaster for three months, because of him. It would be almost another three until the baby came. "We can figure out the divorce later, but for now we need to face what's happening. I'm not really part of your life anymore." Tears filled her eyes and he moved toward her and reached across her desk, but she backed away. "Don't. Let's not make this any harder than it already is."

"What are we going to tell the girls?" he asked, on the verge of tears himself.

"That's up to you. What are you going to tell them about Pascale and the baby?" He still hadn't faced it, as though the day would never come, and his daughters would never know.

"I don't know. I wish I didn't have to tell them so soon. They've never even met Pascale." He had handled the whole thing miserably, and she wasn't going to clean up the mess for him.

"I assume you're going to live with her," Nadia said in a strained voice, trying to be gracious about it.

"We haven't figured it out yet." They had the house in Ramatuelle until September, and she was having the baby a month later. She was going to stay with her mother in Brittany for the last month, and wanted to give birth there, to be near her mother, so she could take care of the baby. Nicolas had promised to be there for the delivery. But where they would live after that hadn't been decided. His life was up in the air. The only stability he had was with Nadia, and now she wanted him to move out. "Let me think about it for a few days, and I'll let you know," he said in a raw voice, and she nodded.

"You haven't been around much. I think even if you pretend to sleep here occasionally, the children know something's up. Maybe not Laure, but definitely Sylvie. I hope you tell them about the baby before someone else does." He was lucky she hadn't. She was leaving it to him. Miraculously, no one else had told them. And Nadia didn't give them access to the internet. They were young enough that his affair with Pascale was the kind of unsavory gossip parents didn't share with children their age. But sooner or later someone would.

"Why would anyone do something like that?" He looked shocked. "Tell them, I mean. They're children."

"It happens. People like to talk about the miseries of others." He got up and left a few minutes later, and Nadia stood on the terrace, thinking about what she had just done. A page had turned. It had taken three months for her to get there. She had asked him to move out. She wanted to feel proud of herself, and thought she would. But she didn't. She just felt sad.

Nadia had to go to her office the next day, and their babysitter called while they were having breakfast. She said she had eaten sushi the night before, and was violently ill. The housekeeper was on vacation, and Nadia thought of taking the girls to the office with her, but it was distracting, and she needed to catch up on her work. She had to schedule a meeting with her client in London. She called the wife of the guardian downstairs, and asked if she could stay with the girls, at least until lunchtime. She was going to bring her work home with her after that. She had no other solution. The guardian's wife came upstairs, and Nadia hurried out five minutes later, and promised to be home by one. They were going to go for a walk in the Tuileries Garden to get some air while she was at work.

Nadia came back promptly, and the apartment was strangely silent when she walked in. She thought they were still out, and was surprised to see both girls sitting on the living room couch with somber faces. She thanked the guardian's wife, who told her the girls were tired from their walk. She said she had offered them lunch, but they weren't hungry. Nadia paid her and a few minutes later, she left. She was kind of an old biddy, always meddling in everyone's business, but she was helpful from time to time.

"Are you feeling okay?" she asked them both, and they nodded. She thought maybe they were still tired from the trip. They were sitting like statues, and Sylvie looked at her with enormous eyes and burst into tears. Her mother rushed over to her and took her in her arms.

"What happened? Was Madame Martin mean to you? Did she tell you scary stories?" People did stupid things sometimes, and by then Laure was crying too.

"Madame Martin said that Papa is having a baby with another lady . . . an actress . . . and you're probably going to get a divorce. Is that true?" Sylvie wailed, and Laure echoed her, then clung to her mother and sister as though they were in a lifeboat and she was afraid of falling out.

"Whoa . . ." Nadia didn't answer for a minute, while she thought about what to do. Nicolas had left her with his mess to clean up, and she was on the front lines now. She knew they would remember what she said forever. "First of all, let's all take a deep breath and calm down. You know that Papa loves you, and I do too. Do you know that?" They both nodded, and she wiped the tears off their faces. "And sometimes even grown-ups do silly things. Papa has a friend right now who he likes a lot. She's very young and very pretty, and it's true, he's having a baby with her. But that doesn't change how he feels about you," she said seriously.

"Are they coming to live with us?" Laure wanted to know.

"No, they're not."

"Is the baby a boy or a girl?" Laure again.

"A boy."

"What's his name?"

"I don't think he has a name yet."

"I don't like boys," Laure said definitely while Sylvie stared at her mother with a ravaged expression, as though the world as she knew it had come to an end. She wasn't wrong.

"Are you and Papa getting a divorce?" Sylvie asked her.

She hesitated for a minute, she didn't want to lie. "Not right now. Things have been very confusing, with his friend and the baby. I think Papa is going to get his own apartment while he figures everything out," or live with Pascale, which she didn't say to them.

"Does he want to marry her?"

"I don't know," Nadia said honestly.

"Do you hate him now?" Sylvie asked her.

"No, I don't. I'm sad that things are confused and difficult, but I don't hate your father."

"Do you hate his friend?" Nadia shook her head in answer.

"Why don't they give the baby away?" Sylvie suggested. It was a somewhat sophisticated concept for a ten-year-old.

"I'm sure they want the baby," Nadia said, trying not to sound judgmental.

"Why did Papa do that, if he has us? He doesn't need a baby." She looked devastated.

"You'll have to ask Papa that." She wasn't going to venture into those waters. Let him explain it, if he could.

"Will we see him if he moves to his own apartment?" Laure was worried.

"Of course. You can visit him there, and he can still come here to see you." Both girls were relieved when she said that it wasn't a full-on war. But everything they'd heard was confusing. They needed to hear from their father now.

She made the girls little thin chicken sandwiches, and they ate them at the kitchen table, then they went to their rooms. She had to call her lawyer then and cancel her appointment. With no sitter, and her children in a panic, she couldn't get to the appointment, and would have to reschedule it later. Then she called Nicolas on his cell.

"Where are you?" she asked when he answered.

"Why? Is something wrong? I'm on my way to see my editor."

"Yes, something is wrong. The guardian's wife told the girls about Pascale and the baby. They've been crying for the last two hours. You need to talk to them. It's face-the-music time." He groaned at the other end.

"Christ, why did that have to happen now? How did she get her hands on them?"

"I needed her to babysit this morning. They looked like they'd been shot when I got home. I've done what I can to calm things down. It's your turn now. Get your ass over here, and deal with it."

"Okay," he said. "I'll be there in fifteen minutes. Nadia, I'm sorry."

"So am I." For once, she didn't sound gentle.

He got there precisely as he said, fifteen minutes later, and she left the girls alone with him, and went to her office in the apartment. She answered emails to distract herself from what was happening. But Nicolas and Pascale had crossed another line, and her kids were paying the price now, not just her, or Nicolas. All she could think of was their ravaged faces in the living room when she got home. She felt sick. And this time, she did hate him for what he'd done.

The girls were very subdued when their father left the apartment. He explained the situation very much the way their mother had. And after he spoke to them, he made a decision to spend two weeks at the château with them. He needed to get his house in order. He invited Nadia to come, and she said she preferred to stay in the city. They should be with him now. He realized at last how serious this was for them. He was quiet and somber when he called Nadia and told her his plans and that he'd pick them up the following morning.

"Will Pascale be there?" she asked in a tense voice.

"No. I want to be with them now, without her." At least he had figured out that much. He knew that Nadia's family was coming out mid-August, and told her that he would give her back the girls then, and she could use the château for the rest of their vacation, until the end of August. "They should probably meet Pascale, but she's going to Brittany in September to stay with her mother until she has the baby. She's having it there."

"Maybe she can meet them after the baby," Nadia suggested.

She packed their suitcases that night, and Nicolas picked them up in the morning. They were happy to see him, and to be spending two weeks with him at the château. He thanked Nadia quietly before he left.

"Thank you for not making it any worse than it already is."

"I'm doing it for them," she said in a whisper. He nodded and after she kissed the girls goodbye, they took off with their father.

She called her lawyer again after they'd gone, for another appointment, and was told by his secretary that he had left on vacation that morning, and would be gone until the first of September. The legal arrangements would have to wait. She didn't want to start from the very beginning with a new lawyer and she liked the one she had. They were physically separated for now anyway, so the meeting with the lawyer wasn't crucial and could wait a month.

And then she called her sisters and told them what had happened. She called Venetia first.

"Oh shit. You were afraid of someone telling them."

"All of France is talking about them. It's not surprising." There were pictures of Pascale pregnant on the front page of every tabloid. And several of them with Nicolas beside her in Saint-Tropez.

"Are the girls okay?" Venetia asked her.

"Relatively. This is a huge blow to them, and a hell of a surprise. They've never even met her. I hope he handles this intelligently while he has them."

"I'm sorry, Nadia. They'll be okay. Kids come through worse. They're resilient." Nadia hoped her sister was right. Athena said pretty much the same. Nadia was glad they'd had a nice vacation before this happened.

Sylvie and Laure called her that night. They seemed happier than when she'd last seen them, and they'd had a nice day with their father. They'd gone for a long bike ride and swam in the pool, then cooked dinner together.

"Papa says he loves us and he loves you too," Laure said as soon as she got on the phone.

"Of course he loves you, silly." She tried to keep it light, but Sylvie sounded more serious and suddenly very grown up. She had been catapulted into instant adulthood by the past twenty-four hours' revelations.

"Papa says he doesn't want a divorce." Sylvie sounded as though she was his emissary. He didn't want a divorce, just a mistress and a baby and a wife.

“Why don’t you forget all that right now, and enjoy your time with Papa.”

“Are you going to divorce him?” She was pressing for answers now. Her whole world had come apart, and she wanted to put it back together as quickly as she could.

“We haven’t figured any of that out yet. Nothing is going to happen right now,” not with her attorney on vacation for all of August. Nadia was frustrated about that. She had missed her appointment with him on the last day before his vacation. But her kids had been hysterical and she had no sitter. Now Nicolas was telling them how much he didn’t want a divorce, so she would end up being the bad guy, and he the victim, in their eyes. “I want you to have fun with Papa for the next two weeks. Try to forget all the rest.” But Sylvie couldn’t, any more than she could.

Nicolas got on the phone after Sylvie finished talking to her, and Nadia spoke to him in a low angry growl.

“If you try to blame me for this, and make me look like the bad guy here, I swear, I will never speak to you again. This is all your doing, even yesterday, because you were never honest with them. You clean this up now, and don’t try to blame me. Is that clear?”

“Yes, of course, I’m sorry, I just thought . . .”

“Good. I’m glad we understand each other,” she said and hung up on him. Enough was enough. She was fed up with his self-indulgence, cowardice, and games.

Chapter 9

While Nicolas was at the château with the girls, Paris in August was peaceful and almost deserted. Everyone was gone. Stores, restaurants, and businesses were closed. It was a skeleton city. Nadia hadn't been there in the heart of the summer for a long time, and she liked it. She walked everywhere. She went to her office and caught up on her files. Factories were closed, so nothing could be ordered, but she felt as though she were cleaning up her life and getting control of it before the fall, after three months of madness since May.

Most of all, she was trying to decide what *she* wanted to do. She spoke to her sisters regularly. Olivia continued to tell her to divorce Nicolas. Venetia told her to fight for him if she still loved him. Athena told her that she would be fine even if she wound up alone. She hadn't spoken to her mother as much recently. Rose was up to her neck in the October issue. The September issue was due out at the end of the month, and Rose was still upset about it. For the first time, she wasn't looking forward to it. All she could think about was the cover feature, with the joint interview and photographs of her son-in-law and his pregnant mistress. She wished they hadn't done the story, but it couldn't be avoided, and she dreaded Nadia's reaction to it, even though she had sweetly agreed to it and said it didn't matter.

Nadia missed her children for the two weeks they were at the château with their father, but it was also a relief not to have to be responsible for anyone, eat at set times, come home on time from the office, and make sure they were happy, safe, fed, and entertained. She had been bracing herself for when they would hear about their father. Now the news was out, and there was nothing she could do about it. It was up to him now. He had to clean up his own mess with them.

In the middle of the month, there was a change of shifts at the château. Nicolas left the day before Nadia's sisters and their families were due to arrive. Nadia planned it so that she would miss him. The housekeeper spent the afternoon with the girls after Nicolas left for Saint-Tropez in the morning. Nadia arrived at dinnertime. Sylvie and Laure were thrilled to see her, and she was equally so to see them. They didn't mention Pascale and the baby until after dinner, and then Sylvie cautiously brought it up.

"Papa says that his friend is leaving the baby in Bretagne with her mother. The grandmother is going to take care of him, so we won't have to see him," Sylvie said, sounding relieved. "Papa is going to visit him, and send him presents, but he won't come to Paris until he's older." Nadia found that interesting. He was intending to be an absentee father to this baby. Apparently Pascale wasn't going to stay with the baby either. Her mother was going to redeem herself by caring for her grandson, to atone for not raising her daughter. Not having the baby with them would give Nicolas and Pascale more time with each other, without being tied down to an infant. Clearly, Pascale had no intention of spending time with her baby, or adapting to motherhood. "Papa says she's having it in seven weeks," Sylvie informed her mother, so obviously he had been talking to them about it. Nadia had avoided speaking to him while the girls were with him, and communicated by text and email when she had to. It was a relief not to hear his voice or see his pleading face when he tried to convince her not to give up on him. For two whole weeks, for the first time in months, she had tried to focus on herself.

When Venetia and her troops arrived, it was like an invading army at the château. Her sons, Jack and Seth, climbed trees and chased each other around the orchards. India tried to keep up with Sylvie and Laure, and was a sturdy little thing. She fell into the pool after lunch on the first day, and came up spluttering, but she didn't cry, and her father jumped in immediately and fished her out. And after that, she jumped in fearlessly on her own, wanting to prove how brave and grown up she was.

"She's going to be a skydiver or a stunt pilot or something when she grows up. She terrifies me, she's fearless," Venetia said, grinning at her daughter.

Olivia and Harley arrived a few hours later, looking very circumspect and somewhat exhausted from the flight. Will was happy to be there. Harley went to take a nap shortly after they arrived, and Will challenged his uncle Ben to a chess game. He had brought his travel set with him and was an expert player. Will was more comfortable with adults than Venetia's sons. Jack, Venetia's oldest son, the same age as Will, usually managed to entice him into mischief eventually, and her younger son, Seth, tagged along. Sylvie loved to tease Seth since he was the same age and she liked him a lot. They blended into a perfect group, with lots of squeals and splashing in the pool, while their parents watched them and chatted animatedly.

The three sisters were happy to see each other, and no one mentioned Nicolas. Ben and Venetia admitted to Olivia that they missed him. He was always a happy addition to the group. They FaceTimed Athena at dinnertime so she didn't feel left out. It was morning for her, and she was on her way to the studio for her show, since their hiatus was over, which was why she couldn't come to France.

"We should rent a house together somewhere next summer, maybe Italy," Venetia suggested, since the château belonged to Nicolas and she didn't know if Nadia would have use of it if they got divorced. And it appeared that they were going to. Nadia was waiting for her attorney to get back to start proceedings.

Olivia went to wake Harley from his nap before he slept too long and wouldn't adjust to the time change. Venetia and Nadia found themselves staring at Will reading at the side of the pool, and the two sisters had the same thought and whispered to each other.

"Every time I see him now, I think of what Olivia told us on the Fourth of July weekend," about Harley not really being his father. Venetia said it so softly that only Nadia could hear her.

"I know. I feel guilty, but I keep thinking about it too. I wish she hadn't told us," Nadia responded.

They joined the others on the terrace shortly after, had a glass of champagne, and then everyone went to change for dinner, and returned in pressed white slacks or clean white jeans. Venetia came down from her room dressed in a bright turquoise silk shirt, with orange satin pants and gold sandals, all of which looked great on her with her tan and red hair. They were a handsome group, and Harley livened up when he joined them. Venetia smiled at what Olivia was wearing: white silk slacks and a navy-and-white silk blouse with a string of pearls and her hair in a knot. She looked years older than she was. Harley was a very distinguished-looking man, but also seemed old for his age. He was only sixty, but the way he moved and spoke and his natural gravitas made him seem older.

They had bouillabaisse for dinner, brought in from a local restaurant, sole meuniére that the housekeeper made, bread and cheese, and a big bowl of fresh berries for dessert. The berries were from the estate and were served with delicate chocolate cookies that melted in your mouth.

Eventually, all the children went to bed, so they'd be fresh for the next day. The adults stayed up late, talking and drinking wine after dinner. It was two A.M. before the adults climbed the stairs to their bedrooms, with Nicolas's ancestral family portraits all around them. It made Nadia feel odd to be there without him, and she was thinking of Nicolas as she left the others and went to her enormous master bedroom. She was grateful that she and her family could spend a week there together, thanks to him. It reminded her of happier times when they'd had house parties with friends for the weekends, and when she had been helping him to restore it. Most of their eleven years of marriage had been happy ones, it was sad to think that it was all ending in disgrace now. It seemed a terrible way to end their marriage. A year before, she would never have expected them to be separated. She tried not to think about it as she slipped into bed between the beautiful Porthault sheets she had bought for all the beds.

They drove to several of the local villages the next day, and then went to walk on the boardwalk in Deauville. The kids loved it. They had a late lunch at a small, noisy local restaurant. The weather had gotten warmer, and they were eager to get back to the pool after lunch.

Nadia had rented a van for the week so she could chauffeur them around. When they got to the château, all the children changed into bathing suits and dove into the pool, while their mothers walked in slowly from the shallow end. Ben and Harley got into a serious political discussion, with similar opinions, despite their differences in politics and age. The two brothers-in-law liked each other, and were a good balance to their wives, who couldn't have been more different too.

Ben and Will finally started a chess game a little later, while Nadia chatted with her sisters on three lounge chairs, and they FaceTimed with Athena again. It was only eight in the morning for her, but she was an early riser. They could hear the dogs barking in the background.

They rented a sailboat big enough for all of them on one of the days. Ben, Olivia, and Harley were expert sailors, and so was Will after years of sailing camp. They went from one day to the next, doing fun things and having lively conversations. They truly enjoyed each other's company and it showed. The children were caught up in the warm family atmosphere too.

Whenever Nicolas called the girls, he told them to give everyone his love. He had been thinking about them a lot, and missing them. He was getting tired of Pascale's jet-set life with endless hangers-on in Saint-Tropez. They were all along for a free ride, and he hadn't had a serious conversation all summer. He was eager to get back to work in Paris, although he had no place to stay now, or to write, if Nadia was serious about his getting his own apartment. Pascale was going to stay in Brittany with her mother until the baby was born, and for a month or two after, until she recovered. She had given up her Paris apartment, so he was camping at a friend's. He was beginning to think he had to get an apartment of his own after all. He had nowhere to stay long-term, and he could no longer count on Nadia letting him stay at their apartment.

On the last day of the vacation, Olivia was watching Will play an intense game of chess with his father, and she leaned over and whispered to her sisters.

"Ever since I told you guys, I feel like I should tell Harley. I hate to be so dishonest with him. Sooner or later, the lie will corrode our relationship," she said pensively, and both her sisters looked horrified.

"Don't you dare tell him," Venetia whispered back. "Harley is much too straightlaced and old school to understand it. You'll break his heart."

"What if he leaves you?" Nadia added, frightened for her sister.

"He wouldn't. He has too big a heart, and he loves Will too much to do that."

"I don't think he'd abandon Will, but he might leave you for lying to him. Harley is pretty rigid," Venetia whispered to Olivia. "You *can't* tell him after all this time. And what would you gain from it? What difference does it make now?"

"It's a matter of integrity," Olivia insisted.

"You should have thought of that fifteen years ago," Venetia said, sounding very definite. "Why would you tell him now?"

"After I told you, I realized how wrong it was not to have told him sooner."

"But you didn't, so just forget about it now," Nadia insisted.

"What if he finds out one day after I die? He'd hate me forever," Olivia said to both of them.

"He's twenty-one years older than you are. That's not going to happen," Venetia said practically.

"It could," Olivia said. It had weighed on her heavily since the Fourth of July, and she thought about it all the time now. Venetia and Nadia did everything they could to convince her to just put it behind her and forget about it. Her window of opportunity was long past.

It was with genuine regret that they said goodbye when the week ended. Venetia and Olivia and their families flew back to New York together. And late on Sunday afternoon, Nadia drove Sylvie and Laure back to Paris in the rented van that seemed so empty now, without the six cousins talking and laughing, the three sisters chatting, and the two men in earnest conversation about a variety of topics. Ben had liked Harley more than ever, with more time to explore the different facets of him. He could see why Olivia loved him. He was an extremely intelligent, very well-balanced man, with deep knowledge of many fields of interest.

Sylvie and Laure fell asleep on the drive back to the city, and Nadia drove in silence, thinking about how much she loved her sisters and how lucky she was to have them. And she loved both of her brothers-in-law, and Athena's long-term boyfriend, Joe. The three men couldn't have been more different, just as she and her sisters were, and their children. They all had distinct personalities and diverse interests. She woke the girls up when she got home, and they helped her carry the bags in, and get them up to the apartment in the elevator. The housekeeper had left food in the refrigerator, but they only wanted a snack for dinner. They ate cheese, cold meats, and fruit they'd brought home from the château.

For the next several days, Nadia had a lot to do to get the girls ready for school. Nicolas had texted her that he wanted to see them and asked when he could come to the apartment. She was grateful for the break they'd taken, being away from each other. Her heart didn't ache quite so acutely. She had started enjoying life again, after their trip to the States, and her family's visit to the château.

Nicolas showed up faithfully the next afternoon, after Nadia had chased around with the children all day, doing errands, buying notebooks and school supplies, and new backpacks to put them in. They found pink ones that the girls loved. They showed the backpacks to their father as soon as he walked in, and he assured them they were terrific. Nadia smiled when she saw him with them. Sometimes for an instant she forgot the chasm that had opened between them.

"Did you have fun with your sisters?" he asked Nadia when he saw her.

"Lots. Thank you for the use of the château. They love it there." She was trying to keep her distance.

"Are you serious about my getting my own apartment?" he asked her when the kids were out of earshot. Pascale had made a big fuss about wanting to live with him, and instead she was going to be with her mother in Brittany for a few months. She'd had a temporary furnished rental apartment in Paris she didn't like, and it was going to be too small for her and the baby, so she had given it up.

"Yes, I am serious," Nadia answered him. "I don't think it's healthy for us to live together, or for you to stay here a few nights a week. If you have your own life, you should have your own place. It's misleading and confusing for them and for us if you stay here." Now that they knew about Pascale and the baby, she felt more comfortable asking him to move out.

He nodded reluctantly. He was in no position to argue with her. "I'll call a realtor tomorrow. Are you still going to see the lawyer?" he asked her cautiously.

"Yes, I am. I think he's back from vacation next week. I just want to establish some ground rules for both of us to follow." They had actually been managing well without them, but he dropped by whenever he wanted, without warning. Lately, he had been calling first, but not always. He still felt as though he lived with them.

"I'll be in Brittany for a couple of weeks in October," he said, and they both knew why, although he didn't say it. He was going to be there for his son's birth. But it didn't sound as though he would be seeing him regularly, if Pascale was planning to leave him with her mother. That way she wouldn't have to hire a nanny or worry about him. She joked about it and said she had never liked babysitting when she was younger, which shocked Nicolas. And yet she had wanted the baby, like a doll to play with when it suited her.

Thinking about it made Nadia realize how difficult it would be to go back to him, if she had wanted to. They would always have his son as a reminder of his affair with Pascale, even if they were no longer together. The child would be a living reminder of the hearts that had been broken when he came into the world. She felt sorry for the baby, with an absentee mother and a father who had another family he felt closer to. She wondered if Nicolas would fall in love with him, as he had with their girls. He had been crazy about them when they were born. Maybe he would with this one too, since he was a boy.

"Where are you staying now?" she asked Nicolas before he left, since she knew that Pascale was still in Ramatuelle.

"I'm staying with a friend. And I'm going to move to a hotel. It seems less complicated." She nodded, and didn't feel guilty about it. It was necessary, and a natural consequence of his actions. Everything seemed to be going smoothly, until he turned around and looked at her right before he left. "I still love you, you know," he said softly. She didn't know what to say at first.

"That's too bad for both of us," she said. She knew he missed the apartment, their shared lifestyle, and their daughters. She wasn't convinced he missed *her*. "You'll get used to it. We both will. It's a big change for all of us," she responded quietly.

"I'm not so sure I will get used to it. I've made some terrible mistakes in the last several months," he said.

"Let's not talk about it now," she said. She was tired and didn't want to dredge it all up again. "It happened. Now we have to live with it." *Forever,* she thought. "Good night." She walked to her room, and a minute later, she heard the front door close behind him.

* * *

The September issue of *Mode* came out, as it always did, in the last week of August. It sat on the corner of Rose's desk, and she didn't handle it with pride this time. She always loved the look of the thick magazine, with all its wonders. She was usually so proud of it, and it represented such a huge collaboration and so much work and inspiration. This time, she cringed every time she saw it. It pained her almost physically to see Pascale Solon on the cover. She was wearing a ruby red evening gown, extraordinary makeup, and the photograph itself was a work of art. The girl on the cover was a beauty, almost like a gem herself. And the photographs taken in Ramatuelle were inside the magazine, with the interview.

Olivia, Athena, and Venetia had gotten their copies, since they subscribed. Nadia always bought hers at a newsstand. She saw it on her way home from work, the day the girls started school. The red dress caught her eye, and she stood staring at it for a minute, not wanting to buy it, but feeling compelled to. It was as though it had beckoned to her. She had promised herself she wouldn't buy it this time, but after standing in front of the kiosk for a full five minutes, she finally reached into her wallet, pulled out the money, handed it to the vendor, and grabbed a copy. She clutched it to her chest like something alive that she was shielding, as though it could leap out of her arms. Once she'd bought it, she hurried home, wanting desperately not to read it, but she knew she had to. It would not let her go now, as though it had tentacles, which held her fast.

She threw it on her bed when she walked into the apartment, sat down and stared at the cover for a long time, looking at every inch of Pascale's face as though she were alive, and then she checked the table of contents, found the page number, and opened the magazine to the feature story. There was a full-page photograph of Nicolas and Pascale sitting on a lounge chair together, his arm casually around her, Pascale in a white lace dress, where you could almost see her breasts but not quite, and the full belly, which was carrying his baby. It nearly choked Nadia when she saw it, and she studied each photograph carefully, then read the interview. The questions were painful for Nadia, and Pascale's answers were innocuous. Nicolas's more artful answers were even more so. He had tried to glide through each question they had asked him, and in every image of them, he appeared happy. Looking at it, Nadia wondered why she had hesitated to divorce him. He appeared to be so in love with Pascale, and so bewitched by her. She finished reading the article and had to admit that none of it was actually tasteless. At one point she could see that they had pressed him about his marriage, and they had printed his response, "I love my family very much," and then he had changed the subject. He said he was excited about the baby, but that was all he'd said about it. The rest of the time, he had talked of their working together on the film, what a powerful experience it had been for everyone in the cast, and what a talented actress she was. He had thrown many compliments her way for her acting, and he had spoken as little as possible about their relationship. He had handled it artfully, and defused most of the loaded questions. Pascale had spoken almost entirely about herself. All roads led to Rome with her. She was the classic, young narcissistic actress, and Nicolas almost seemed like a backdrop for her, a piece of stage scenery put there to enhance her. He didn't seem stupid so much as deluded, and Nadia didn't find her touching or innocent or *sympathique* in her responses. It was what you'd expect from a girl her age, who had recently exploded into stardom. She was very taken with herself. And the poses she melted into were invariably sexy. Nadia glanced through the photographs again until she'd had enough, and then she called her mother in New York. It was lunchtime for her, and Nadia got her on her cell.

"I know how terrible you feel about the interview, Mom," she said simply, and Rose made a groaning sound, almost as though she was choking, or the interview was stuck in her throat. "I just wanted to tell you that I think it was done very tastefully. It's better than I expected. It hurts to see him with her, but it's nothing I don't know, and he was careful and respectful with his responses." She wanted her mother to know that she had survived it and had suffered less than her mother feared.

"Do you really think so?" her mother asked, amazed, and deeply grateful for the call.

"Yes, I do," Nadia said, relieved that it hadn't been worse. She thought it would rip her heart out, but it hadn't.

"I was so worried about how you'd feel about it. It made me sick to publish it. The last thing I wanted to do was hurt you, but there was an incredible amount of pressure about it."

"They're the hot topic. You did it as elegantly as ever, Mom. I'm proud of you. I know it can't have been easy to pull it off without being sleazy. It's a pretty cheesy story to work with." Rose had sat on the writer relentlessly, and had edited it herself several times. She felt as though Nadia had just lifted a thousand-pound weight off her shoulders.

"Your call means the world to me," Rose said gratefully.

"I just wanted you to know that it's fine, I'm okay, and I love you."

Each sister had a different reaction to it. Venetia told her husband and her sisters that she thought it was disgusting and the writer was a little bitch. Athena thought Pascale looked like a whore in the lace dress. And Olivia read Nicolas's responses and called her mother and said he was a "sick fuck" and she was embarrassed to know him. When Nicolas read it, and saw the photographs of him and Pascale, he sat and cried, knowing how Nadia must have felt when she read it. The only one who was okay with it was Nadia, because she had expected something so much worse, and she could see how hard her mother must have tried to rein it in and keep it clean and aboveboard. Rose was just grateful that Nadia didn't hate her, and it hadn't broken her heart, again. Like Nicolas, she just sat at her desk and cried, but hers were tears of relief. She would rather have died than hurt any of her daughters, and was so relieved that Nadia didn't hold it against her.

Chapter 10

The day after Nadia read the interview that she'd been so terrified of, she felt strangely free, as though she didn't have a care in the world and everything was going to be okay. It was the first time she had felt that way since May. She walked to her office, and was smiling when she got to work. Her assistant, Agnes, had read the article the night before too, and didn't dare comment on it to her, not sure how she might react. She noticed Nadia's good mood immediately.

Nicolas called her on her cell and she didn't take the call. That felt good too. Somehow, she had turned a corner, and she couldn't wait for her attorney to get back. She was ready to make a move. It had taken her three months, but she felt like herself again. She knew there would be hard times ahead, but nothing could be as bad as what she had lived through since May, when she read about his affair in the tabloids and then learned that Pascale was pregnant with his baby. It had been a nightmare, but she was finally waking up.

Venetia called to check on her, and Nadia told her she was fine, and her sister could hear it in her voice.

"You're a better woman than I. I wanted to kill him when I read it last night," Venetia said, still upset about it. Ben hadn't liked it either and thought that flaunting the affair was in bad taste. He didn't blame Rose. He blamed Nicolas for the whole thing. Rose had a business to run, and an editorial board and owners to satisfy. All Nicolas had to satisfy were his ego and his mistress.

"Poor Mom was so stressed out about it. I called and told her that I was okay, and I really am," Nadia said cheerfully.

"I know she's been worried sick about it. As long as you're all right, that's all any of us care about. And fuck him," Venetia said, and Nadia laughed.

As soon as she hung up, her assistant told her there was a call for her, from a man who had called twice that morning before she arrived. "He was referred by a Mrs. Archer in London. He said she was a client. It must have been before my time." Agnes had only worked for Nadia for a year, after studying interior design in London and New York. She was bright, young, and energetic, and loved working for Nadia, although Nadia hadn't been at her best for the past few months, and business had been slow. "Do you want to take the call?" Agnes asked her. "His name is Gregory Holland."

"Sure," Nadia said, feeling revitalized. "Mr. Holland, Nadia Bateau. What can I do to help you?" He explained that he was an old friend of a previous client of hers in London, who had recommended her. He had just moved from New York, to run an American investment bank with a Paris office. He said he had rented a house in the sixteenth arrondissement and was hoping she'd have time to decorate it for him. His friend had warned him that she was busy.

"I'm afraid I don't have the talent or the time," he said with a deep voice.

"How big is it?" she asked, grabbing a notepad and a pen, and jotting down his name.

"Four hundred square meters. I believe that's roughly four thousand square feet."

"That's a pretty big place," she said. "Is your family with you?"

"No, I'm divorced. No wife, no kids. I'm originally from Texas. We like things big," he said, and she smiled. "Could we get together and talk? I'm staying at the Ritz until I get settled. Would you meet me for a drink?" She had to get the sitter to stay late, but he sounded like an interesting prospect.

"I'd be happy to," she said smoothly, wishing she had worn something fancier to work. She was wearing a plain Dior black pantsuit, but it was simple and professional and looked good on her.

"Six o'clock? The Bar Vendôme at the Ritz?" he asked.

"That sounds perfect. How will I recognize you?"

"I'll be carrying a book and a red rose, and wearing a black hat." For a minute she was afraid he was a nutcase, and then he laughed. "I'm six feet five, and have white hair," he said easily, and she liked him even before meeting him. She hoped he had good taste, but if not, she could educate him.

"I'm five-feet-two, have dark brown hair, and I'm wearing a black pantsuit."

"I've seen your photograph on your website. I'll recognize you. See you at six."

She was busy for the rest of the day. She spoke to several of her clients, had Agnes check on outstanding orders now that factories were reopening after the summer, and got an Uber at five-thirty to take her to the Ritz. The traffic was heavy crossing over to the Right Bank, but she arrived right on time, and walked up the stairs of the venerable hotel. It had always been her favorite hotel in Paris, even since the remodel. She knew it was the most expensive one, more so than ever after its facelift. So if he was living there, his budget for the apartment was likely to be a healthy one.

She glanced around the bar as she walked in, wondered how she'd recognize him if he wasn't standing, and saw who he was immediately. He had well-cut white hair, was wearing a dark blue suit, an impeccable white shirt, and a navy Hermès tie. He stood up as soon as she approached his table, and he was as tall as he had said. He appeared young and athletic in spite of the white hair, and she guessed him to be in his early forties, if that. He had blue eyes, a wide friendly smile, and a cleft chin. He had movie star good looks.

"Thank you for meeting me on such short notice. I just got the final paperwork on the house this weekend, and I'm anxious to get started. It's in a great location, the building has full concierge services, which is convenient for me. It's actually a house within a building." As soon as they sat down, a waiter came to the table. Nadia ordered white wine, and he had scotch. He was a classic American, the best of his breed. Handsome and in great shape. He looked like someone who went to the gym regularly, and probably had one of his own. His suit was perfectly cut. He was businesslike, efficient, had an impressive job, and sounded like a straight shooter. She could hear a faint hint of Texas when he spoke, but very little, and he wanted the job finished yesterday.

"That's a big house for one person," she commented, as he showed her the plans and the pictures he had brought with him. They looked interesting.

"I like a lot of space, and I entertain frequently for business. I need the name of a good caterer, by the way." He was all business and no frills, and she liked dealing with clients like him. They knew what they wanted, didn't get emotional about it, and rarely made mistakes.

She wrote down the name of the best caterer in Paris, and a smaller one that was good for intimate dinners, and handed the slip of paper to him. He took it and put it in his jacket pocket.

"I lived in London for five years," he told her. "I'm looking forward to Paris. That's the advantage of no wife and kids. I'm free to move around. I don't have to worry about schools, or anyone complaining about leaving home. How long have you lived here?"

"I've been here since I was twenty. I came to go to the Sorbonne, and stayed. I was . . . I've been . . . I am," she corrected herself, "married to a Frenchman."

"That sounds a little vague, past or present?" he teased her, and she blushed in embarrassment.

"Sorry, it is a little vague at the moment. We're separated." She didn't want to tell him her personal life, which was unprofessional, but she had fallen into it.

"That's too bad. I've been divorced twice. It's not fun. Fortunately, no children. I married my high school sweetheart the first time, and she turned out not to be such a sweetheart," he said with a grin. "The second time I married a powerhouse in finance. Brilliant woman, lousy wife. She cheated on me with my trainer. That's a little low rent for me. Actually, we got divorced and she married him. And now I'm here." He seemed very matter-of-fact about it. She didn't tell him about Nicolas and Pascale. "Do you have kids?"

"Two girls." She smiled. "Seven and ten. Now let's talk about your house. Tell me about your dream house. If you had a magic wand, what would you want?" She liked giving people their dreams and improving on them.

"Everything," he answered. "A huge living room, which it has. I like big furniture, I'm a big man. Fabulous bedroom, a gym. A dining room I can entertain in. Big table for anywhere from ten to twenty-four guests. A cozy den where I can work at home. The place has everything I need space-wise, but big rooms can look cold if you don't do them right. That's where you come in."

"Colors?"

"Dark blue, hunter green, deep red, good lighting for the art." He had very definite ideas, which in some ways would make it easier, in others harder, if he wasn't open to new ideas. "I like charcoal gray too."

"Modern?"

"Traditional, classic," the way he dressed. "I'd like to show you the space when you have time. I'm pretty tied up this week. Maybe on the weekend?" She knew she'd have to get a sitter, or maybe Nicolas would take the girls for a few hours. That was the hard part of being alone now, juggling her work schedule and her daughters, but that wasn't the client's problem, it was hers, and she wasn't going to make it his. He didn't look like the kind of man who would put up with it. He'd expect her to be available when he was, and since he didn't have children, he wouldn't be sympathetic to hers. She had other clients like him, and as long as you delivered what they wanted, on schedule, it all went well. And she liked working with businessmen like him. They were decisive, knew what they wanted, and didn't waste time.

At seven o'clock, he paid the check, wrote down the address of the house for her, and they agreed to meet at noon on Saturday. Then they stood up and walked out of the Ritz together. He was all business, but she liked him. He was smart, fast, and efficient, and the client he had mentioned knowing had been a pleasure to work with too. He said he was on his way out for dinner.

They shook hands in front of the Ritz, and the doorman got her a cab, while Gregory Holland got into his car. He drove a sleek black Bentley sports car. He wasn't showy or vulgar, but he clearly had money. And as long as she came up with ideas he liked, and delivered on time, she thought she had a new client. She couldn't wait to see what his "house within a house" looked like and to get started.

She felt alive again on the way home. For the past four months she had thought of nothing but Nicolas's affair. She had let her business slide, and fortunately much of that time had been during the slow summer months, and in August, almost everything in France was closed. She had felt dazed with her children, depressed about the collapse of her marriage, indifferent to her clients, and now she suddenly felt back on track, and ready to take life by the horns. Gregory Holland heralded a new era in her life. For eleven years, she had been married, putting everyone else's needs first, making her schedule work with theirs, worrying about Nicolas's career with each new book, delicately giving him advice when she read his early manuscripts, being available at all times, at work, at home. Now it was just her and the kids. It was true that at times it would be more of a balancing act without another adult present, especially on weekends, but she also had one less person to drop everything for and take care of. At times, especially when he was writing, Nicolas had been needy and demanding, almost like a child.

Meeting with Gregory Holland had infused new life into her work. She had a feeling that his house was going to be amazing. Even more so if she got to work on it. She had no other big projects at the moment. The house she had installed in Madrid in May was a huge job, and the client had spent a fortune on it. The installation was why she hadn't been able to join Nicolas at the Cannes Film Festival, and their life had imploded after that. She had done a fabulous vacation home in Punta Cana in the Dominican Republic right before that, and had juggled both projects for over a year. But since Madrid, there had been a lull. She had time to tackle a big job now, and it would be easy managing it right in Paris, and not abroad.

One of her clients was looking for a new larger home in London, but they hadn't found what they wanted yet, and she had a new client in London for a small pied-à-terre she could do easily, so Gregory Holland's job was welcome. Her work was always feast or famine. Either five of her clients had new homes, half of them in different cities, or they had a quiet spell, which never lasted long. Her reputation carried her along, and eventually brought in new clients by word of mouth. A particularly showy project, with a client who wanted it photographed in every magazine, helped to build her business. She had done extremely well in the past ten years, and was one of the youngest, most successful decorators in Paris.

Nicolas had agreed to take the girls out for a few hours on Saturday, although he said he was going to Brittany that night to help Pascale settle in, and he was going to stay there for a few days. He told her he had rented a small furnished apartment in Paris that week. He didn't sound enthused about it, but she was relieved that he had taken her seriously and was moving forward. Her life felt more on track now too. She had told him she had an important meeting with a prospective new client, and he was willing to accommodate her.

Nadia arrived ten minutes early for the appointment and stood outside the impressive stone building with tall ornate glass and metal doors that required a code to enter. She peered into the courtyard and saw a security guard, a parking attendant, and a guardian, all properly dressed in black suits, and giant marble urns with palm trees at the entrance to the courtyard. Gregory Holland drove up as she was looking in, used a remote control, and the heavy doors opened and he drove in. She followed his car in on foot, and he unfolded his long limbs out of the car, then turned it over to the parking attendant. It was extremely rare to have that kind of personnel in a residential building in Paris, unlike New York or L.A., where it was commonplace.

She noticed as soon as she walked into the courtyard that there was a beautifully proportioned private home nestled there. Gregory said good morning to Nadia and walked toward it.

"That's it? The house?" She looked surprised. She had only seen a house tucked away like that once before. It was like a magical surprise behind the doors of the building around it. They were on the front steps by then, and he took the key out of his pocket.

"The building is all large floor-through apartments. The house is really more of a home. There's a swimming pool, a wine cellar, a gym, and a movie theater in the basement, most of which I won't have time to use, except for the gym and pool. It's kind of a giant bachelor pad. It has a master suite on the top floor, one guest room on the floor below, and a study, which I'll use a lot. The reception rooms are on the main floor. I really lucked out," he said, as he opened the front door. "It's just what I need, and totally protected in this courtyard, with a great deal of security in the building, and surveillance cameras everywhere. I put some of my art in storage before I came here, but the building is so safe, I'm shipping it over." She had looked him up on the internet after their meeting, and it said he was an important collector of contemporary art, but it hadn't listed the artists. She realized as she followed Gregory into the house that a plum had fallen into her lap.

The main floor of the house had a vast entrance hall which fed into a huge living room, dining room, and state-of-the-art kitchen, with a view of an enclosed garden. He could easily give a cocktail party for two hundred people there, or a dinner for twenty or thirty. As he had described, up a sweeping marble staircase was a beautiful guest suite, and an office for himself, and the master suite on the top floor with a dressing room and an enormous round bathtub. The way the house had been renovated had a sleek, stark, almost masculine style, which suited him. It didn't have all the little feminine touches that a woman might have liked, or that the house may have had before the renovation. He was right. It was the perfect bachelor pad, and a dream house for any man. It was made for him, and what Nadia sensed about his style from what she could see and what experience had taught her about people and homes. Although there were always some surprises, which was what she liked about her business.

"So what do you think?" he asked her after they had toured the entire house, even the wine cellar and the gym.

"I think you have found an absolute gem. I've heard about these courtyard homes but only seen one, and it was small and dark. The renovation here was brilliantly done," and there were skylights in several key places, "it's a truly beautiful home."

"Originally, I wanted something smaller. But five years is a long time, and I would miss my art, so I'm having it sent out now. The house lends itself perfectly to the kind of art I collect. It has all the space I need, will be great to entertain in, and I have a guest room if I need it. It wouldn't have had enough closets for either of my wives," but there were two good walk-in closets for him, which was more than he required. Nadia liked the strong, masculine, clean feeling to it. There were no little fussy details or precious spaces that annoyed most men, except if they were trying to please their wives. Since he'd spoken of his two wives and marriages with a certain sarcastic irony, he didn't seem to her like a candidate for marriage, and she had the strong sense that he expected to live there alone and wasn't unhappy about it.

Everything about him personified to her American businessman at the top of his field. He was more than just a bank president, he was an investment expert, and clearly had done well with his own.

"So what do you think?" he asked her again. He got straight to the point on every subject. After living her whole adult life in Europe, she wasn't used to men like him. Even her wealthiest and most important European clients had a softer edge to them than Gregory. And yet she found his whole demeanor fascinating. He was like a brilliantly constructed missile, designed to hit the most minute target with infinite precision. She could tell he didn't like wasting time and wanted everything handled rapidly and immediately. And she liked how direct he was. Clients like him were a pleasure to work with. "What's your vision?" he asked, and the way he said it made her feel that he expected a full-on presentation of what to do, twenty minutes after she had walked into the house with him. He was presenting her with a major challenge. She would have to work fast, deliver the goods, meet every deadline, and come up with creative solutions that appealed to him. She suspected that she'd never had a client quite as tough or clear, and who had set the bar as high for her. It was stressful, but also very exciting, and she wanted to satisfy him and prove to him and herself that she could.

"I'd like a little more time to think about it." She smiled at him. "But off the top of my head, with these vast open spaces on the main floor, I'm thinking white, maybe some charcoal gray, black—but not too much—a dark, intimate dining room with modern silver gleaming. Either some striking sculptures, even enormous ones, and possibly one in the garden, or some fabulous piece of carved Chinese jade, contrasting old and new," which she knew would cost a fortune. "We could go brighter, but the white would lighten it all up. Browns in the study if you're comfortable with that, various shades of chocolate or hunter green, since you mentioned it. A silver blue-gray in the bedroom, which would be restful. We can work with some textures to give it relief and a great piece of art. We can go neutral in the guest room, beige or gray, whatever you prefer, maybe a gray flannel. We can look for a fabulous rug for the main floor, or have one made. I have some very good resources in India. We're talking six months, or at worst a year. And I'd like to see the artwork you're bringing over, because in some cases, we should be guided by them." She was squinting as she said it, imagining it, and he looked at her with growing interest and frank admiration.

"You're hired. Martha was right. You're amazing. I like every single idea you just shared with me. Would you take the job, after I see an estimate for your fees?" But she had the distinct impression that cost wasn't going to be an obstacle, and the woman in London who had referred her had said that Nadia wasn't cheap but she was very good.

"Of course I'd take the job." She smiled at him. "That's why I'm here. I think it will be fun to work with you. How soon would you like a presentation? And I'll include a time and fee estimate with it," she said, respecting his businesslike get-right-to-the-point style.

"Does a week from today sound too unreasonable?" he asked her. "I'm better dealing with something like this on the weekends." A week was going to be a race against time to gather all the materials she wanted to show him, and enough options to excite and inspire him, but not overwhelm or confuse him.

"I can make it work," she said with a look of determination. She was going to have to ask their babysitter to work for a few hours on Saturday mornings, until she didn't need weekly meetings with him.

"Great." He smiled broadly at her and seemed to relax. He held out a hand and shook hers. He had a firm handshake, and a gentler look in his eyes than he had at first. "You seem like a powerhouse, Nadia. At least your separation or divorce hasn't slowed you down any, from what I can see. I was a mess for two years the first time. I felt dead inside. The second time took me about eight months to get back on my feet. The world lost all its color for me for a while." It was hard to imagine his being overly emotional and upset by anything. He seemed to be in full control of his life.

"It was a difficult summer," she admitted, "but I'm better now." She didn't want him to think she was falling apart just when he needed her. "It was all a bit of a surprise."

"It usually is," he said with just the thinnest razor-sharp edge of bitterness in his voice. "Somebody told me you don't know the people you're married to until you get divorced. I think it's true. Some people know it's wrong right from the beginning. I never did. I got blindsided by my own stupidity, I guess. Anyway, I hope your situation goes okay. I'm sure it's even harder with kids involved, emotionally speaking. The economics can be pretty ugly either way." She could easily imagine that greedy women would have wanted a fortune from him. He seemed like he came from old money, had made a fortune on his own, and had a big job on top of it. It was a recipe for people wanting to take advantage of him, which wasn't her situation with Nicolas. There were no vast fortunes involved, and what Nicolas had inherited from his parents was entirely his, and she had no problem with that. She had a successful business of her own. It wasn't about money with Nicolas. She imagined that Gregory lived a lonely life in a rarefied world, which wasn't her situation. Gregory Holland was all business.

"I'll have everything to present to you next week," she said with a smile, and they took a last run-through to make sure they hadn't missed anything. She would need a set of blueprints from him if he hired her. Nadia made a few notes and then he set the alarm, and they walked out together. She could hardly wait to get home and get started over the weekend. He got in his car and left, and she walked out to hers on the street.

Two hours after she'd left home, she had an enormous new project, which she thought could turn out brilliantly, and a new client. She went to meet Nicolas in the park to pick up the girls. She was going to do errands with them that afternoon.

"How did it go?" Nicolas asked her. He was having fun with the girls, running around and letting them chase him. His eyes lit up when he saw Nadia. He thought she looked beautiful in a red sweater and jeans, with black Hermès riding boots that were just broken in enough to look chic.

"It went great. I think he's going to hire me. He found a beautiful little house in a courtyard. He's a typical American businessman, probably very tough, but smart, sharp, honest, direct, no games, and lots of money."

"That type of guy scares me to death." Nicolas had the soul of an artist, and had been writing since he was a child. In better times, he was sensitive, gentle, and funny. Gregory Holland wasn't any of those things. Her new client didn't seem to have an artistic nature, but in some ways it was a relief. She didn't have to massage his ego or play games with him. All she had to do was work like a dog and make the interior of his new home beautiful. A tall order, but one she felt she could achieve. And the house had good bones. It was a lot easier than dealing with the mess her husband had foisted on them.

She left with the two girls then, and Nicolas said he'd be in touch when he came back from Brittany in a few days. He said he wasn't staying long. Pascale's mother's house was tiny, with one bathroom, and there was barely room for all of them. Nicolas was accustomed to bigger spaces and more comfort, and he wasn't crazy about her mother. Nicolas found her brassy and common. But she was useful, and had promised to take the baby off Pascale's hands to make up for her own past sins with her daughter.

Nadia began working on concepts and drawings for Gregory Holland on Saturday night, and again on Sunday night after Sylvie and Laure were asleep. By Monday, she was on a roll and knew what direction she was heading in. She pulled fabrics from the mills she liked to work with, and included a few photographs of sculptures on her suggestion boards. She computerized drawings and photographs to show him what it could look like.

On Tuesday, she finally got to see her lawyer, whom she hadn't seen since late July. She told him what she was thinking about the divorce, and their current separation.

"You want to file the divorce, Madame Bateau, or wait until he does it?" That idea didn't appeal to her. It put the controls back in his hands, on his schedule. If he didn't want a divorce, he could drag it out forever, or for a very long time. And if their marriage was truly over, she wanted to close the door for good and be free.

"He just got a small apartment last week," she informed her attorney. "He hasn't moved his things out, but I'm sure he will soon."

"It sounds like he's still got a foot firmly planted in your camp, and probably wants to keep it that way, while he makes up his mind," the attorney said wisely.

"He says that he doesn't want a divorce, and wants to come back. But he's still with his mistress, and they're having a baby."

"Are you sure you want a divorce, Madame Bateau?" he asked her pointedly. He had had plenty of clients change their minds. Sometimes it was just too hard to let go, and he suspected that she was still in love with him, despite her brave words about how "done" she was.

"I believe so," she said quietly. "For now I would like a legal separation that officially acknowledges the fact that we're not living together, and I don't want him staying at the house, or even pretending he is to my children. We can always get divorced later. I see it happening more in stages, at least that's what's comfortable for me." She wanted her freedom, but at a dignified pace, which she thought would be better for the children too. They had all been shocked enough.

"We can start the wheels turning now for a legal separation. We can always turn it into a divorce," the lawyer said. Nadia knew that she needed time each step of the way to adjust, as the air got thinner. Like mountain climbing. For now, she realized that she could handle it better, and not panic, if they did it in stages. They still had money and custody to work out, and she knew that Nicolas wasn't ready to discuss that either. She thought she might do better with him with the sensitive issues after the baby, rather than stressing him out even more while he was already unnerved about having a baby with a woman he barely knew. He said he had been in love with Pascale at first, but Nadia wasn't so sure. He was enamored with Pascale, and wanted her body, even pregnant. He had never seen a more gorgeous female body, but that was very different. She had a mouth and a mind and ideas which conflicted with his, even though he was choosing to ignore it so he could be with her. But to Nadia, his relationship with Pascale seemed more like lust than love.

The separation she wanted wasn't a solution to everything, but she felt better after she saw the lawyer. They were on a path now, moving slowly, but there was nonetheless some slight but definite forward movement toward the dissolution of their marriage.

She felt strangely peaceful that night, and in the morning she went back to work on her proposal to Gregory Holland. True to her extraordinary work ethic, Nadia was ready for him the following Saturday when she met him at the house. She had a beautifully put-together proposal, with just enough options, but not so many she'd confuse him. She had good instincts with most of her clients about where that line was, particularly with men, who couldn't tolerate too many decorating choices before their minds turned to mush and they refused everything to escape making any decisions.

Gregory Holland was not afraid of making decisions. He made them every day in his office. Nadia handed him the folder and they sat on the stairs leading up to his bedroom and study. He asked very few questions and said nothing as he went through it. There were fabric samples attached throughout, paint chips, and photographs of paint finishes she thought would make the rooms more interesting and give them some texture. He looked at her when he was finished and handed it back to her. She wasn't sure what that meant for a minute. If he was rejecting her proposal in its entirety or felt too confused to choose anything.

"Fabulous," he said, as he sat close to her on the stairs.

"What part?" she asked him.

"All of it. You're a genius." And he had glanced at her fee estimate without comment.

"Can we pick some options?" she asked him cautiously, and handed the folder back to him. They went through it item by item, while he selected his favorite in each case. The process was fast, simple, and efficient, and in several instances, he loved all of her suggestions. She had never had a client as easy to deal with. In less than half an hour they were finished, including the explanation of why she thought some of the options would work well. And he thought her gray flannel guest room was the epitome of chic. He had even picked several upholstered pieces, large couches for the living room, oversized chairs in dark green leather for his study, and a dining table that seated thirty. With the choices he'd made, the house was going to have a decidedly masculine look, which suited him. He had emailed her images of the art he was having shipped from New York. They were all from major artists, Rothko, Pollock, Warhol, and a stunning Picasso they were going to put in the living room.

"I don't think I've ever been able to do this part of the process as quickly," she said, smiling at him as they left the house. "It's terrific. I'll get everything ordered by Monday." She hadn't promised him, but she was promising herself to have his house finished by Christmas, which was only three months away. She had given him a date further out, so he wouldn't be disappointed if everything didn't arrive as quickly as she hoped, or if they ran into problems or delays.

"You're a whiz, Nadia," he said admiringly. "Do you have time for lunch?" It was a rainy Saturday, and both of her girls were out with friends. She had begun to organize her Saturdays for their morning meetings.

"Actually, I do," she said easily.

"Do you like Costes?" It was trendy and popular, a lot of fashion people and models went there, and they had a year-round covered garden and good food. It was only about a block away from the Ritz in a small boutique hotel. The restaurant was jammed most of the time, and particularly during any of the fashion weeks. It was fun people-watching there.

"I like it a lot." You could have anything from a salad to a major meal, and the food was more international than just French, so Americans loved it.

When they got to the hotel, there was music playing in the hallway leading to the restaurant, and the garden looked bright and cheery under a canvas canopy. The outdoor space was heated, as dozens of sexy young waitresses buzzed around in miniskirts waiting on tables. The headwaiter led them to a quiet table in the corner at Gregory's request. Compared to most popular restaurants, it was busy but not too loud, so they could talk.

Gregory ordered a Bloody Mary, and they ordered spring rolls and salads for lunch. He smiled as he sat back and looked at her. "It's funny, Nadia, you seem so French to me. I forget you're American. Are you part French too?"

"My mother is half English and half Italian, which is a bit of a conflict. She is incredibly organized, and at the same time very creative. I think I inherited it from her."

"Is she an interior designer too?" He could tell from how efficient

Nadia was that she had years of experience, despite the fact that she looked very young.

"My mother is the editor-in-chief of *Mode Magazine,*" she said with a hint of pride. "She's incredibly good at what she does." He smiled as her face lit up when she said it.

"So I've heard. I didn't realize she's British."

"I've been here for all of my adult life, including college, so I guess a lot of that has rubbed off too. I have to admit, I don't feel very American anymore. It's kind of a disconnect for me. My husband was . . . is . . . French, and so are my daughters. I'm just very comfortable here. I always feel a little out of place now when I go back to the States."

"Do you go back often?" He was interested in her, who she was, what she thought, and what made her so talented, because it was clear to him that she was.

"A few times a year," she answered. "I have three sisters there. Two in New York and one in L.A. We're very close, and as different as night and day, or 'chalk and cheese' as the British say. We don't even look related. One of them is a fashion designer, Venetia Wade, my next oldest sister is a superior court judge, and my sister in L.A. is a TV chef and food guru."

He was amused. "That's quite a variety. It must have been fun at your house when you were growing up. What did your father do?"

"He was in finance, and grounded all of us. That's a lot of female energy under one roof. He handled it very well and was very supportive of my mother's work. We still have a great time when we get together. Two of them just came over for a week in August with their families. My oldest sister, the foodie, has dogs instead of children." He laughed.

"Smart girl."

"I take it you're not crazy about kids." She was intrigued by that. He made occasional negative comments about children and marriage.

"I wouldn't say that," he said, pensive for a moment as their food arrived. "I've just never wanted any." He wasn't a warm, cozy person, but he was obviously very smart, which she did find appealing. He was so quick in his responses and thought processes. "I grew up in a scientific household. My father was a research scientist and worked for a big pharmaceutical company in Texas. My mother was a doctor. They wanted me to be a doctor too, but I've always been attracted to business. I find investments fascinating. I love entrepreneurial ventures. What does your ex-husband do, or shouldn't I ask?" It jolted her when he called Nicolas her ex-husband, but she realized she had to get used to it, since he was going to be.

"He's a writer, a novelist." Gregory was intrigued by that.

"That must have been interesting. Bestsellers?"

She nodded. "He's very well known here. It's a pretty dull story otherwise. Several of his books have been made into movies. He had an affair with the star on his last one. The usual tabloid trash. They're having a baby in a couple of weeks."

He winced when she said it. "Wow, I bet that hurt. You filed for divorce, I assume."

"I'm working on it. I just started the process. It took me a few months to catch my breath."

"I'm sorry, Nadia. That must have been nasty to live through. My last divorce was small potatoes compared to that, although finding her getting it on with my trainer wasn't a happy moment for me either. I moved out that night. I gave her the apartment. You can see why I'm not too keen on marriage. You do get over it, but it leaves scars." She nodded, well aware that hers were still raw, even if she was feeling better.

"People have affairs here all the time. It's the one part of French life I've never adapted to. I don't see the point of being married and cheating."

"How are your kids doing?"

"We're getting through it. It's an adjustment. And they're not too happy about the baby. It's a boy, which will be a big deal for my husband, since he's French."

"It sounds like you've been through the wringer," he said gently, and touched her hand. When he did, it surprised her and she looked across the table at him, and smiled.

"Thank you. It's been hard, and the whole thing was a shock. I couldn't have gotten through it without my sisters. They wanted him burned at the stake. I still have to deal with him. He's my children's father."

"That's another reason not to have kids. It ties you to the bad spouses forever. I'd rather cut my losses and run. All I lost in the divorce, other than money, was a dog. I miss him, but he's happy with her. I can always get another dog. I might get one here." He didn't seem emotionally tied to anyone or anything.

He was so different from the men she knew, so unattached and unencumbered, and he seemed to like his life that way. She wondered if he got lonely but didn't know him well enough to ask, and he was a client after all.

"Do you have brothers and sisters?" she asked, wanting to know more about him too.

"No, I'm an only child."

"So is my husband, and one of my nephews. It's very different. My nephew is very adult for his age, he's never around kids except in school."

"That's how it was for me too. I liked it. I thought other kids were silly. In retrospect, I think I never really had a childhood. Maybe that's not such a bad thing. It gave me a head start as an adult. I didn't waste a lot of time on beer bongs and frat parties. I was already an adult when I got to college." He certainly was one now. She realized that that was what was different about him. He wasn't playful, and there wasn't a boyish side of him, despite his good looks. He was an adult through and through. In a way, she felt sorry for him and wondered what he did for fun. He was so disciplined and focused on his work. Every meeting had a purpose, even their lunch. It was so he could get to know her better, because she was his decorator. She served a purpose in his life. If she weren't his designer, she was sure he would never have taken her to lunch. She was certain he was smart in business, but she wondered how intelligent he was about life. The difference between French men and American men was that the French liked to play and have fun. They loved talking to other people. When she had guests over, they stayed late into the night to talk philosophy or politics, or about life. It wasn't just about eating at night, working by day, set on a straight path like a robot.

Gregory was almost like a very handsome bionic man. There wasn't much fantasy there. If he had spare time he probably went to the gym and worked out. He didn't call a friend and meet for coffee. American men were different. French men were warmer and more appealing to her.

She loved the way she and Nicolas could talk into the wee hours, chasing an idea, or arguing over an abstract concept. Nicolas was a philosopher, an observer of the human condition, until he went mad over Pascale. Gregory was all about money, how to make it, how to keep it, how to invest it and make it grow. It was a different mindset. On the other hand, he was probably more disciplined and reliable than any of the men she'd known. As he said, he was an adult, and had been all his life.

They lingered over lunch, then he paid the check, they left the hotel, and walked to the Place Vendôme, where he headed to the hotel and she hailed a cab.

"Thank you for a lovely lunch and time with you, Gregory," she said warmly.

"Call me Greg. I loved it. We're going to do a great house together, Nadia."

"I think so too." She smiled at him.

She slid into the cab, and he waved as the taxi pulled away, to take her back to the Left Bank. The girls weren't home yet, and she walked into her office and sat down at the desk. Greg was fascinatingly American. He had none of the tousled, casual, slightly off look of French men. He was so clean-cut and straight as an arrow. Nadia couldn't imagine him doing something silly or childish or making a fool of himself. There was something sexy but stiff about him. And whatever he was, he seemed like a nice man. She couldn't imagine herself dating him, even once she got free of Nicolas. She was nowhere near that yet. She couldn't envision herself dating anyone, and certainly not a client. But for now, no matter what she told herself about him, or how unworthy he was, she still felt married to Nicolas, and wondered how long that would last. Her ties to him still held her fast. But in time those ties would dissolve. That was her mission now, to sever all the ties she had to Nicolas. She had already started the process.

Chapter 11

Nicolas didn't come to see the girls in the first two weeks of October. He was in Brittany with Pascale, waiting for the baby to come. They had given up the house in Ramatuelle, and had had a good summer there, despite the superficial people she gathered around her. It was part of her life as a star. But now, in her mother's tiny crowded home, she was getting down to the business of having a baby, and Nicolas had promised to stay with her until it came. He found the tiny town her mother lived in painfully boring. He and Pascale sat around playing cards every night or watching TV with her mother. He missed Sylvie and Laure and called them often, but he knew he had to be there with Pascale no matter what happened later, and he wanted to be at his son's birth. He knew it was a magical moment, no matter what the circumstances. He had had no contact with Nadia since he left Paris, and felt he owed Pascale this time. Talking to Nadia would have been too awkward. They both knew why he was there.

Pascale and Nicolas went for long walks by the sea every day and ate her mother's country cooking. Pascale felt heavy now, and uncomfortable at night, although she was as beautiful as ever. She couldn't wait for her pregnancy to be over. She said to him at times that she felt as though aliens had taken over her body. The baby was fighting for space, and finally, three days after her due date, she went into labor. Her mother and Nicolas took her to the hospital. Pascale had insisted she wanted a natural delivery and wasn't prepared for how painful it was. By the time she couldn't stand it anymore and wanted drugs, it was too late to have them. She screamed piteously and Nicolas felt sorry for her. They did their best to help her stay calm, and in the end, no matter how she fought it, the baby tore through her and appeared. She lay crying afterwards, and refused to hold him. Nicolas was the first one to hold his son. He was a big, strapping baby with a lusty cry, and he looked just like her. It shocked Nicolas to realize that Pascale's mother was younger than he was. She had had Pascale at sixteen, and was now a grandmother at thirty-eight.

The oddest thing was that Nicolas was sad not to be able to share this moment with Nadia. The baby hadn't brought him closer to Pascale. It didn't create a bond between them, which surprised him. And he felt sorry for the baby. Pascale had no idea how to be a mother, and no desire to learn. And he was a reluctant father. He'd been roped into it, duped by his lust for Pascale, but with no deep feelings for her.

Pascale looked at her son as though he belonged to someone else, and it reminded Nicolas that becoming a parent took more than just giving birth. You had to want to be one, and she didn't. She had wanted a baby, but had no idea what that meant. She felt separate from the baby, and her mother said she had felt that way too when Pascale was born. They weren't maternal women, and their children weren't born from their love for the baby's father, as his children with Nadia were. Pascale wanted to free herself of the baby and take her body back. It hadn't been the magical experience she thought it would be. It was long and painful and hard. It was too much for her. All she wanted to do afterwards was sleep, and she refused to nurse him. Her mother helped take care of the baby in the hospital, and Nicolas did too. But it was different from what it had been with Sylvie and Laure. He and Nadia had been so excited to share them. His son had come into the world with a mother who was still a child herself, and a father who felt guilty every time he looked at him. Nicolas had feelings for him, but the baby wasn't part of Nicolas's family. He was a separate entity. When Pascale went home to her mother's house, Nicolas spent a few days with them, feeling like an outsider, and then went back to Paris to his rented apartment. All he wanted to do was get away. He knew he didn't belong in Brittany with them. He wanted to see his daughters, and to show them photographs of their brother when he saw them. He was sad about the life the baby would live, with Pascale and her mother. Nicolas was going to provide for him and already had, but it took more than money to parent a child, and Nicolas didn't intend to be a full-time presence in his son's life. He couldn't be.

They had posed for photographs Pascale's mother took, with Nicolas holding the baby, and within days, they appeared in the tabloids. Nicolas was sure that her mother had sold them to the press. He was wearing doctor's scrubs, and smiling into the camera, as he held his son. The tabloids announced the baby's birth, and Nicolas hoped that their interest in the baby's arrival would end there. It provided a conclusion to their love story, and not a fairy-tale ending. They named the baby Benoit, which was the name Pascale had wanted. Nicolas acknowledged him by allowing him to use his last name, and intended to provide for him generously. He had made all the arrangements, and Pascale supported her mother so Benoit would lead a comfortable life. But somehow the infant didn't seem as much his child as Sylvie and Laure had, because he didn't love the boy's mother in the same way. In the end, Nicolas discovered, it did make a difference. It was a relief to get back to Paris, after two weeks in Brittany. His time there seemed surreal, despite the arrival of his son. The baby wasn't integrated into his life and never would be.

When he got back, he took the girls to the château for the weekend. It was beautiful there in the fall, and he filled his lungs with the familiar air of Normandy, thinking about the infant he had left in Brittany who had no place in his Paris life, which seemed sad to him.

He took the girls to the beach, even though the sea was rough and the weather chilly. The girls suddenly seemed so big and grown up to him. They were filled with tales about school and their friends. He'd seen Nadia when he picked them up and she waved from the distance. She was busy. The girls told him that she was doing a big job for an American.

He'd had a letter from her lawyer when he returned, asking him to acknowledge their legal separation. And this year, when she had the traditional Thanksgiving dinner she had every year to keep the girls in touch with their American connection, she didn't invite him. He hadn't expected her to, but he was disappointed anyway. They had agreed to share the girls during the holidays. She was getting them for Christmas Eve, and the week before. He would pick them up on Christmas Day, and have them until New Year's Day. He made arrangements to take them skiing in Val d'Isère, where he had many friends. He didn't know yet what Pascale's plans were, or when she would return to Paris. They'd spoken on the phone and he had told her he would be with his children over Christmas, and she didn't seem to mind. She seemed less interested in spending time with him now that the baby was born, and she had plans of her own. She told Nicolas she was going to St. Barth's with friends to get some sun, and didn't suggest he come along, which he couldn't have done anyway.

She came to Paris when the baby was a month old, and had left him with her mother in Brittany, as she had planned. She didn't look as though she'd had a baby. She had her figure back, and was starting her next movie in January.

She had her life back too, her mobility and independence, and Nicolas was less a part of it than he'd been before. He spent a night with her in his new apartment, but everything was different. The magic was gone, and it was clear that their blazing, white-hot romance was over. He was a man she had had a baby with, but he could tell that she wasn't as in love with him. She had conquered him and was ready to move on. And his feelings for her had dissipated. His heart had remained with Nadia, not Pascale. He had to face the consequences of what he'd done. And he didn't want his son to pay the price for his foolishness.

Nadia congratulated him when she saw him a few weeks after the baby was born, but she was cool and distant with him, and he thanked her politely. The girls weren't asking to meet their half brother. After seeing the first photographs of the baby, they didn't mention him again. They could tell that they hadn't lost their father to him, which was all that concerned them, and it was obvious that he loved them as much as ever. He didn't talk about the baby either. He didn't want to upset them.

At Nicolas's request, he and Pascale were going to arrange some kind of visitation schedule when Benoit was older, and he was paying her enough in support to amply cover all his expenses, including a nanny to help her mother. He expected to pay for Benoit's education. And according to French law, since Nicolas had acknowledged him legally, Benoit would inherit equally with his half sisters from Nicolas's estate one day. It was all about details now. But physically, the child wasn't really part of his life, or Pascale's either, which worried Nicolas, but didn't bother Pascale at all. Nicolas didn't go to Brittany, and the baby was too young to visit him in Paris.

Shortly after Pascale got back to Paris in November, he wasn't surprised to see her in the tabloids with a new man, the male lead in the movie she would start in January. He was a hot young French actor, twenty-four years old. Nicolas didn't call her after that, and she didn't call him either. Their relationship was over, but their bond through their son had only just begun.

"Are you still with her, Papa?" Sylvie asked him about Pascale one day when they were at the château. He thought about it and shook his head. He wasn't, and hadn't talked about it until then with anyone. The whole episode was embarrassing, especially with them.

"No, I'm not," he said quietly. Their affair had lasted less than a year, just long enough to have the baby, who would grow up with his grandmother now, with occasional visits from his father, and a mother who was a movie star. Nicolas intended to visit him, but living apart he would probably never be as close to Benoit as he was to Sylvie and Laure, and he was sad about it. It wasn't the fate he would have wanted for his son, but it was what had happened, given the circumstances. He would provide him a good life, and comforts he wouldn't have had otherwise, but his father wouldn't be close at hand as he grew up. He was the product of their passion and their indulgence. Nicolas regretted it, whenever he thought about it, and wanted to do as much as he could for Benoit to make up for it.

A letter from Nadia's lawyer in December told him that the divorce was going forward. Nadia wanted support for the girls, and none for herself. She wanted their apartment put in the girls' names, and the use of it herself, as long as she wished to live there, which was customary in French law. She was taking nothing for herself from the marriage. The château was his and would belong to the girls one day too, with a third equal share for Benoit now. Nadia's requests in the divorce were very restrained and seemed very cut-and-dried to Nicolas. There was nothing greedy about her, she wanted no revenge for the pain he'd caused her. She was an entirely honorable woman. All she wanted was to end the marriage as quietly and fairly as possible, which was typical of her, and made Nicolas feel even worse about his own behavior toward her. He had to live with that now. She barely spoke to him anymore except when she had to about their daughters.

It was a dark winter for him, and he wrote all the time, whenever he wasn't with the girls. He was writing a book about a passion that had burned everything and everyone in its path, and had destroyed a marriage. He learned a lot about himself, and how selfish he had been, as he wrote it. He missed Nadia every day, but didn't feel he had the right to intrude on her. He had hurt her enough.

A week before Christmas, Nadia accomplished what she had worked so hard for. The final installation of Greg Holland's house was complete. She didn't let him visit for the final days, and placed everything where they'd agreed it should go. It looked spectacular. She made him close his eyes when they walked in, and then told him to open them. He almost cried it was so beautiful, and so exactly what he wanted. She was smiling broadly as she watched him.

"Do you like it?" She'd been so busy she had hardly seen him for weeks.

"Oh my God, it's incredible. How did you get it done so quickly?"

"Magic." She laughed, and he went upstairs to see his bedroom, and then the floor with the gray flannel guest room, and his study with the dark green leather chairs, his desk, and a fireplace. She could imagine him working there late at night. Every inch of the house was exactly as he had envisioned it.

"I'm going to give a housewarming after the holidays, Nadia. You have to be here." He had spent a fortune on the house, and she had earned a handsome fee, but it was worth it, and his Picasso in the living room was stunning. She had designed the whole living room around it, the lighting, the comfortable couches, the textures, the colors. She had even found the perfect rug for the room, and the huge central hall had the white couches and rug that he had wanted. It looked like a magazine cover, and it would be one day, with Nadia credited for the design.

He was going home to Texas for the holidays, and she was going to New York to visit Venetia, her mother, and Olivia between Christmas and New Year's, when the girls would be skiing with their father. Venetia's wish for a fourth child had come true, and she had gotten pregnant at the château in August. She was four months pregnant now. They knew it was another girl, which was exactly what she'd wanted, so she would have two girls and two boys.

Greg was leaving the next day. The house had been finished just in time, and had required endless hours of work on Nadia's part to achieve it.

"Now I don't want to leave," he said, and put an arm around her. They had become friends while she worked on it, but he had never gone beyond the line of friendship, and she didn't want him to. She found him incredibly attractive to look at, but she wasn't attracted to him. She wasn't drawn to any man. She found that Nicolas had vaccinated her. She was content with her children and her work. She didn't miss having a man in her life, knowing now how wrong it could all go, and how devastating it could be. She'd been too badly hurt to want a relationship for now.

"I'm taking you to dinner to celebrate when I get back. Nadia, you made all my dreams come true. You created a real home for me. I can't wait to get back." Greg had told her he hadn't dated anyone since he moved to Paris. He hadn't had time. Now he had a real home. Even Nadia thought it needed a woman's touch to soften the masculine strength of it. As they stood in his living room, admiring his

Picasso, he turned to her and kissed her. She couldn't tell him, but she felt nothing. She was still too broken inside to want anyone, and he sensed it immediately.

"Too soon?" he asked her, and she shook her head.

"No, maybe too late." She wanted to feel more for him than she did, but she didn't, and didn't know if she ever would again. There was a piece of her missing now. She wasn't heartbroken. She was empty, and she knew that Nicolas had taken the missing piece with him, and it had gotten lost somewhere. It was as though her heart had been so shattered, it had been removed.

She and Greg sat down on the dove-gray velvet couch in his living room, and he pulled her close to him. It felt good sitting with him, she just didn't know how much more of her there was to share with him. Her affection for him had been expressed in the home she had designed for him.

"I love being with you," she said softly, "I just don't know how much I can connect with anyone right now. I think he broke something deep inside me."

"That's how I felt after Sharon," Greg said quietly. "The feelings come back. They're just different."

"I liked myself better before," she admitted to him. "I feel alive with my kids now, and my work. The rest of me is just dead, or gone, or buried somewhere. I can't seem to find it, or turn the switch on."

"You will," Greg said confidently. "I'm not going anywhere. I've never met another woman like you, and I'm not going to lose you, Nadia. What you did with my home is an incredible gift." He had paid for it, but he knew you couldn't pay for the love and talent she had poured into it. She had given herself to him in all the little details she had thought of, the touches she had added that would give him so much pleasure for years. He wanted to share it with her. He knew with certainty that she was a woman who would never cheat on him as others had. She was a woman of honor to her very core.

"Thank you for loving the house." She smiled at him and nestled next to him as they sat there admiring it.

"How could I not love it? You're an extraordinary woman, and eminently lovable. I'm sorry he hurt you so badly. You'll get over it one day." And if she didn't, she wasn't sure she minded anymore. She was content. She felt fulfilled. She had her work and kids and friends. She was no longer in pain. Seeing the look on Greg's face in his new home was enough for her. She didn't need more than that for now, or even want it.

They left the house together, hand in hand. He dropped her off at her place, and he was going to go back to his new house and spend the night. She had had the bed made up for him with new Porthault sheets in case he wanted to sleep there before he left for Texas. It was his kingdom now, his domain. Her job, she knew, was giving others the joy of a home they loved. She couldn't think of anything better, or anything she loved doing more.

She kissed him on the cheek before she got out of his car, and he didn't try to kiss her again. He knew better. She slid out of his car with a wave and he watched her go inside. Then he drove back to the house she had turned into a magical place for him. Nadia was the magician, and his friend.

* * *

After Nadia turned Greg's new house over to him, she took four days off to be with her girls. Their Christmas Eve was warm and cozy. She was going to miss them for the week they'd be away with their father, but she was looking forward to seeing her sisters in New York. Athena was flying in with Joe, during a break in the show. There was no place like New York at Christmas, except maybe Paris, and she felt blessed to have both cities in her life. The girls loved New York at that time of year too. They had been there before, but their week of skiing in Val d'Isère was going to be fun for them, and Nadia kept everything light and happy and fun before they left. It was their first Christmas season without their father at home. She made Christmas Eve dinner for the three of them. She had turned down all the Christmas parties she'd been invited to. She didn't feel ready to see their friends yet. The affair had just been too public, the fallout too enormous, and the baby was the final blow. She felt fine again, but not ready to face people who were still happily married or in couples and felt sorry for her. Their pity was more than she could bear. She could see it in their eyes when she ran into them, and she didn't want to have to put on a show of how great things were. Things were good, and she was grateful for that, but not great yet. Greg was probably right. It would take time. But she wasn't sure that time would change how she felt about him. He had become a good friend while they'd worked on his house, but in a funny way, he still seemed too American to her, too stripped clean of eccentricities and Gallic charm. There was something about French men that made her feel like a woman, or made her heart dance like Nicolas used to. If she ever fell in love, she wanted to feel like that again. Or maybe it was just too late and that part of her was dead. She wondered if she'd ever know.

* * *

Nicolas arrived on time on Christmas morning to pick up the girls. She noticed that he was thinner, and pale, and she could tell that he'd been writing. He looked that way when he stayed home for days and weeks on end, writing and editing and rewriting. She wondered who read his manuscripts now. His editor probably.

"Merry Christmas," he said solemnly, and she smiled at him.

"Merry Christmas," she said, and hugged the girls tightly before they left. Laure turned back for one more hug, and then they ran to catch their flight to Chambery to get to Val d'Isère. Nadia was leaving for New York that afternoon. She had given Agnes and her other employees the week off and closed the office. They had worked like demons until all hours of the night for weeks, getting Greg's house installed. They had earned the time off. Nothing would happen over the holidays anyway. Their clients were all busy, and new ones wouldn't surface until mid-January.

Nadia had a date in January to appear in front of a *notaire,* which was similar to an attorney with some powers like a judge, to confirm their divorce agreement, since it was being handled *à l'amiable,* on friendly terms. Because there was no dispute in their divorce, according to recent laws, they didn't have to go to court and could deal with it in the *notaire*'s office. And after that, it would be final in roughly two months. It was a simple procedure as long as there was no disagreement about the terms. Nicolas had finally stopped saying he wanted to come back, which was a relief to her. Nicolas had understood at last that Nadia had no desire to resume their marriage and wouldn't let that happen. Nicolas was crushed but didn't try to argue with her. Sylvie and Laure were getting used to the idea, and so was she. She was going to be a divorced woman, which reeked of failure to her. Failure to keep her husband's interest, to keep him out of someone else's bed, to keep him from having a baby with a twenty-two-year-old girl. In some ways, Nadia blamed herself. He had done it, but she felt that she must have set the stage for it to happen, maybe by being too busy, working too hard, or assuming that he would love her forever no matter what. As it turned out, love was a fragile flower that didn't live as long as one hoped. For some it did, but not for all. They hadn't been among the lucky ones who made it until the end. She accepted it now. And out of respect for her, Nicolas had to accept it too.

She left for the airport an hour after the girls. She checked her suitcases. She was bringing presents for everyone. They were going to spend a weekend at Venetia's, and Nadia couldn't wait to see how pregnant she was. She was having this baby at forty-two, which Nadia thought was heroic, and Olivia thought was insane. Athena was just happy it wasn't her. Rose worried about her daughter's health, and if childbirth at forty-two was dangerous, and kept warning Venetia of danger signs to look out for. Venetia had just had an amnio, and everything seemed fine. She said the greatest risk she had was that Ben would kill her if she got pregnant again. But she had wanted one more child so desperately that he had given in. It hadn't been an accident. They had conceived it during their week at the château, which seemed a tender way to Nadia to end her own tenure there. A new life conceived at the home she was giving back to Nicolas, after they had been so happy there. But the château was part of his heritage and belonged to him. They had alternated there that summer, but once divorced, she no longer belonged at his family château. He would go there with the girls, and whatever woman was in his life. But Nadia's days there were over. She accepted it, and didn't allow herself to look back at the past. She had to look forward now, and was determined to have a good life without him.

The flight to New York was easy and she slept most of the way. She had worked so many late nights that she was more tired than she realized, and felt refreshed when she got to New York after the long flight. She was staying at her mother's apartment while in New York, and Rose was delighted to have her. After Nadia left, Rose was going to Palm Beach for a few days over New Year's Eve to see friends. The magazine was essentially closed for the holidays, and she needed a rest too.

They hit commuter traffic on the way into the city, and everywhere Nadia looked there were lights and Christmas decorations, Christmas trees in front yards, and lit-up Santa Clauses on top of houses. She loved the kitsch quality of it, and then the more elegant trees that decorated the city when she approached her mother's address.

Rose was waiting for her at home, and they went to Olivia's for dinner that night. Harley looked tired and was in the middle of a trial that had just gone to the jury, so he was on call, waiting for the verdict. Olivia was thin and pale too. Nadia had forgotten about the frenetic pace and how ravaged by the winter months people were in New York. The intensity of it was electric. When Venetia and Ben arrived, they were full of life and healthy, and Venetia's pregnancy already showed. She was wearing a bright red dress and looked terrific. She was blossoming and radiant, and she and Ben were both happy about the baby.

Both sisters observed Nadia carefully to see how she was, and decided that she looked well. She told them about Greg's house and showed them photos on her phone, and they were vastly impressed by how beautiful it was.

"I know who he is," Venetia commented. "Ben did a deal with him a few years ago. What about him as a prospective date? I think he's from Texas, and rich as hell." Nadia shook her head.

"I know. He's a terrific guy, and we're friends. He's just not exciting. Something's missing." He wasn't Nicolas, but she didn't dare say it, given how that had ended. "I'm not ready to date."

"Please don't tell me you're waiting for another French cheater to show up," Olivia said in her usual blunt way.

"Maybe so," Nadia admitted. "Maybe American men are too wholesome for me." She was still trying to figure out what was missing for her with Greg, and hadn't yet.

They spent a warm, cozy evening together, and Will joined them for dinner. He chatted with his uncle Ben and his grandmother, and then left the table before dessert to read in his room.

The evening ended at midnight, and Nadia went home with her mother. The three sisters were having lunch with their mother the next day. Rose was treating them to lunch at La Grenouille and Athena was arriving from L.A. that afternoon. After that they were going to Venetia and Ben's home in Southampton. Rose was joining them for the weekend, before going to Palm Beach for New Year's. It was going to be a family-filled week, which is what they all wanted.

They never tired of each other. At breakfast the next day, Rose looked at Nadia, and spoke quietly over her morning tea.

"Are you all right? Is everything okay in Paris?"

"I'm fine," she said softly.

"Have you seen much of Nicolas?"

"Not really. He's writing a new book, and he picks up the girls downstairs and takes them to his place or out to dinner. We're perfectly friendly when we meet." But something in her eyes told her mother that she was not healed yet after everything that had happened. It worried her.

"Does he see the baby?"

"I honestly don't know. Pascale left him in Brittany with her mother, so Nicolas must not see him often. I don't know if he goes to Brittany to visit. Maybe he will when he's older." She didn't need to think about it and tried not to. It wasn't her problem. It was his.

The girls had fun at the luxurious lunch with their mother, and with Athena the night she arrived and the following day, and then they all left for the Hamptons. Nadia was happy to see that her mother was well and looked terrific. Age never seemed to touch her, and she never slowed down. It made Nadia think that she might be fine without a man too. But her mother was thirty years older, and had been widowed at sixty-two. She hadn't given up on men at thirty-six, so Nadia realized she might be premature in planning a life of celibacy, which Venetia pointed out to her when they all went for a walk on the beach. Nadia loved the Hamptons in winter. There was a rugged beauty to it that suited her mood.

Two days later, Rose left for Palm Beach, the others were planning to spend New Year's Eve together except Olivia and Harley, who went back to the city for a New Year's Eve party with friends. The others stayed in the Hamptons and saw the New Year in together with a delicious dinner cooked by Joe and Athena, and excellent French champagne. It was Nadia's last night with them. She had to fly back to Paris on New Year's Day, which would land her in Paris late that night so Nicolas could return the girls to her the next morning. She was letting him have them on New Year's Day. Athena and Joe were staying longer. She was going to tape one show in New York with a famous chef before they went back to L.A.

Nadia was having breakfast with Venetia and Athena in the kitchen on New Year's Day, before she had to dress for her flight. Olivia called Venetia on her cellphone, and Venetia looked shocked at whatever Olivia had said. She asked a series of rapid-fire questions, and it sounded to the other two as though Will had run away, judging by Venetia's questions: "When did he leave? . . . Did you see him go? . . . Do you know where he went? . . ." She promised to call Olivia back later, ended the call, and stared at both her sisters in disbelief.

"Olivia had too much to drink last night, and she said that what she told us on the Fourth of July has been weighing on her ever since. She told Harley about Will last night. He locked himself in his study and wouldn't talk to her afterwards. He was gone when she got up this morning. He didn't leave a note. She doesn't know where he went. He left her, and he told her last night he would never forgive her for lying to him about something so important, and for cheating on him. . . ." Venetia looked panicked for her sister, and the other two stared at her, too shocked to speak for a minute.

"Oh my God," was all Athena could say, as Nadia glanced at her watch.

"Oh shit . . . I have to dress for my flight. What is she going to do? And what did she tell Will this morning?"

"I have no idea. She's panicked. She thinks Harley's going to divorce her."

"He might," Athena said solemnly, "he's a pretty rigid guy. I'm not sure he can recover from a blow like this. A lot of men wouldn't." She couldn't imagine him swallowing it. The others didn't disagree with her, and they sat staring at each other, then Nadia rushed up the stairs to dress. She hated to leave them in a crisis, but she had to get back to Paris for the girls. She knew that Nicolas was leaving for London the next day to see his publisher there. All Nadia could hope as she dressed in haste was that Harley had somehow made his peace with Olivia's confession and would come back, and forgive her. If not, Olivia would be getting divorced too. She thought it was a terrible mistake to have told him. They had warned her not to. And now there was no telling what would happen. Nadia felt sorry for both of them, Harley and Olivia. She could only imagine how Harley must feel. What a god-awful mess. She felt terrible about it, but she had to leave.

She called Olivia from the car on the way to the airport, but it went to voicemail. Will was out with friends by then. Olivia was lying on her bed, after crying for hours, convinced that Harley would never forgive her. And knowing how stern and uncompromising he could be, and how moral he was, all of her sisters were afraid she might be right.

Chapter 12

Nadia tried Olivia again when she got to the airport, and that time, she picked up. Olivia was crying when she answered.

"I was so stupid, Naddie, I shouldn't have told him. But it's been driving me crazy. After I told you all last summer, I realized that our marriage has been a lie, and he had a right to know. You don't know how moral he is. He thinks cheating is as bad as murder. He doesn't talk about it, but he's a very religious person. He told me he would never feel the same way about me again. He wouldn't even talk to me after that. I've been calling him all morning and he's not picking up. I don't think he'll ever speak to me again. We've been married for fifteen years," she sobbed. "I love him so much. I'll die without him."

"You won't die," Nadia said in a stronger voice, so her sister would hear her. She hadn't died from losing Nicolas. Things happened in life. People died, broke promises or each other's hearts, or ran off with someone else. She realized now that you couldn't count on anything or anyone staying the same forever. And whatever happened, you had to get through it. Even more so if you had kids. You had to stay alive and keep on going for them. It was what she was doing now with Sylvie and Laure. She had to be okay for their sakes, no matter how broken she felt inside, or how hard it was.

"If he's that religious, he'll forgive you," Nadia said. Though maybe not. She hadn't forgiven Nicolas, and she wasn't going back to him. But his sins were fresh, and he had humiliated her publicly. She thought that made a difference. What mattered to Harley was that his wife had slept with someone else, not who knew it. On the contrary, Olivia's transgression had been her darkest secret, especially from him, and even from her sisters until that summer. She bitterly regretted telling them now, because their reaction had made her realize that she'd been wrong not to tell him. She could see now, from his reaction, that her first instinct not to had been right. And it was too late to confess to the lie fifteen years later.

"What if he never comes back?" Olivia asked. Nadia didn't want to say that Harley wasn't as young as they were. He would probably die before her, and she'd have to survive without him one day. And if Harley took an extreme position to her confession, Will would need her more than ever. But Harley wasn't a cruel man. Nadia doubted that Harley would never forgive her, or reject Will for his mother's sins. He loved him too much to do that, no matter who his father was.

"I think he will come back," Nadia said. "Give him time. He probably needs to sit with it for a while. This is a huge shock for him. He's a very straightlaced, serious guy, but he loves you, Ollie. He probably feels like he'll die without you too."

"He says he'll never believe another word I say. He asked me how many other men I slept with. I've never, ever cheated on him again."

She was wracked with sobs again after she said it, and Nadia's heart ached for her.

"I believe you."

"I wish I hadn't told him."

"In the long run, you probably did the right thing," Nadia tried to reassure her, although she wouldn't have told him, and had tried to convince Olivia not to. Nadia had thought it was too risky, and she wasn't happy to be proven right. Harley had reacted just as severely as she'd feared.

They talked for over an hour before Nadia got on the plane. Will came home after the movie, and fortunately didn't ask where his father was and went to read in his room.

"You have to pull yourself together for Will," Nadia told her. "You don't want to have to explain this to him." There was no mistaking how distraught she was. She was acting as though Harley had died. But maybe their marriage had. Nadia recognized it as a distinct possibility, and so did Olivia.

"God, no. And Will is so damn smart, he always figures things out." But not this time. How could he possibly guess what his mother had told Harley? He couldn't.

Nadia called her one last time before the flight took off, and Olivia sounded more composed, although she was morbidly depressed, and every five minutes she had tried to call Harley. She had texted him too. He hadn't responded to her pleas and apologies and sobbing messages.

"I'll call you when I land," Nadia promised. It was a six- or seven-hour flight to Paris at that time of year, depending on the weather, but she knew that Venetia and Athena would be checking on Olivia too. They hadn't told their mother yet, and didn't want to spoil her time in Palm Beach. There was nothing she could do anyway. What would happen next was up to Harley now. Only he could decide Olivia's fate. The future of their marriage was in Harley's hands.

Nadia thought about her sister as she settled back in her seat and the plane headed northeast to Europe. She had her own future to think about now too. She and Nicolas would be filing their agreement soon with the *notaire* for the divorce. Neither of them had been unreasonable, and Nadia was surprised by how simple the process had become, in uncontested divorces. French law had eased up considerably when both parties agreed. Her lawyer had explained that most divorces got mired down in lengthy disputes over money, custody arrangements, or property. But since neither of them was taking an adversarial position, and the only thing Nadia wanted was use of the apartment, which he had agreed to immediately, and child support, they were among the lucky few who could get through the process quickly. Her attorney had pointed out that it sometimes took years where tangible assets were concerned. Sometimes the children were adults and had left home by the time they resolved it. He cited one case he'd had that had taken nineteen years, but he said that was unusual. But most divorces weren't as bloodless as theirs, or as simple. He said that if nothing changed before they signed the agreement, they could be divorced in one or two months after they signed. As Nadia thought about it, she realized they would be divorced before next summer. A few tears rolled down her cheeks, thinking about it, and Olivia's situation, and then she fell asleep.

She woke up halfway through the flight, and tried to watch a movie. She couldn't concentrate on it and didn't want a meal. She hoped Olivia had been able to reach Harley by then, and could talk about what had happened, and that ultimately he would forgive her, although it might take a long time. She had discovered herself that love didn't die as quickly as one thought it would. It died slowly, like a living being as its lifeblood leaked away, shifting its weight occasionally, moving slightly, so you knew that it was still there, dying, but not dead yet. Nadia felt that way about Nicolas. She still loved what he used to be, and the marriage they'd had, not what he had turned it into, and they'd become. Wrapping up the memories and burying them was painful, but cremating them in the white-hot fire of hatred was probably even more so. Nadia was still waiting for her love of Nicolas to die a gentle death. The embers were still warm, and not fully out yet, and she accepted the possibility now that maybe they never would be. Sadly, when she thought of their marriage ending, she thought of how gentle and loving he had always been, the happy times, the things they had in common, and everything she loved about him. But when she thought of staying with him, she thought of him cheating, and was sure he'd do it again. It didn't leave much room for someone new to take his place, but she didn't want that anyway.

The only serious candidate who had crossed her path was Greg, and she wasn't in love with him. She knew she never could be the way she had been with Nicolas, in the beginning. But maybe a love like that only happened once in a lifetime. That was a possibility she accepted too. Maybe the people you loved after that were more like friends or companions, people to travel through life with, on parallel tracks, always with a little distance, but not interwoven or entwined. She and Nicolas had been part of a single fabric, their threads forming a single design. He had torn what they had in half, and shredded their marriage, and there were only tatters left.

She wondered if she could ever truly love Greg. He was a good person, a smart man. He wasn't interested in becoming involved with her children, which might be a good thing. He wouldn't interfere, and Nicolas was their father and was staying closely engaged with them. Greg was a possible companion for her, an intelligent, caring partner she could share a life with. He was civilized and not passionate. She wondered if that was what she needed now. But it felt more like a business alliance than a love relationship to her. And eventually, he'd go back to the States, New York or Dallas or somewhere, and she didn't want to live there. It would be a big change for her girls. She didn't want to take them away from Nicolas now. They needed to see him, and to have him close by. And she couldn't imagine living in the States herself, and leaving France.

She wondered too what Nicolas was going to do. It didn't seem as though his relationship with Pascale was continuing or prospering, even with the baby. She wasn't a deep person and was content to have someone else carry her responsibilities, like Nicolas. The baby was an add-on, an accessory, to pick up and put down at will. And she seemed to feel that way about Nicolas too. Sylvie had told her that she thought it was already over. But if not Pascale, there would be another woman in his life eventually. He said he still loved Nadia, whenever he had the chance to tell her, but what did that mean and how long would that last? How soon would he cheat on her again? Twice in eleven years was twice too often. He was a passionate man. He loved women, and he would fall in love again. He didn't keep his emotional life on a low simmer in full control at all times, like Greg, never letting it heat up too much. It was less dangerous that way, which was why Greg did it, having been burned himself.

Part of Nicolas's appeal was how he threw his heart into everything, with total abandon, giving his whole soul to whatever he was doing, or whomever he was loving. She had benefited from that for sixteen years of their loving each other, and Pascale had only been around for a few months. Maybe the next time would be forever. Or as close to it as he could get. Maybe he was a man who needed different women for different stages of his life, different decades. She couldn't really expect him to be the same man at fifty or sixty that he had been in his thirties. Or the same man now at forty-two that he had been when they were students and he was madly in love with her, and they stayed in bed for hours instead of going to class. But oddly, she could see him doing that into the future. She wondered if he was going to remain a boy for the rest of his life. Greg was decidedly and indisputably an adult, to the very core of his being. There was no whimsy in him, but that innocent, magical side of Nicolas is what had led him astray and into Pascale's arms.

She thought about it until they landed, got off the plane, and headed to baggage claim. She took an Uber into the city, and texted Nicolas that she had arrived. He answered that the girls were excited and couldn't wait to see her in the morning. He had had a wonderful time with them, but they were ready to return to their mother. She was home to them. He was the outsider now, and he knew it. And even more so with his wife.

It was cold in the apartment when she got home. She turned the heat up in their room, so it would be warm in the morning. There had been a severe cold spell while they were gone. The housekeeper had bought groceries, so she'd have enough to make them breakfast. They were going back to school the day after, so they'd have a day together. She was back in her role as mother, always thinking about them first. She left her suitcase in the front hall, and walked around the apartment. She was wide awake with the time difference from New York. She was proud of herself. It had been her first Christmas vacation when she wasn't with them the entire time, and she had gotten through it. She'd had a nice time with her mother and sisters, although it was odd being with her niece and nephews without having Sylvie and Laure with her. She went to bed late, after calling Olivia, but she didn't respond. She called Venetia, who had no news either.

Nicolas arrived early the next morning. The girls threw themselves into her arms. She had hot chocolate ready for them, and offered Nicolas coffee. He took a cup from her with a smile. It felt good to see her, and was warm and familiar. He had missed her. He always did now.

The girls bounded around the apartment, happy to be home, and Nicolas lingered for a few minutes. She came back to the kitchen, while the girls settled in. She loved having them home, the apartment always seemed empty to her when they were with him.

"Laure is going to be an amazing skier one day," he said with a smile. "She's fearless. Sylvie is more cautious, and sensible. She's more like you. Laure will probably throw herself off a lot of cliffs one day. Like me." He hesitated, and then looked at her seriously. "I know we have our date at the *notaire* in a week. I just want to check in with you . . . is that what you really want? A divorce?" She nodded. She wondered if he was going to try to fight her on it now. She hoped not. She wanted to get this behind her, the last of their painful memories. She wanted closure. Olivia had told her it was for the best and she'd be glad she did it. Nadia wondered how she felt about that now, with Harley walking out on her. Nadia suspected she was probably asleep. It was early in New York. She hoped Olivia had heard from Harley by now.

"Yes, it's what I want," Nadia confirmed to Nicolas. "It's not how I wanted our life to turn out. But it did, and we have to face it."

"Why? Why can't we turn it around and try to fix it?" he asked. Nadia knew she'd feel like a fool if she did, and everyone would think less of her for it, if she put up with what he'd done and went back to him now. And she didn't want to.

"The divorce is the right thing for a lot of reasons. Most of all, because I'd never trust you again. I don't want to live like that. Nor would you. You'd feel like a criminal on parole," she said seriously.

"I could live with it. Maybe one day you'd forgive me," he said hopefully.

"I doubt it."

"Have you tried? To forgive me?" She shook her head in answer.

"No, I haven't. I've put all my energy into getting over you, not forgiving you," she said honestly.

"That's not very nice of you," he said, looking hurt and boyish, which was so Nicolas. It was the part of him she loved, and also that infuriated her at other times.

"What you did wasn't 'nice,'" she reminded him, and he looked embarrassed, and nodded. It had been hideous, and agonizing for her. Crushing.

"I thought you were more French than that," he said ruefully, and she laughed. He was ridiculous at times, which she had loved about him.

"It turns out I'm not. I thought I was more French too, but not on this subject. I don't want a husband who has a mistress, or a little quickie affair to break up the boredom of marriage from time to time, or a big affair, which breaks my heart."

"I was never bored with you," he said, serious again. And she was never bored with him either.

"And it was no little fling," she reminded him. "It was a wild, passionate, crazy love affair, all over the press, and you had a baby with her. It couldn't have gotten much worse." He hung his head, knowing he couldn't argue with her. He felt deeply remorseful for what he had done, even if it was too late now, which it seemed to be for her.

"I just don't want us to end in divorce," he said so sadly that it tugged at her heart. She didn't want it to either, but there seemed to be no other right answer. "That's so ugly and so sad, and so final."

"I don't feel like I have any other choice," she said, and he could see he couldn't sway her. She couldn't forgive him. He had wanted to give it one more try before they met at the *notaire* a week later. If there was any chance at all of turning the tides, he wanted to try and convince her while he saw her face-to-face. He had nothing to lose now, but he could see that she was immovable on the subject. He had pushed her too far, and been too foolish, even heartless, with what he'd done. Now he had to face the consequences. He had lost her.

He didn't let her see the tears in his eyes when he left.

Venetia called her at 8 A.M. in New York. "Olivia found out where he's staying," Venetia filled her in. "He's at the yacht club."

"Did he call her?"

"No. She checked, and he's registered there. He still hasn't answered any of her calls and texts. She had an anxiety attack last night and had to go to the emergency room. She's okay now, they gave her a Xanax."

"How is she explaining this to Will?"

"She told him that it's work-related, that she has a big trial starting tomorrow, which isn't true. And that Harley is in Washington for a conference that starts tomorrow. Apparently Will called him and he confirmed it, and he's talking to him."

"That's something at least. God, what is she going to do if he leaves her?" Nadia asked, worried about her.

"She'll get through it. You did," Venetia said simply. "I hope he doesn't, but he might. He's a very old-school guy. He deals with criminals every day, and hands down sentences and punishments. So I guess that's what he's going to do here."

"She's not a criminal, for chrissake," Nadia defended her. "She did something really stupid, and yes, she told a terrible lie. But did it really hurt him in the end? Or Will? This is not a hanging offense." Why did life have to be so harsh and cruel at times?

"Maybe to him it is," Venetia said, and Nadia sighed. "How are the girls?"

"Happy to be home. They had fun with Nicolas but they seemed thrilled to see me. I am too." She smiled. "But I had a nice time with you."

"Did you see him when he brought them back?" Venetia asked her.

"Yes."

"How was it?"

"Sad. He gave it one last stab before we sign the final agreement next week. He still wants us to get back together. I can't."

"Let me ask you something," Venetia said, sounding matter-of-fact. "Do you still love him?"

Nadia hesitated. "That's beside the point. Yes, I still love him. I probably always will. He was my first love. That doesn't die overnight or maybe ever. If he were dead, I'd still love him. But it's over. It's not a viable marriage. He'd probably do it again."

"Then you leave him again. I just don't see why you want to divorce him, if you still love him. Maybe you could breathe life into your marriage again after all." Venetia was always the most practical among them, Athena the most compassionate and forgiving, and Olivia by far the toughest and least forgiving. It was ironic that she was in the situation she was in now, begging her husband for forgiveness for her own crimes, and not being forgiven so far.

"What about my self-respect?" Nadia countered. "Do you realize what an ass I'd look like? My husband had the most publicized affair in recent history, has a child with someone else, and I take him back? Everyone would think I'm an idiot."

"No, they'd think you love him. And who cares what people think? Do you really give a damn about that? Nadia, if you love him, you have to think about it, for your sake, not just his."

"He has to be held accountable," Nadia said insistently. She had gotten tougher since it happened. It had made her stronger, which wasn't such a bad thing. And more decisive. She wasn't as soft and shy and accommodating as she'd been before.

"Then make him wear a hair shirt or something, or put him in shackles. He was a good husband for a long time, and you're great parents together. What he did was terrible, but I suspect he loves you. If this is fixable and you love each other, you should think about it. Think about Olivia. She's a hanging judge. She kept pushing you to divorce him right from the beginning. What if Harley does that to her now? What do you think about that? Do you think he should forgive her?" Nadia was silent for a moment, considering it.

"Olivia's deal was more of a sin of omission about Will, rather than the cheating part. Nicolas's sin was insanely, flagrantly outrageous. He made a complete fool of me!"

"Is that what you care about, that he made a fool of you?" Venetia asked her.

"No." Her voice was a low growl of pain. "He broke my heart. That's what I care about."

"So do I, for you. I hated him for what he did to you. But hearts can be mended. Not always, but sometimes. That's what you need to figure out before you end it forever. Can your heart be mended? Only you know. I guess that's what Harley is trying to figure out right now too. You two have a lot in common." Nadia hadn't thought about it like that. Venetia always had a way of presenting things to her in a way that made sense. She was hoping, for Olivia's sake, that Harley would forgive her, because she didn't want her sister to be hurt. But she was guilty too. She had lied for fifteen years. Nicolas hadn't. The two cases were both similar and different.

They promised to stay in close touch about Olivia, and hung up a few minutes later. Venetia had given her a lot to think about. She thought about it all day while she was with the girls and lay awake considering it for hours that night. And in the morning when she woke up, she knew what she had to do. She was going to divorce Nicolas. She was sure. Accountability. She couldn't let him off the hook. He had hurt her too much. She wondered if Harley felt that way about Olivia too.

Chapter 13

Olivia continued calling and texting Harley day and night for three days. She left a letter for him at the yacht club, pouring her heart and soul out, begging his forgiveness. He didn't respond to that either. She heard nothing from him.

On Friday, at lunchtime, she walked to the federal courthouse on Centre Street after she adjourned her own court. She walked into his chambers, which were open, waiting for him to leave the bench and call a recess for lunch. She was sitting quietly in a chair when he walked in and gave a start when he saw her. His face was expressionless and unreadable. He didn't look happy to see her.

"I couldn't stand it anymore. I had to see you. You haven't answered anything," Olivia said grimly, her face sheet white.

"I was thinking . . . deliberating." He sat down at his desk, to keep his distance from her. He looked tired, and she could see the toll it had taken on him. He seemed five years older in just a few days. She was thinner and pale too. Having him walk out on her was the most terrifying thing that had ever happened to her. "Why did you come here?" he asked her coldly.

"I came for sentencing, Your Honor," she said, and he didn't smile. Normally, he would have.

"Sentencing happens thirty days after conviction, Counselor. Or have you forgotten that? Along with decency, morality, honesty. I expected more of you, Olivia." He sounded like her law professor again, and she had clearly gotten an "F" in Marriage. She couldn't debate the point with him. She had lied to him. A terrible lie.

"I have no defense, Your Honor, except youth, stupidity, and fear. I didn't want to hurt you, or lose you," she said, standing in front of him, as she fought back tears. He didn't appear moved by them. He was every inch a judge as he spoke to her, in all senses of the word. He had judged her, and found her behavior criminal.

"You managed to do both. Lose me and hurt me. You just postponed it by fifteen years by not telling me."

"I probably should never have told you," she said miserably.

"No, you should have been honest right in the beginning."

"What would you have done?"

"I probably would have divorced you then. And missed out on fifteen great years with you. So maybe you were right not to tell me. It doesn't change anything for me with Will. He's my son in every way that matters. But how do I trust you again? What else have you lied about that you haven't told me?"

"That's the only thing. I didn't want to lie about it anymore. So I told you the truth."

"And what did you think I'd say?"

"I was hoping you'd forgive me," she said in a small voice.

"I don't know if I can." She nodded and didn't argue with him. He was staring at her long and hard from the other side of his desk. "How could you look at me every day and lie about something so important? I thought you were an honest woman."

"I am," she said with tears brimming in her eyes. "And I didn't lie to you every day. I made a terrible mistake. I was young and stupid. Maybe I should have had an abortion when I wasn't sure who the father was, but I didn't want to do that either, in case he was yours. After the amnio and the DNA test, it was really too late. I was five months pregnant." And neither of them favored abortion.

"Thank God you didn't. Will is the best thing that ever happened to us. And he's nearly a genius. Whoever his father is, I love Will as my son." She nodded. She knew that. "I need to think about this."

"I love you, Harley," she said softly. "I don't suppose that makes a difference to you now. I'd plead for clemency, but I guess I don't deserve it." She turned away to leave. She could see that she wasn't going to convince him. She had said what she needed to, and it was obvious that he couldn't forgive her. As she walked to the door, she didn't see the tears roll down his cheeks, or see him brush them away.

"Olivia . . ." he said to stop her, and she turned to see him stand up and come around his desk. He walked straight to her, still wearing his robes, and pulled her into his arms. They were both crying as he held her, and she wasn't sure if it meant that he forgave her, or if he was saying goodbye to her forever. "I love you," he said in a choked voice, enveloping her in his strong arms. "I love you," he said again, and then he looked down at her through his tears. "It says in the Bible that we have to forgive seventy times seven. That's four hundred and ninety times. I warn you, I don't have another four hundred and eighty-nine times left in me. Don't *ever* lie to me or hide anything from me again."

"I swear I won't," she said fervently, smiling and crying at the same time. "I haven't lied to you since then. And I never will again."

"I believe you," he said solemnly, and then he looked pensive for a moment. "Technically, by law, I should adopt Will now, to establish paternity. But if I do, he'll figure it out. I just have to stay alive until he reaches majority, and then it won't matter." He had been thinking about that for days.

"You'd better plan to stay alive for a hell of a lot longer than that. I don't intend to lose you after all this." He smiled and kissed her, and then took off his robe and grabbed his coat.

"Let's go for a walk and get some air."

"I thought I'd lost you," she said as she looked up at him. "I thought it would kill me if I had."

"I'll kill you if you ever lie to me again. I sentence you to spend the rest of your life with me. That should be punishment enough." He smiled and held the door open for her, and they left his chambers holding hands. They went for a long walk around Foley Square before they both had to be back on the bench. They didn't say a lot. They didn't need to. They had come through their trial by fire, and Harley knew what he needed to know and should have known all along. They both knew how much they loved each other. It was a win-win all around.

As she walked back to her own courtroom afterwards, she sent the same text to all her sisters. "He forgives me. Thank God. Thank you for being there. I love you. Ollie."

In the Federal Building, Harley was smiling as he took his place on the bench. He was going to pick up his things at the yacht club when he adjourned for the day, and go home to his wife and son.

Nadia had dinner with Greg the night before she had to sign the agreement for the divorce at the *notaire.* She was quiet and tense, but he had just gotten back from Texas and was eager to see her. He told her how much he had missed her. She was happy to see him when he picked her up. She thought it would be a good distraction, so she didn't worry too much about the meeting the next day, but she could hardly think straight, and couldn't follow anything he said.

"Are you okay?" he asked her. He had taken her to a beautiful restaurant, and she barely ate.

"I'm sorry, Greg. I'm nervous about the meeting tomorrow, more than I thought I would be."

"Why? You said it's all been amicable, and he's not opposing anything you want. It'll be a relief when this is over and you're not married to him anymore. Divorcing him is the right thing to do, after what he did. You don't have any doubts, do you?" He was searching her eyes after he asked the question.

"Not doubts. It's what I want to do, but it seems like a very big step. Just as important as marriage. Unmarriage is a big deal too." She looked very young to him as she said it. And pretty in a sapphire-blue dress the color of her eyes.

"'Unmarriage' is a very big deal, but a necessary one sometimes. It sounds like you had a pretty good run for eleven years before it all went south. That's more than a lot of people get. Neither of my marriages lasted eleven years. The first one lasted for three years of total misery. And my second wife cheated on me two days before our second anniversary. So you're way ahead of the game, and you got two nice kids out of it. You're smart to walk away before he lands you in the middle of a public scandal again. I can't think of anything worse."

"It was bad," she conceded. "Very, very bad." It had been hideous.

"He sounds like an immature guy who let his dick run away with him. That's not husband material, Nadia." It was one way to look at it, and he was right. He made it all sound so simple, but it didn't feel that way. It felt hard, like tearing off an arm or a leg. It seemed excruciatingly painful to her, and she didn't want to talk to Greg about it. He was pleased that she was getting a divorce. He had told her he didn't go out with married women, or even separated ones, and he had made it clear that he wanted to date her. She thought they'd have fun together. But she wasn't looking for a date. She had loved being married to Nicolas, and their family life. It was never going to be the same again. It already wasn't.

She managed to get through dinner. Her heart wasn't in it, and Greg knew it. He didn't try to kiss her, wished her luck for the next day, and took her home.

She lay in bed awake after that for several hours, thinking about Greg and the things he'd said about divorce. She thought about Nicolas, and the memories of the past came flooding back to her. Of when Sylvie was born, and how excited they had been, and Laure. Of reading his books, and the thrill it was for both of them when one of his novels was number one on the bestseller list for the first time. The trips they had taken, the time they spent with her sisters and their families as a group, the summers at the château. She finally fell asleep an hour before she had to get up, and woke up with a start, afraid to be late for the meeting at the *notaire*.

She looked ragged by the time she got there. The babysitter had spent the night so she could take the girls to school. Nadia kissed them both and flew out the door. She took an Uber so she wouldn't have to park.

Nicolas was just ahead of her as she walked into the building where the *notaire* had his office, and he stopped to wait for her. He could see how nervous she was, and he was no better. "This is like taking exams when we were at school," he whispered, and she smiled. They arrived at the *notaire*'s office together and both their attorneys looked surprised. Hers leaned over to her once they were seated in the conference room.

"Has there been a change of heart?" he asked her.

"Of course not. We just met outside so we walked in together."

"It happens sometimes, you know." She shook her head, and the *notaire* walked in, looking serious.

Their divorce would become official once he stamped their papers and sent them on to the court to complete the process.

The *notaire* questioned Nadia first. They were his first appointment of the day.

"Madame Bateau, when did your husband leave the family residence?"

"He moved out in September."

"And you are separated?"

"Yes, we are."

"Have you reached agreement about your financial affairs?"

"We have. The Château de Champfort belongs to my husband

solely, as his inherited property. I make no claim to it or the use of it. I would like my daughters to own the apartment we live in, on the Quai Voltaire, and for me to have the use of it, *usufruit,* as I wish. And we've agreed to visitation every Wednesday night for dinner, alternate weekends, two Friday nights a month on the weekends he doesn't have them. That comes to ten days a month, and one month in the summer." It was all very cut-and-dried, and her attorney handed over the financial declarations and the file. The *notaire* was a serious older man, and nodded as he glanced at the papers. Nadia wanted no financial settlement and they had agreed on an amount for monthly support for their daughters.

"And you are in agreement with the visits, Monsieur Bateau?" he asked Nicolas, who said that he was. "And the monthly support?" Nicolas agreed to that too. It was a generous sum, since it was the only money Nadia would accept from him.

Because it had been done *à l'amiable,* amicably, with both parties in full agreement, there was nothing to add to it except the confirmation from the *notaire* and his stamp and signature. There were no gray areas of dispute, so he took out a stamp and pounded it on the top sheet of all the paperwork, and forty minutes after they had arrived, they left the conference room.

"I guess that's that, then," Nicolas said as they stood in the hallway looking lost for a minute. Nadia felt dazed, and he glanced at his watch. "I have a train to catch," he said. "I'm going to Brittany for two days, I'll be back in time for dinner with the girls on Wednesday," now that their visitation was set in stone with the courts. He had hoped to avoid that. But now the wheels had been set in motion, and there would be no stopping them, unless they canceled the divorce. It was clear that Nadia wanted it as much as ever. She had confirmed that to the *notaire*.

He kissed her on the cheek, hurried out, and made it to the station in time. He had told Pascale he was going. She was in London, on location for her new movie and said she didn't mind. She was going to be there for three months. The producers had gotten her an apartment. But her mother didn't speak English, and the baby was only three months old, so she had decided not to bring them to London, and left them in Brittany, which was easier for her. She had more time to play without her mother and the baby there. Having an infant had turned out to be more complicated than she thought it would be, and less fun.

Nicolas caught his train and was in Brittany that afternoon. He went straight to see Isabelle, Pascale's mother. His business was with her, since she had the responsibility and was the deciding voice. They sat in her kitchen, drinking coffee, and she was startled by his plan. He wanted her to come to Paris twice a month for a night with the baby, so he could get to know his son, and the baby would know him. He didn't choose any of the nights the girls would be with him, so they weren't intruded on. But it had become clear to Nicolas that Pascale was going to lead the life of a single twenty-two-year-old girl, while the child would grow up in Brittany with her mother. And he didn't want to just drop in on them. He wanted more, and to give Benoit more. He wanted to set up regular visits, and when Benoit was older, he wanted them to come to Paris on the weekends he didn't have the girls. He didn't want to simply forget about his son, and never get to know him, just because the relationship with Pascale hadn't worked out. He had been thinking about it a lot lately, and he liked the solution he had come up with. So did Isabelle. They were contemporaries, only a few years apart, and she approved of what he was trying to do. He didn't want to just send a check every month, he wanted Benoit to be part of his life, and even more so as the boy got older. Isabelle loved the idea of coming to Paris. It sounded very glamorous to her. She could do what she wanted when Nicolas was with Benoit, and take him to the park when Nicolas was working. She might even meet a man while she was there. She was still young. She was two years older than Nadia.

There were two guest rooms in his rented apartment, for the girls, and she and the baby could stay with him easily. The apartment wasn't large or fancy, but it was adequate. Isabelle thought it an excellent plan and admired him for thinking of it. He was hoping too for his girls to come to love their brother, if they got to know him.

"So, little man, you're coming to Paris to see your papa?" he said as he held him aloft and the baby smiled and giggled. He took him out for a long walk in his stroller that afternoon. He helped Isabelle give him a bath and gave him his bottle and put him to bed. The next morning, Nicolas left and went back to Paris. Isabelle Solon was coming to Paris with the baby in a week. She thought Nicolas was a good man. She was sorry that Pascale hadn't stayed with him. She knew about Pascale's new actor boyfriend, but thought he smoked too much dope and didn't care about the baby. She thought Pascale was a fool for not staying with Nicolas, but Pascale said that writers were too dull, and Nicolas was too old for her. At least he was taking his paternal responsibilities seriously. He had Pascale's permission for the baby to visit Paris every other week with her mother. She thought it was fine. It was a year since they had gotten involved with each other on the set of his movie, and it amazed him how such passionate feelings had dissipated so quickly. He thought it was a huge mistake to have had a baby when they had such flimsy knowledge of each other, but the baby was here now, and he wanted to make the best of it for himself and the boy.

Pascale didn't find it unusual or unfortunate that she had a child now by a man she was no longer involved with and would probably rarely see in the future. She was perfectly satisfied to have him deal with her mother. Isabelle Solon had done the same thing when Pascale was born and left her with her own mother when she was sixteen. But now, as a grandmother, she was more attentive to Benoit than she had been to Pascale, and Nicolas was satisfied that he was in good hands. He was happy to spend two nights a month with the baby and Pascale's mother, and in time two nights a week. Eventually, Benoit would be able to come and visit him alone, or with a nanny. Isabelle already had a nanny for him now, a few hours a week, so she could get some things done. Nicolas had been paying for it since Benoit was born.

Venetia called Nadia to see how the *notaire* meeting had gone, and she said it was fine, and very anticlimactic. A few questions, their financial statements, the visitation schedule, the *notaire* stamping what they had agreed to, and it was over.

"What happens now?" The divorce seemed so sad to her, especially if Nadia still loved him. She admitted she did, but not enough to go back to him, or forgive him.

"Sometime in the next two months, we get the papers in the mail, and we're divorced. The way we did it, there's no drama."

"That's something at least."

Greg called to check on her too, and invited her to dinner, but she said she was too busy. She had a new client and had to get started with the preliminaries, but she promised to see him soon. On the heels of going to the *notaire* to end her marriage, she didn't feel ready to throw her arms open to Greg, and something about him always stopped her. She didn't know what it was. He was too unemotional, or too businesslike. She kept shying away from starting anything with him, although she knew she was interested in him, but not enough. And in an odd way, she still felt married to Nicolas, and as though she'd be cheating on him. She wondered how long it would take for that to go away, and to feel like a fully free woman. Maybe when she got the papers. But just as paperwork didn't make the essence of a marriage—as Athena and Joe had amply demonstrated—papers alone didn't end a marriage either, as Nadia was discovering.

She was working late on her first big proposal for her new client, who had bought a beautiful house in the seventh arrondissement and was a friend of another client, when her cellphone rang. She picked it up without looking. She was staring at a drawing on her desk of the kitchen she envisioned for them with a glass sun roof that could be opened on warm days over the garden. It made it feel like a country home, not just a city house. She was startled to hear Nicolas's voice.

"Are you awake?" He sounded serious.

"I'm working. Is something wrong?"

"Yes . . . no . . . I don't know. I guess the answer to that has been yes for the past year. I'm downstairs. Can I come up?"

"I've got a presentation tomorrow, so you can't stay long. We can't talk on the phone?" She would have preferred it. They were almost divorced now.

"No," he said firmly.

"The girls are asleep. Don't ring the bell, I'll buzz you in." She sighed and put her pen down. The drawing still didn't look right to her. There was something cumbersome about it.

She buzzed him in a minute later, and he came upstairs fresh from a cold rainy night. He left his coat in the hall, came to sit across from her desk in her office, and glanced at her work, as he had a million times before.

"It's top-heavy," he said. "The roof of the glass house needs to be lighter. In a peak maybe?" She looked at it and realized he was right.

"Thank you. I couldn't figure out what was wrong."

"I thought our meeting with the *notaire* was really depressing."

"It would be more so if we fought about it for ten years. I was surprised at how easy it was," she said.

"Too easy. Is that what you want, Nadia? You open an envelope one day in the next few months, and that's it. It's over. We're divorced. Why can't you give us another chance? Why can't you put me on probation? Punish me. Have me followed. Give me a lie detector test once a week."

"I'm not a policeman, and I don't want to be. I went through hell. Now it's peaceful. I don't want to go through that again." She was definite about it. It was a decision of the head, not the heart, which would have said something different. She didn't trust her heart either, any more than she did his actions.

"I've learned so much from it. Doesn't that count for something?"

She hesitated, not sure what to say to him. She had made up her mind and wanted to stick to it.

"It might," she finally said softly. "But I couldn't go through that horror again. I don't want to take the chance. I'd rather have no life, with just my work and the girls, than have you break my heart again. What did you do in Brittany, by the way?" She was curious.

"I'm having the baby come to Paris twice a month, so we get to know each other." It touched her that he cared, even though his relationship with Pascale was over and the baby had been an accident. He had always had a soft side that she loved. He liked children and was so good to them. She had loved that about him.

"That's sweet."

"I am sweet." He smiled sheepishly at her. "When I'm not being an asshole." She laughed. "Nadia, please, don't give up on us. I don't want those papers to come and just erase everything we had."

"They won't. We have all those memories of the good times," she said with tenderness in her voice and a lump in her throat. "Nothing can erase those."

"I'm glad you think so," he said with a sigh, and then he walked around her desk, gently pulled her into his arms and kissed her. He didn't know what else to do or say. He loved her, and she didn't believe him or didn't care or didn't want him anymore. But the pull between them was so powerful and the force so magnetic, that without even thinking about it, she kissed him back, and they kissed for a long time. She made a soft moaning sound when they stopped.

"Oh, Nicolas, please don't . . . don't do this to me, to us. I've tried so hard to put 'us' behind me, to stop loving you. Don't torture me." She was almost in tears.

"I love you, Nadia. I don't want to put it behind us." He kissed her again with even more passion, and she held on to him in just the way she had missed for months now.

"You have to go." Her voice was hoarse and sexy. "You're a menace," she said, smiling at him. He had always been the most handsome, sexiest man she'd ever known. He was almost irresistible, but she was resisting, or trying to.

"Will you think about it?" he begged her, as she walked him back to the front door and he didn't resist her.

"No! . . . Yes, dammit. You're impossible."

"You can't divorce me while you still love me. That's insane."

"No, it's not. It's probably the sanest thing I've ever done."

"You don't divorce someone you love," he argued. "I'll tell them we have a dispute, and I don't agree with your proposals. I'll recall the papers."

"You can't. They've already been approved by the *notaire* and they're being processed by the judge."

"I hate you. Goddammit, don't be so sensible. Nadia, this is our life, our marriage. It's not a business deal. Yes, maybe we'll make a mess of it, or I will, but can't we at least try?" As he said it, she thought of her sister, confessing her sins fifteen years later, and Harley walking out on her. Somehow he had forgiven her. Maybe she could forgive Nicolas too. It was the first time she had really thought about it and wondered if they should try. "I know I don't deserve you, Nadia. But I love you, I really do."

"Harley and Olivia almost broke up recently. He actually left her for a few days."

"Harley? Why?" Nicolas looked shocked.

"She did something she shouldn't have fifteen years ago, and she decided to confess it to him, and he took it badly. Very badly. But he forgave her, and they're working it out," she said, thinking about them, and how happy Olivia sounded now.

"I'm sure whatever she did wasn't as bad as what I did, but at least he forgave her. Could you take a lesson from him?"

"I think it just boiled down to the fact that they love each other. And I suppose we do too." She looked at him helplessly standing in the front hall of their apartment, and suddenly it just seemed like too much work to fight him. Maybe Venetia was right and if they loved each other, to hell with what everyone thought they should do. If it went wrong again, they could still divorce each other, or leave the papers in place. Suddenly trying again didn't seem like the worst thing that could happen to them. He made her laugh. She had never known another man who could have fun the way he did, or make love like he did, which she had been trying to forget for the past eight months. She hadn't made love to anyone else since, and hadn't wanted to. Greg was a very attractive man, successful, interesting, smart, had great taste, but he didn't excite her. Nicolas did. "Why don't you stay here this weekend, and we'll see how it goes? I'll send the girls to friends. I don't want to get their hopes up and then disappoint them."

"We won't," he promised her, and then crushed her against him in an embrace. "Oh God, Nadia, thank you . . . thank you . . . I'll be a saint for the next fifty years. I promise."

"That sounds incredibly boring." She grinned at him. He knew what he had to do and not do. Now it remained to be seen if he could maintain it. "If you have another affair, I'll divorce you so fast you won't know what hit you."

"I know," he said. "I wouldn't blame you. It will never happen again."

And then she thought of something. "Are we going to have Pascale hanging around to visit her baby?"

"She's not interested in the baby," he said. "He's going to live with his grandmother. I can go to Brittany to see him if you want me to. But I do want him to come to Paris for visits. He needs his father." Even more so with a mother he would probably see very rarely.

"No," she said carefully. "He's your child. He can visit us here. I'm just not ready for that whole family."

"Neither am I. I think I should see him, and I want to, but he'll have a life with them, and visits with us if he's a decent kid. Pascale isn't part of it. She doesn't really want to be part of his life, let alone ours."

"That's sad for him."

"I'm going to keep an eye on him, and the grandmother loves him."

Nadia nodded. It sounded workable. Nicolas was trying to walk a fine line between benevolent supervision from a distance, and participation to a degree that was comfortable but not overwhelming, which was all she could ask of him. They'd have to see how things developed as the boy grew. He might not even want to be with them, or he might fit in very well. Nadia respected what Nicolas was trying to do.

"See you this weekend," she said with a cautious smile. She was nervous about it, like a first date. She had never had those feelings about Greg, the butterflies in the stomach and sweaty palms. But Nicolas always gave her all those feelings and more. He still did.

He kissed her one last time before he left. She stood in the hall for a minute after he was gone, wondering what she'd done, and if she was crazy, but it felt right to give him another chance and try. Much better than getting divorced, or trying to feel something for Greg that she knew she didn't, and never would. Or for someone else she loved less than Nicolas.

She went back to her office to call Venetia and tell her what had happened. This was what her sister had suggested when they talked about it. Nadia thought she'd be pleased.

She picked up her phone to call her, and the phone rang in her hand. She saw that it was from Venetia, and she laughed as she answered it.

"You're psychic. I was just going to call you. Nicolas was just here and we were talking." As she said it, she heard a terrible groan at the other end, and she suddenly realized that her sister didn't sound well, she sounded like she was in pain. "Are you okay?"

"No . . . they think I might be in labor. I'm having terrible pains. Ben is getting dressed to take me to the hospital now. Don't tell Mom. I just wanted you to know. I don't want Mom to worry." And then she started to cry with the next pain. "I'm so afraid I'll lose her. I'm only five months pregnant. She wouldn't survive."

"Just take it easy. Go to the hospital and see what they say. Are you bleeding?"

"A little." That didn't sound good.

"I wish I were there."

Ben helped her stand up then, and Venetia had to go. He half carried her out to the Uber he had called. Fortunately, they were in the city.

Nadia spent the next two hours waiting to hear from her, and talking to Olivia and Athena. She didn't hear from Venetia until four in the morning in Paris. She sounded slightly drunk and said they had given her something to stop labor, and it had worked.

"They're putting me on bed rest for a month or two and we'll see what happens. How am I going to run my business?"

"You can do designs just as well in bed at home. You don't have a choice," Nadia said firmly.

"I know." Her voice was very small and she sounded very scared. Nadia talked to Ben after that and he said the baby looked fine on the monitors and sonograms, they just had to keep it in now until it was cooked.

They kept Venetia in the hospital for a week to observe her and do tests. After that, Ben drove her home. She was lying down on the back seat of their SUV. As soon as they got there, he carried her straight to bed. They had a live-in nanny, so she was covered for childcare, but running her business from bed was going to be hard. Venetia wasn't easy to keep down. She had her finger in every pie, came in and out of design meetings all day, and looked over everyone's shoulder. They decided to put a video screen up in her office, with another screen in her bedroom, so she could see people and participate in meetings. Ben called and checked on her half a dozen times a day, and she was afraid to spend too much time out of bed. As soon as she did, she started having contractions. They had to keep her from having the baby for four more months. It sounded like an eternity to Venetia. With three young children and a booming business, it was going to be a huge challenge to stay in bed.

When Venetia felt better, Nadia told her that she and Nicolas were going to try to work things out.

"I don't know if it will work, or if it's too late for us. But you're right. We love each other. I don't want to throw that away yet." Venetia was happy for her. It was what she had hoped would happen all along.

Chapter 14

Nadia flew to New York to see Venetia for a few days. Venetia had been in bed for a month, but she was busy too and had several new clients. She was doing one presentation after another. And things were going well with Nicolas so far. He was walking on eggshells, but they were both starting to relax. She told Venetia about it when she brought her Thai food on a tray.

"It's not like it used to be, but it's getting there," Nadia told her. She hadn't seen the baby yet, and Nicolas didn't push her to. He still had his rented apartment, and had Isabelle and the baby stay there for their visits. The girls had gone to see him and thought he was very cute. Nadia said she hadn't heard from Greg Holland again since she told him that she and Nicolas were giving it another try.

Nicolas was on his best behavior. They had spent several weekends at the château with the girls, and Nicolas and Nadia had gone to Rome alone for a weekend. He was writing full steam ahead again, and it was flowing. They were both busy and working hard. And he was staying at the apartment with her and the girls. She had told her mother about it and Rose said she was cautiously optimistic. He was going to have to prove himself to her.

Olivia and Harley were doing well too. Venetia thought they were even closer than they'd been before. But the explosion between them had been brief. Nicolas and Nadia had been apart for many months, and the damage had been more extensive.

Rose was relieved that they were back together, and hoped it worked. Everyone was wishing them well.

They had been together for three months when Nadia came home from the office one day. The girls were at their gym class with the babysitter, and she opened the mail that had been left on her desk at home. There was a thick unmarked envelope that she opened last. She had brought work home from the office, and had a dozen things on her mind. Nicolas was back in the room he used to write. When she pulled the letter out of the envelope, she stared at it, shocked. She sat down and read through it, and then got up and hurried down the hall to his office. He was correcting some pages he had written the day before on the computer and looked up in surprise when he saw her. She hadn't knocked. She didn't say a word. She walked over and handed the papers to him and he stared at them in shock, as she had.

"Shit. How did this happen? I meant to ask you about it a few weeks ago, if we were supposed to do something to stop it, and I forgot. What do we do now?"

"I don't know. I think it's too late to reverse it. It looks official," she said, staring at him. They were divorced. The divorce had gone through. They had signed the papers three months before, and had never stopped the procedure. “Oh my God, I’m not married to you anymore.”

“You’re a free woman.” It was kind of a creepy feeling, like a ship that had slipped its moorings and was drifting out to sea.

They both called their attorneys and were told the same thing. It was too late to reverse it or cancel the proceedings. Their marriage had been dissolved, and the only thing they could do was get married again, if they didn’t want to be divorced. But for now, they were in fact divorced.

They met in Nadia’s office at home after talking to their lawyers, and spoke in whispers. The children were home by then and they didn’t want them to know. Nadia was sure it would panic them, and she felt slightly panicked herself.

“Do you want to get married again?” he asked her, unnerved by it too.

“I think so.”

“You *think* so? What do you mean by that?”

“What if getting married again screws things up, or jinxes us or something?” She looked worried and he laughed.

“This is ridiculous. We went through hell and we were married. Now we’re back together, and we’re accidentally divorced. Personally, I don’t like it. I like being married to you. I *want* to be married to you.”

“So do I. I feel a little silly telling people we forgot to cancel our divorce, so now we’re not married.”

“Let’s fix it. We don’t even have to tell anyone beforehand. We can just invite everyone to the château for a long weekend, surprise them when they get there, and do it," he suggested. Nadia liked that idea too. They agreed not to tell anyone about the papers that arrived. They laughed about it in bed that night. "Actually, it's kind of sexy making love to you and not being married. I'd forgotten what that's like."

"Well, that's a relief. We can't get married until at least June," she reminded him.

"Why not? You have something more important to do?"

"No, Venetia does. She's not due till mid-May, if she makes it till then. She's on bed rest, and she won't be able to travel until the baby is a month old." He had forgotten.

"Fine. We'll get married in June. Invite everyone then. I can't believe I'm planning a wedding with my own wife."

"I don't know how I forgot to cancel the papers. I think I was afraid to."

"And now?" he asked her. "Are you still afraid?"

"No, I'm not," she said and kissed him. Things had been perfect between them, better than she had expected. Maybe even better than before.

"Are you happy?" he asked her seriously.

"I am." She nodded and nestled peacefully into his arms. "I can't believe we're divorced, though."

"That's what happens when you play with fire. You're the one who wanted to get divorced. That was your idea."

"I was trying to get over you," she reminded him.

"Well, you did a lousy job of it, fortunately," he said, pulling her close to him. He loved sleeping with her again and waking up next to her, talking to her late at night and in the morning. The girls were happy too. It was as though the nightmare of the year before had never happened. She was so precious to him, he knew he would never be unfaithful again. She still had to meet Benoit, but she felt ready to now. What had happened wasn't the baby's fault. And Nicolas had no contact at all with Pascale anymore. Only with her mother. He and Pascale weren't on bad terms, she was just pursuing her own life and doing what she wanted. Nicolas had been a moment in her life, and for her the moment was over. For Nadia she had been an explosion, a bomb that had hit them. She didn't like to think about it, but she did at times, and marveled at the fact that they had recovered from it, and been able to get back together.

"How are we going to do this?" she asked Nicolas about their remarriage. "We just go to the *mairie,* and have lunch afterwards?" The *mairie* was the city hall of each district of Paris and each small town outside Paris.

"That's a little dry, don't you think? We could do it at the *mairie* for the legal ceremony, and have a church wedding the next day, the way normal people do it."

"I'm not sure how 'normal' we are. We're divorced. Are you telling me you want a real wedding?" She looked amused.

"I think I do," he said, mulling it over. "Why not? We have a lot to celebrate. We could make it one-stop shopping. Benoit hasn't been christened yet, and I suspect they'll never get to it. We could have him baptized at the wedding, and have him at the château for the weekend. Or is that too crazy?"

"Definitely crazy. I think we're starting to border on the seriously eccentric. But I guess we could, as long as his mother doesn't show up."

"She won't. We won't tell her."

"Don't ever tell me that I'm still too American. I'm going to marry my husband, whom I accidentally divorced, while we christen the baby he had with his mistress, who was the reason for the divorce in the first place. In America, they put you in psychiatric hospitals for this."

"I don't think it's actually done in the better social circles here either, but I don't care. Do you?"

"Actually, I don't. What the hell. Why not baptize the baby? I hope my mother is up to this."

"Your mother is pretty cool."

Nadia had an idea then. She wanted to discuss it with Venetia. She had come back to her marriage still in love with Nicolas, but with a stronger sense of herself, more self-confidence, and an independence she'd never had before. She had survived the worst blow that could hit a marriage, and had come out the other end, whole, and strong, and happy. Her sisters had noticed it too.

She called Venetia the next morning and confided in her. She was the only one she was going to tell. She wanted to surprise everyone else.

"How did you manage to get divorced without noticing it?"

"I just forgot about the papers, and then we got back together and that seemed more important."

"You're probably right," Venetia said, bored out of her mind. She had a drafting table over her bed in the daytime, so she could continue working. "So what do you want me to do?" Venetia thought the whole thing was funny.

"I want you to design a fabulous dress for me. A total fantasy. I wore such a serious one last time. It was beautiful, but I want to have fun this time." She had worn an ivory peau de soie gown with a lace coat over it and a ten-foot train, which they got at Bergdorf's. "I want you to go crazy with it."

"Well, we could go little farm girl, or Heidi, if you're going to do it at the château, or we could go totally nuts with a giant tulle ball skirt," she suggested off the top of her head, but she could envision it on Nadia.

"That sounds better. I want to look and feel like Cinderella."

"Oh my God. Are you on medication? Maybe you should be. Now you're divorced, then you want to give a fantasy wedding. Are we dressing Nicolas like Elvis, or Prince Charming?"

"He can wear a white linen suit. He has ten of them. I want my dress to be special. Lots of tulle skirt, I think Galliano did one like that once for Dior. I think it was yellow or pink or something."

"Are we doing white or a color?" Venetia was beginning to enjoy it and doodling as they spoke.

"White. And cute little white organdie dresses for the girls."

"I can't wait for this wedding," Venetia said, giggling. "I have to figure out what to tell my workroom about who this is for. I'll pick some fabulous rock star. I'll send you a sheet for your measurements." They talked about it for half an hour, and afterwards, Venetia continued to text her questions, which she answered, about how the bodice should look, sleeves or no sleeves, how long the train should be, pearls or tiny rhinestones. Nadia texted back "Both." No veil since it was a second wedding. Venetia thought a tiara. She was having as much fun with it as Nadia was. It took the sting out of having discovered the day before that she was divorced. Nicolas had decided that was funny, but it still made Nadia uneasy. What if they never got around to getting married again? She didn't like that idea at all.

She and Nicolas picked the third Saturday in June, and they were able to book the small country church near the château. The priest faltered for a minute when Nicolas told him they were divorced, and he explained that divorced people could not get married in a Catholic church, and Nicolas explained to him that it was a technicality, and they were marrying the same people as the first time.

"Ah, like a renewal of vows."

"Exactly." It was the brief ceremony at city hall that would actually bind them together legally again. The church ceremony was more about religious tradition, and Nicolas mentioned to him that there would be a baptism too.

"The bride and groom's baby?"

"Actually, the groom's, not the bride's." The priest decided to ignore that. Nicolas reported to Nadia that everything was in order with the church. She had to go off to meet clients then, and she could hardly keep her mind on the project at hand. Suddenly, their unorthodox, very eccentric wedding seemed more exciting.

Nadia sent Venetia her measurements, and the gown got under way. Venetia sent her emails showing her the sketches for it. They were going to make the bodice out of six layers of white organdie, and she'd be corseted in tight, with gossamer sleeves, and the tulle ball skirt was in fact enormous, with a hoop under it, so it would swing like a bell when Nadia walked.

Nadia had extended the weekend invitation to her sisters and their partners and children, and her mother. Rose wanted to know if they were having a big party or a family event. And Nadia responded that it was a family party.

"What do I wear?" she wanted to know.

"Something summery and dressy."

"Long or short?"

"Whatever you like."

Nicolas had hired a local quartet to play chamber music, with a violinist. Nadia was going to do the flowers herself the morning of the wedding.

They had everything lined up by the first of May, when Venetia called her at two A.M. in Paris, eight P.M. in New York. "I'm in labor. They said they're not going to try and stop it this time. I'm only three weeks early. I didn't even think I was in labor, I thought it was something I ate. But it's getting bad now."

"Are you okay?"

"Yes, just scared. I hope she's going to be okay."

"She'll be fine," Nadia said in a strong, encouraging voice. "You've done this three times, you know how to do it."

Venetia called Athena and Olivia too, and she kept calling Nadia every half hour to report in, until Nadia saw the sun come up. It was one in the morning in New York by then, she'd been in labor for six hours, and had finally stopped calling. Nadia walked into the kitchen and made herself a cup of coffee, waiting to hear from her, when Nicolas walked in.

"No news yet?"

"I hope she and the baby are okay."

"I'm sure they are." He knew how close she was to her sisters. They were always there for each other. Olivia was at the hospital with Venetia, and Rose was waiting to hear at home.

Venetia finally called at eight-thirty. It had taken longer than they expected. The baby had been turned the wrong way and they had to shift her, and she was a big baby, considering that she was born early. She weighed eight pounds and Venetia sounded like she'd been beaten up. But she was euphoric, and said the baby was beautiful. They were calling her Valencia. Ben sent a photo of her a minute later. The girls had already gone to school, and Nadia promised to show them later.

"Congratulations!" Nadia said with tears in her eyes.

"I think I'm going to stop at four," Venetia said, exhausted. "Four months in bed was way too long." But she had gotten a healthy baby out of it. And Ben sounded happy too when they talked to him. Nadia called her mother and congratulated her. She had seven grandchildren now.

"I can't wait for your party next month," she told Nadia.

"It's just family, Mom. But we wanted to make it a special occasion. We all have a lot to celebrate." Olivia and Harley's marriage had been saved. Venetia and Ben had a new baby. And Nadia and Nicolas were back together after the worst year imaginable, and a divorce they were planning to trade in for a wedding, even if no one knew it yet.

Chapter 15

The timing in June turned out to be perfect for everyone. The network let Athena take the time off. Seven weeks after Valencia's birth, Venetia was back on her feet and feeling fine. She was almost back to her normal weight, and looked beautiful. Olivia and Harley had planned a trip for right after the weekend at the chateau. Nadia finished installing an apartment in London a few days before. Planning for the September issue had started but wasn't insane yet for Rose. And this year's September issue would be a breeze compared to last year.

Nicolas had rented two vans to get them to the château, and everyone was in high spirits when they got there. He had sent their regular nanny to Brittany to bring back the baby with her. He had found some of the family christening gowns in a cedar chest at the château. They were beautiful, ornate, handmade gowns, and Nadia picked one that fit Benoit. It was the first time that she had seen him, and she held him for a few minutes as he cooed and smiled at her. Seeing him was the final hurdle she had to clear after the last year. She made it over smoothly, as Nicolas watched her hold him.

"Thank you," he whispered to her. She had made it possible for Benoit to be there, and being able to baptize him at the château on a special day for them meant a lot to him. He looked like a little prince when they tried the christening gown on him. He was fair like Nicolas, with a fine peach fuzz on his head, and big blue eyes. Pascale hadn't objected to the baptism when he decided to call and asked her. She said she wasn't religious and didn't care. He did. It seemed more respectful to ask her.

Neither he nor Nadia had commented when the Cannes Film Festival happened in May. He didn't have a film there this year, and neither of them wanted to go. It brought back bad memories and probably always would of his year of insanity.

Nicolas had brought the marriage license with him and had it in his pocket. Nadia's dress had arrived in a crate that had to be specially built and sent to the château by truck. The wedding was scheduled for Saturday. Everyone arrived at the château the day before, and spent the day relaxing at the pool, and played Marco Polo with the children. Nicolas took Benoit in for a few minutes and he loved it, then he squealed with delight while Sylvie and Laure fussed over him. Valencia was too young for the pool and was asleep in her pram. They all had a big family dinner that night, to celebrate just being there together. It was the first time they had been with Nicolas since he came back. He slipped back into his place in the family very quickly. Nicolas and Nadia looked relaxed. No one knew about the wedding until breakfast the next day, when Nicolas announced it, much to everyone's surprise. Harley was worried that he hadn't brought a proper suit, and Nicolas said he could lend him one, but he didn't need it. His summer navy linen blazer and white linen pants were fine.

Rose looked amused when they made the announcement. They were certainly going all out to reforge their bond to each other. "You mean you're renewing your vows?" They'd been married for twelve years by then.

"Not exactly," Nicolas explained in answer to her question. "We had a little administrative glitch a few months ago. We appeared at the *notaire* for our divorce papers, and subsequently when we got back together, we forgot to cancel the divorce. In April we were advised that our marriage had been dissolved. So we are getting married today, for the second time." There was a babble of comments, jokes and laughter, and everyone was excited to be part of it, and loved that they had done it as a surprise.

"What if one of us couldn't come?" Athena asked, stunned by the plan. For fourteen years, she had refused to marry Joe, and her sister was marrying the same man twice.

"We made sure you all could come when we set the date," Nicolas told her. "But if not, you would have missed a terrific dinner tonight, and seeing Nadia in the gorgeous dress Venetia made for her. I haven't seen it yet. But the crate it came in is the size of this house." The chatter continued for another hour. And they were all told that they had to be at the town hall at noon for the legal ceremony. They had a reservation at a local restaurant at one. The church ceremony was to be at six o'clock, with dinner afterwards at the château. They all scurried off then to put their outfits together and be ready on time.

Rose watched them go and smiled. It was certainly unorthodox, but if Nadia was happy, it was all she cared about. And if Nicolas cheated on her daughter again, she was going to kill him herself.

Everyone was standing at the vans outside at twenty to twelve, and they set off to the little town where the town hall was located. Nadia was wearing a very pretty simple white cotton dress she had found at the Bon Marché, by a designer she didn't know but Venetia did and approved. She was wearing her dark hair in a neat ponytail, and high-heeled white sandals. She was carrying a small bouquet of white flowers that Sylvie helped her pick. They had their papers with them, and everything went smoothly. Ben and Venetia were their witnesses, and at twelve-thirty they were standing outside, congratulating the bride and groom. Nicolas looked relieved that they were legally married again. The rest was window dressing after this.

The food at the local restaurant was simple bistro fare, but very good. There was even a vegetarian meal for Athena. Joe loved the traditional French dishes, and went to the kitchen to compliment the chef, explaining that he was a chef too, and so was Athena.

They were back at the château at three-thirty, and everyone went to their rooms to rest or outside to lie at the pool. Nadia finished arranging the flowers, and a local caterer was doing dinner.

She bathed and did her own hair and makeup, and at five-thirty all three of her sisters and her mother came to help her put on the enormous dress. It almost filled the room, and Venetia smiled broadly when she saw it on her. It fit perfectly, even without fittings and only her measurements to go by. Nadia really did look like Cinderella, and Sylvie and Laure gasped with wide eyes when they saw their mother.

"You look like a princess, Mama," Laure said in wonder.

"No, she doesn't. She looks like a queen," Sylvie corrected her. Rose dabbed at her eyes watching the scene, and kissed all of her daughters. It was a very different story from what it had been a year before when she was fighting to keep Pascale and Nicolas off the pages of *Mode* and lost the battle. It was testimony to the human spirit and what people could come through if they had the courage to do it. A year before, Nadia had been mourning her marriage, now they were celebrating its rebirth, stronger than ever, with a depth to their relationship they hadn't had before, and a greater understanding of themselves and each other. Nadia had gotten stronger and was more sure of herself. Nicolas had grown more serious and had greater respect for Nadia than ever before.

They had to turn the ball skirt sideways with Venetia's help and open the double doors to get Nadia out of the room. Harley, Joe, Ben, Will, and Nicolas had gone ahead to the church to wait for the others. Venetia's children went with her, Olivia, Athena, and the nanny holding Benoit in his antique christening gown that Nicolas thought his grandfather might have worn, from photographs he'd seen.

And Nadia, Sylvie, Laure, and Rose rode in an old Rolls they kept in storage on the estate. It was from before the war, in perfect condition, and was a museum piece that had been the pride of Nicolas's father and they normally never used. The gardener knew the car, had cleaned it, put gas in it, and was driving it for them in his best suit.

Sylvie and Laure were sitting on little jump seats and looked at their mother with awe.

They had discussed over lunch who should give Nadia away. Her brothers-in-law all volunteered, but she asked her mother to do it. They were going to walk down the aisle together, side by side, toward Nicolas at the altar, in the small, ancient church.

There was a throng of women and children around her, as Venetia fluffed up the skirt, Rose straightened the tiara Venetia had brought with her, borrowed from Fred Leighton, the jeweler in New York. Strangers watched her progress into the church. And finally, the family walked in, leaving Rose and Nadia outside with her daughters, while people stared at her from a distance and smiled. They had never seen such a magnificent bride.

Laure walked into the church first, with Sylvie right behind her, hissing at her to slow down, and Nadia and her mother came slowly down the aisle. Rose had bought a pink silk suit that was perfect on her, and Nadia's skirt swung as it was supposed to, and filled the aisle. She looked toward the altar and saw Nicolas waiting for her, with tears streaming down his cheeks. The past and the present blended together and all he could see was her, the wife who had stood by him, and was giving him another chance. He was filled with love and gratitude.

Harley and Olivia were holding hands in the front pew. And Ben stood beside Nicolas as his best man. Nicolas had been restored to them, like the prodigal son, and was back in the fold, profoundly grateful to be there with all of them.

Rose stood beside her daughter until the priest asked who gives this woman in marriage and she said "I do," and then took her seat next to Joe, with her daughters around her, and her grandchildren in the pew behind them. It was a simple, traditional ceremony, more touching than the big social wedding Nadia had had twelve years before, when her father and Nicolas's parents were still alive.

As they said their simple vows, promising to love, honor, and cherish, all of the family had damp eyes, knowing how far they had come to reach this moment. The love they had shared had almost died, and they had managed to breathe life into it again. And Nadia and Nicolas had discovered that what they had was stronger than what he'd done.

The priest baptized Benoit at the end of the ceremony. Nadia held him and then handed him to the nanny. The priest then pronounced them husband and wife, as Nicolas and Nadia looked at each other. She was radiant in the spectacular dress. Nicolas had never been prouder in his life. In the end, the affair meant less to them than their marriage. This was a new beginning for them.

Then they all went back to the château, drank champagne, and ate caviar, lobster, and sole, and a wedding cake Nicolas had thought to order from the local bakery. It had a bride and groom on top, and two little girls, which delighted Sylvie and Laure. Benoit and Venetia's baby slept peacefully through the festivities.

The quartet played and they danced, as Rose watched her daughters, Nadia in particular. They had all learned valuable lessons, how at one moment you could be in darkest despair, and yet celebrating a year later. It was a perfect example of the beauty and unpredictability of life, the strength of the human heart to endure and prevail, and the love which made it all possible, as it had for them.

Danielle Steel

Have you liked Danielle Steel on Facebook?

Be the first to know about Danielle's latest books, access exclusive competitions and stay in touch with news about Danielle.

www.facebook.com/DanielleSteelOfficial

FINDING ASHLEY

Bestselling novelist Melissa Henderson withdrew from her successful New York life when her young son died of a brain tumour. Distraught, she abandoned her career to renovate her beautiful Victorian home in the Berkshire mountains of Massachusetts. And she hasn't spoken to her sister Hattie for years, after her shocking change of ambitions from an aspiring Hollywood actress to retreating to convent life as a nun.

But both have long-buried secrets. Pregnant at fifteen years old, Melissa was sent to a convent herself to have the baby, which she was forced to give up for adoption. She never forgave her parents and she would always yearn for the little girl she lost. And Hattie has her own secret. She was abused and blackmailed by a powerful producer – the true reason for her decision to leave Hollywood.

Now, both women find that it is time for forgiveness and to heal old wounds. As they re-connect, Hattie vows to find Melissa's daughter lost all those years ago.

Coming soon

PURE STEEL. PURE HEART.